Amaranth Dawn

DAUGHTER OF ZYANYA: BOOK ONE

MORGAN J. MUIR

This is a work of fiction. Names, characters, places, and incidents either are the product of the author's imagination or are used fictitiously. Any resemblance to actual persons, living or dead, events, or locales is entirely coincidental.

Copyright © 2016 by Morgan J. Muir

All rights reserved. No part of this work may be reproduced or used in any manner without written permission of the copyright owner except for the use of quotations in a book review.

Cover & book design by Morgan J. Muir
www.Morganjmuir.com
Cover art by Joelle Douglass
smojojo.deviantart.com

ISBN-13: 978-1-7338906-3-2

For my grandparents
who gave me space to imagine.

ALSO BY MORGAN J. MUIR

Daughter of Zyanya
Aura of Dawn – a Prequel
Amaranth Dawn – Book 1
Aeonian Dreams – Book 2
Abiding Destiny – Book 3 (*forthcoming*)

Short Stories
Nadir: A short story of Motherhood
Control: A short story of Courage
Burdened: A short story of Choice
Heartfelt: A short story of Loyalty
Unnamed: A short story of Hope (*forthcoming*)

Paws: Sheltie Stories (graphic novels)
Paw Prints
Paws of Power (*forthcoming*)
Path of Paws (*forthcoming*)

Available at Amazon.com

Prologue

KALÁIRA WALKED in the peace of the dream world. The quiet space around her whispered of Freedom. It teased her with the idea of slicing through the bands of anger that weighed her down and the resentment that held her back. Imagined images of her upcoming wedding flickered across the dreamscape, her random thoughts made momentarily manifest. The wind toyed with her hair. Full of the warm scent of flowers and rain, it whispered secrets in the language of her fathers. Si'a, the little spirit bird with his deep black wings and golden chest, danced brazenly among the winds. Kaláira smiled at him.

With closed eyes, she took a deep breath, imagining the sweet air that filled her lungs pushing the anger deeper into her belly, where it could not escape. She turned her gaze toward the stars, brilliant through an impossibly blue sky, and ignored their murmuring. She would not think about her mother. Si'a twittered at her, a sound suspiciously similar to laughter.

What would you know about it? she asked, giving him a wry look.

In response, he dropped something at her feet. Narrowing her eyes at the playful bird, she dropped to pick it up. *Tu'uma?* The precious red stone was warm in her hand. What did her spirit guide mean by giving her this? Si'a chirruped and flitted overhead as she straightened, and even the wind seemed more agitated than usual, pushing her forward. Kaláira closed her eyes and allowed herself to be led. It was not often the spirits of the dream world were so insistent. There was both power and meaning to be found here, even when the spirits were calm. Unbidden, a smile pulled at her lips. Perhaps this time she would see a true vision, like the elders, and earn a place of respect among the tribe.

She allowed herself to be carried by the winds, gliding like a ribbon of sand before a storm. Si'a flew alongside, chirping urgently. Setting her feet on the ground, she opened her eyes and drew in a sharp breath. The wind had taken her to Ouktaa, the place of shameful death. Kaláira scowled. There was no reason to be here.

Her anger darkened the dream world around her and dropped her from the wind's embrace like a rock over a cliff. Landing roughly on the ground, she glared at the dark, carved mouth of a cave. It was a blight on the land, an abomination in both the physical world and the ethereal. The aura of the place hung thick with stale fear and old pain, tainting each breath with the tang of bitterness. The entrance had been carved with strange pillars and harsh shapes. Perhaps it had been meant to look lovely, but to Kaláira it was naught but foreign.

Her mother was in there somewhere, no doubt. Hiding from her pain, from her life. Kaláira rubbed her forearms absently. Her mother had not run away when Kaláira's baby sister had been killed, nor when her father or brothers had died. Shadowed images of her memories flickered by to the whispered accompaniment of her family's silenced laughter. But the loss of Kaláira's younger brother lingered. She remembered the transparent image of her mother kneeling, with her empty eyes over the body of her youngest son. It had broken her.

Kaláira waved the image away.

In Kaláira's moment of greatest darkness, when she needed her mother the most, her mother had left, run away to Ouktaa. Kaláira clenched her fists. Her mother, Ka'i, had abandoned her. She had abandoned her duties as a mother and as eldest daughter to her own mother, leaving all the responsibility on Kaláira's slender shoulders. The weight of that responsibility settled over her again, tight and biting across her shoulders and stabbing through her chest. She turned to leave this place of misery but the winds enveloped her, filling the heavens with storm clouds, and would not let her pass.

I want nothing to do with her! Kaláira shouted, fighting her way through the wind. *She left me! Let me move on!*

The dream winds pushed against her harder but only hardened her resolve.

If that is the way you want to be about it, she snarled. *I'll leave the other way.*

Only by killing her could they stop her from waking. She began the descent back into her own body. Si'a fluttered down to perch on her shoulder, and she paused for her friend. The bird's glinting chest and black-feathered hood drew her unwilling eyes. He cocked his head at her, and she could not help but see beyond him as the figure of a woman, clearly ill and emaciated, stumbled out of the gates of endless death. Si'a's golden plumage brightened and his blacks deepened as Kaláira's anger turned to fury.

No. She glared at Si'a, who now hovered before her.

Si'a cocked his head.

I don't care. Kaláira turned her back to the woman who held so tightly to herself as she staggered through the storming darkness.

Si'a looked unblinking into her eyes.

She chose her path. Let her die. Kaláira walked away from her mother, the air around her suddenly calm.

Teeth jaguar sharp prey prey prey. Si'a trilled as he circled around her head.

What did you say? Kaláira stopped in her tracks and looked at the bird. He never spoke to her.

Si'a flapped playfully before her, a golden light in the gathering darkness. *Sun bear Moon, Jaguar cub cub cub.* The bird flared his wings before her, and in them she saw the wild cat's teeth bathed in the moonlight, crunching through the net that bound her people. As the jaguar's powerful jaws crunched through the blood-sucking *thing* that held them, a drop of moonlight fell from Si'a's wings into Kaláira's hand. She looked down and found the tu'uma stone she'd picked up earlier, bathed in iridescent moonlight.

Her breath caught in her throat. She, Kaláira daughter of Ka'i, had been given a vision. But of what?

Freedom, the wind whispered in her ears.

And the cost? she asked, not looking up from the stone.

Forgiveness, the voices echoed in her mind as she opened her physical eyes. She opened her hand and saw the stone that Si'a had given her, brought to the physical world. The anger and bitterness congealed inside her into a solid rock of stubbornness. It was time to save her mother.

Chapter 1

JULY 1740 - MARACAIBO

THE WORLD AROUND Mariah came to a standstill as she stared down the sights of the flintlock pistol held in her hand, pointed squarely at Antonio Gonza. Moonlight bathed the garden in its pale glow and the distant music of the wedding dancing floated over the hedge. Mariah's mind raced, flitting around, and she could feel the trembling start in her gut. She had already killed one man tonight; surely the universe would not make her kill another.

The weight of Miguel's arm over her shoulder steadied her, even as she held him up. His leg had given out and the blow to his head frightened her. Only moments ago, he had been proposing to her. How had this happened? She took a cautious step back, her heeled boot crunching against the gravel. She needed to get Miguel back to the house. How would she get out of this?

"I'd have rather had you alive, but I'm just as happy crushing Álvarez this way." Gonza stepped closer, his raspy voice grating against her senses. "And believe me, your father will be crushed."

Beside her, Miguel muttered an unintelligible mix of English and Castilian. Weight crushed against her chest as her breathing came in short, unfulfilling gasps. She needed to do something, and now. Everything within her urged her to shoot Gonza. He was dangerous and bent on destroying her father, and if she didn't find help, Miguel might die as well. She couldn't run for help and carry him. Nor could she leave him for Gonza's non-existent mercy.

Pain seared her heart; she didn't want to kill anyone else. She'd had so much death in her life already. He wasn't even armed. Could she scare him off? But she had only one shot. If she wasted it... The trembling reached her arm.

Gonza sneered at her hesitation, stepping forward again. "You're far too much of a coward like your mestizo-loving father to shoot me, girl." He leveled his own pistol at her.

Mariah froze. Where had he gotten a gun? He wouldn't actually shoot her. How could she die now? She wasn't even eighteen yet. This couldn't be happening.

Miguel growled, and the pistol jerked in her grip, his hand covering hers. An explosion of light and sound set the world in motion again as Gonza dropped before her. Her blood ran cold as Miguel's arm fell from her shoulders and he collapsed beside her, the pistol still tight in his grip.

***

The carriage rolled through the dark streets as the inevitable rain of tropical Maracaibo pattered against the windows. Mariah kept her seat easily in the gently rocking cabin, her arm threaded through Miguel's. His solid presence stilled her lingering fears. *My fiancé.* The thought made her smile. Perhaps she would never stop smiling.

A jarring bump in the road made him groan and lean forward to rest his head in his hands. His dark hair cascaded over his fingers and obscured his face.

Mariah rubbed her hand across his broad shoulders, the fine linen of his shirt bunching beneath her fingers. Once they were back within the walls of the *hacienda* they would all be safe and everything would be fine. "We're nearly there, Miguel. I wish I could help more."

He sat back and smiled at her. "It's fine, *mi morena.* I'm sure I'll feel as good as new after some solid sleep."

Mariah frowned at how thickly his English accent came through. At least he'd started speaking Castilian again, and in coherent sentences. It reassured her more than the healer's words had. "You'd better be." She gently tucked his hair behind his ear as the carriage turned, entering the wide gates of the *hacienda.* "I don't intend to announce our engagement without you beside me."

"You sure?" Miguel squeezed her hand. "You seemed to do just fine today, ordering the Casa de la Cuesta staff around like you owned the place. I can only imagine the look on Sergio's face when you walked in, demanding to speak with your father."

Mariah ducked her head, blushing. "I only did what needed to be done." The events of the last few hours swirled through her mind. They had been enjoying the wedding festivities of her dear friend, Betania, the daughter of her father's business partner, Sergio Díaz, and Miguel had proposed. Mariah absently touched the brooch on her shoulder, a sweeping, worked-silver vine with three dark enameled roses to one side, now pinned right side up—a sign for any who saw it that she was now an engaged woman.

But the perfect night had been shattered when her father's nemesis, Antonio Gonza, had attacked them and Miguel had been injured in the struggle.

The carriage pulled to a stop outside the main doors of the *hacienda's* main house. Mariah smiled up at the large white building, trimmed with dark wood and surrounded by grounds overflowing with greenery.

"We're home," she said softly to Miguel, who had returned to holding his head. The carriage rocked when the footman leapt down and opened the door. The warm, damp wind of the storm blew her hair across her face, and she pushed it from her eyes. With a worried glance back at her fiancé, Mariah stepped down into the courtyard.

"He may need some help in, Dom," she said quietly to the man who stood beside her, as her father's steward took the umbrella he held to protect them from the rain. "Gonza attacked us at the wedding. He was injured, but disappeared. Papa says to secure the *hacienda,* and he will return later tonight on horseback."

"I'll see to it, *señorita.*" Dom nodded and motioned another forward to help Miguel down.

Mariah watched, concerned, as Miguel attempted to stand straight, nearly a head taller than her, and tried to shake off the footman's hand.

"The señorita insists," the footman said, refusing to be shaken off.

"Well, if the Lady says," Miguel replied in English with a roll of his eyes.

Mariah bit her lip and led them into the main house. "Take him to his room and see that he sleeps," she said as they passed under the arched walkway and through the doors.

"No." Miguel nodded toward the sitting room, his speech slipping back to Castilian. "We should wait for your father."

They moved to the sitting room, and Miguel sank into a seat. The warm familiarity of the room put Mariah further at ease. The walled *hacienda* had stood as guardian to Mariah her entire life. It, as much as her father, Ciro Alvarez, was immovable and unconquerable.

Mariah sat across from Miguel, spreading out her damp, red skirt. "Do you realize every time something bad happens, I'm wearing a red dress?"

"Sometimes good things happen, too." Miguel turned in his seat to put his feet on the cushions and leaned back over the armrest, his arm draped over his eyes.

"That doesn't offset the fact that bad things still happen. If it's not the dress, then it's me. I've a curse of bad luck." Mariah worked her fingers through her black, windswept hair, setting it back into a semblance of order.

Miguel laughed. "Yes, terrible bad luck. I could use some more of it, I think."

"What do you mean by that?" Mariah tossed a throw pillow at him, hitting him in his covered face.

"What did I do to deserve that?" he asked, shoving the pillow beneath his back.

"You never addressed the infestation of flying pillows in this house." Mariah sat back. "Now, what did you mean about my luck?"

"Well, your dog died, right?"

"And it was my fault he got run over by a wagon." The stab of pain in Mariah's gut at that truth had lessened over the two years since she'd lost her sweet Alistair, but it still came. She took a deep breath, willing it to pass.

"But I first saw you from my ship the night you set him to sea on his little funeral barge. So it was good luck for me. Good luck for me, too, that you went back the next morning and we ran into each other."

Mariah crossed her arms. "It was Elisa who saw you first."

"Oh, I think we're all well aware of that; she never stops pointing it out. But it was you who encouraged her to talk to me." Miguel shifted his weight, wincing as he adjusted the pillow behind his back.

"Only because I was cross."

"Nevertheless, your so-called bad luck was really good luck for us both. I will never forget being greeted by four angels as I stepped onto the docks of Maracaibo. Or when the darkest of the four, with her shining black hair and dark, serious eyes, suggested I could find work with a certain merchant who turned out to be her father." He raised his arm from his face and turned his head to look directly at her. "The rest of it isn't bad luck or your fault, it's just life."

A silence filled the space between them. She didn't want to say it, but she had to. "My mother's death was my fault. She died because I was born."

With an effort, Miguel pushed himself upright and gestured for her to sit beside him. She moved across the floor and sat beside him on the couch, and he took her hand. "Mariah, that was nearly eighteen years ago. You can't keep blaming yourself for that. Both your father and Nana, who were both there, have told you it wasn't your fault. Why can't you believe them?"

Tears stung at her eyes, and suddenly all the emotions of the night filled her, pushing against the wall she used to push them back. "It's late, Miguel. I'm tired, you're tired, and neither of us are thinking straight. I'm sure Papa will get everything straightened out and will want to talk to us in the morning."

"Don't cry." He touched her jaw and turned her face toward him. "You're right; everything will turn out fine. And I believe I owe you a kiss."

For a few, beautiful moments, all of Mariah's cares fell away, and nothing existed except herself and Miguel. A knock on the open door pulled her back to earth, and Mariah sat up, pulling herself from Miguel's arms.

"If you're quite finished." Nana swept into the room as though she owned the place. Mariah's nursemaid, and a faithful servant and friend of the family since Mariah's mother had been a child, reached out her hand to help Mariah off the couch. "Dom told me what happened, and a messenger just arrived with further instructions. Your father will spend the night at Casa de la Cuesta and wishes you two to get some rest."

Mariah nodded, gesturing to Miguel, who had lain back on the couch. "He may need some support getting to his room."

"I can sleep on the couch," he muttered.

"I'll see to it, *chica*." Nana smiled. "And congratulations, from both myself and your father."

Mariah gave her a quick hug, glad for the woman's stalwart presence. Between Nana and her father,

Mariah's world was stable and strong. Now that she had Miguel as well, what could possibly shake it?

Chapter 2

MARIAH WALKED through fields of gently waving grass, and the stars overhead shone through the blue sky. The sounds of the jungle that blanketed the distant mountain sounded unnaturally close, comforting her with their presence. Behind her lay Lake Maracaibo and home. A gentle breeze flowed around her, tugging playfully at her hair and whispering secrets she couldn't quite understand. Mariah turned her face to the cloudless, star-strewn sky. It would rain soon, but it always rained here.

A whine and a pressure against her leg drew her attention. Mariah looked down to see Alistair beside her with his large, lopsided smile. She dropped down and hugged her dog. *I've missed you, you rascal,* she said, scratching his ears. *Can you believe it? Miguel proposed to me!*

Alistair barked and jumped on her shoulders, knocking her backwards. She laughed as he licked her face, and she pushed him off. *I'm glad you approve.*

***

The soft sound of rain against her window woke Mariah the next morning. She reached under her pillow and pulled out the pin from the wedding, smiling as she turned it over in her hands. Despite his injuries, Miguel had escorted her to her room, relying on Dom to steady him as he walked. When Miguel tried to stand guard at her door Nana had chased him off so that he, too, could rest. Mariah smiled at the memory and the sense that she again felt secure in her world. She was still in bed studying the silver brooch when Nana came in with her breakfast, the old woman's white hair coiled severely on her head.

"Bah! Still in bed? Youth is wasted on the young, I always say," Nana grumbled, setting down the tray and bustling around the room.

Mariah cheerfully threw off her covers and set her feet on the cool, tiled floor. "It's a beautiful morning, don't you think?"

"Only if you're in love." Nana pulled out a grey and green dress from the wardrobe.

"What of it? I am unapologetically in love and will soon be married to a wonderful man," Mariah dropped the dress over her head.

"*Felicitaciones,*" Nana said dryly as she worked the laces closed.

"*Gracias.*" Mariah started brushing her long, black hair, but Nana took the brush and gestured Mariah to the waiting breakfast of fruit and a boiled egg.

"Have you heard any more from my father yet?" Mariah asked between bites of her breakfast as Nana worked through her hair.

"*Si*, he arrived not too long ago, too weary for breakfast. He thinks he's still the young man he used to be, but this life, it has allowed him to go soft."

Mariah smiled at the thought of her father, Ciro Álvarez Bosque, being soft. To her, he was tall, strong, capable, and unconquerable. "I'm sure he knows his limits." Mariah shrugged.

"Men his age know no such thing. Their youth sneaks away from them while their head is turned, and when it comes time for them to run, they find they can barely walk. But a man like your father, his spirit is still that of the man he was twenty years ago, all fire and strength, capable of fixing all that is wrong in the world." Nana's voice had turned sober as she twisted up parts of Mariah's hair into a knot, held in place with a tortoiseshell comb, and letting the rest falling in gentle, dark curls down Mariah's neck. "He still sees himself as he was, but, mind me now, he will soon go out expecting to do what has been done before, but this time, his body will fail him, and he will not succeed."

Mariah felt a twinge of foreboding as a silence fell between them. She shook her head, refusing to let the feeling linger. What would old Nana know about such things?

Mariah finished eating and had Nana hold up her hair for her while she tied on her mother's necklace. Her father had presented it to her the previous year, explaining that the stone had been particularly precious to her mother. She touched the cool pink stone where it rested on her throat. Her father had it set in silver, surrounded by a dozen diamond chips, and strung on a rope of pearls. Her father rarely spoke of Mariah's mother, Ayelen Cordova, a Spanish woman with some French heritage. Most of what Mariah knew, she'd wheedled out of old Nana. One thing had always been clear to her, though: her father had loved her mother.

Mariah checked herself over in her mirror, tucked a red carnation into her hair beside the comb, and left her room with no particular direction in mind. The scents of earth wet from the morning's light rain and flowers from the *hacienda's* gardens filled the halls of the main house. Soon, she found herself in her father's study, sorting through papers that hadn't been seen to the day before. The cozy room reminded her of her father, from the warm wood accents of the walls and the bright morning sunlight that slanted down through the windows, to the orderly stacks of books and papers that filled every shelf and bookcase in the room.

"*Buenos días,*" Mariah said absently when Miguel came in, her mind entirely focused on the papers before her. "How are you feeling?"

"*Buenos días,*" Miguel said, joining her with the paperwork. "My ribs still feel like they've been kicked by a horse, but otherwise, I feel as good as new."

She gave him an appraising look. He'd changed into clean clothes, his standard well- worn and comfortable looking pants, a linen shirt, and a light jacket, despite the warmth and humidity of the climate. His customary cutlass hung from his hip, and Mariah had no doubt he'd stashed his knives and at least two pistols somewhere on his person. He'd chosen his old, worn boots, likely for their comfort more than anything else, and had pulled his long dark hair into a queue at his neck. But his green eyes were clear when she met them, and he seemed alert enough. Even his English accent was minimal this morning. She moved a file from her stack and set it in front of him. "If you say so."

She watched him sign his name to one of the documents. His normal flowing script seemed a little more forced today as the pen spelled out his adopted surnames.

"Miguel?" Mariah asked. "Are you sure you want to keep the surnames we gave you? Blanco del Mar? Wouldn't you rather go by your real family name, whatever it is?"

Miguel's smile held a touch of sadness in it. "I left that behind me when I stepped off that ship. A new place, a new name, truly a new start."

"Will you ever tell me what it was?" she asked, taking his hand.

"Perhaps some day. But I prefer to let dead things be. I am happier here than I've ever been in my life. Would you want to be someone other than Mariah Alvarez Cordova? Should we follow English tradition, and you can drop your family names to take mine?"

"And erase my family history? Not a chance." Mariah shook her head at the absurdity of it. "I am proud to carry my father's name of Alvarez, and I have precious little of my mother's. I could not think of giving up her name of Cordova."

"It is the same for me, *mi morena*. Miguel Blanco del Mar is the only name I want." He squeezed her hand gently, and she let it go, turning back to her work.

The third time he sat back, rubbing his eyes, his face pale, she set down her pen. "You're supposed to be resting. Go sit over there. I can handle this on my own for now."

Miguel rose, the pain in his movements apparent despite his attempt to hide it. He sat gingerly on the overstuffed chair and closed his eyes, turning his face away from the morning sunlight. She continued to work, but after several minutes she rose and shut the blinds to the window, casting the room into an almost twilight gloom. Miguel returned to the desk, insisting he felt better without the bright light.

They worked together, Mariah managing the figures and Miguel sorting things, until Don Ciro came in, looking a little worse for wear despite having bathed and donned fresh clothes. He sat at his desk after greeting them, watching as they continued through the accounts.

"I don't know how I managed all these years without the help of you two," he said with a chuckle. Mariah smiled and Miguel shrugged. When he didn't get more of a response Ciro tried again. "Is there any news I need to be made aware of?"

"Nothing out of the ordinary," Mariah flipped through the portfolios and pulled one out of the stack. "The Ortiz account is behind again—"

Ciro heaved a dramatic sigh, and Mariah looked up at him with a raised eyebrow.

"That can wait," Ciro said. "I'm sure there is another recent development that ought to be made official?"

"Oh, that." Mariah set down her papers and sat back. A giddy feeling grew in her chest, and she couldn't help the small smile that formed on her lips. "Miguel?"

"Don Ciro." Miguel took Mariah's hand. "Your daughter and I have decided to be married. We would ask for your blessing, but it would appear you've already given it."

"Indeed I have." Ciro's hearty voice boomed, and Mariah felt Miguel flinch. "I am happy for you, *mi querida.* For you both, Miguel. I think you will do well together. Now, when shall we plan for this happy event to occur?"

"I will need at least a year to save enough for a modest estate," Miguel said tentatively.

"Nonsense, Miguel. Mariah is my only heir, and all that I have will pass to her. This *hacienda* is hers when I die, and all that goes with it. I would rather you continue on with me, both of you, to take it over in the next couple of years." He chuckled and added, "That way I can retire and spend my time playing with my grandbabies."

Mariah blushed at the implication as Miguel stood and enthusiastically shook her father's hand.

Miguel's smile nearly split his face. "I would be honored, Don Ciro."

"Miguel, just 'Ciro,' please. My congratulations to you both, again. A year is a respectable enough length for an engagement, but you might be wiser to wait a year and a half, as there is always less rain in January. That is, of course, if that is acceptable to you, Mariah."

"Of course, Papa."

Ciro gave her a strange look, then pulled her out of her chair and gave her a huge hug. "I'm so proud of you, *mi querida*. I can hardly believe you're old enough to be married. I love you."

"I love you too, Papa." She hugged him back as tightly as she could.

"Now, I think this demands some celebration. Mariah, would you go let the cooks know to make something extra special for tonight? Perhaps, also send an announcement to Don Sergio and his family inviting them to supper."

"Certainly." She smiled. Today was going to be a wonderful day, and if she had to deal with Elisa a little, well, that wasn't going to spoil things. Mariah had never really gotten on well with Elisa Díaz Palomo, Betania's younger sister. Elisa was only a year or so younger than Mariah, but Mariah couldn't help thinking of her as a child. At the same time, however, she didn't mind the girl. Mariah had practically been raised with Betania and Elisa. Doña Olivia Palomo Mingo, Señora de la Cuesta, had insisted on taking the motherless Mariah under her wing. The formidable woman had taught Mariah much, but it was old Nana, the Wayuu woman with the long, silver hair and a penchant for teaching Mariah the native's legends, who was the closest thing Mariah had to a mother.

Mariah left the men to their work, reminding them both that the healer had ordered Miguel to rest, and did as her father bid her. The cooks were excited at the prospect of a party and often made treats for themselves as well, a habit Ciro encouraged. He believed that servants who enjoyed their lives were not only a great asset, but also better cooks.

Once the messenger was dispatched, Mariah went in search of Nana. She found the Wayuu woman elbow deep in a sudsy wash bucket, working on laundry beside a mestizo servant girl a couple of years younger than Mariah. Mariah didn't recognize her and thought she must be new to the *hacienda*. Gonza had called her father a mestizo-lover, and had meant it as an insult. While it was true Ciro Alvarez hired more than his share of mestizos—people of mixed heritage—as well as full-blooded Wayuu, Mariah could not consider it a bad thing. Ciro took care of his employees, Wayuu, Mestizo, or Spaniard alike. She had grown up watching her father treat them as equals, regardless of the opinion of Society. And she would never be anything but proud of him for it.

"What is it that you want, child?" Nana asked Mariah, handing her a wet shirt.

"There is to be a celebration tonight, Nana!" Mariah grinned and began wringing and hanging the clothes Nana handed her.

"Bah, I'm too old to enjoy celebrations. They mean more work for these old bones."

"Nonsense. It will be fun. You haven't asked what we're celebrating."

"I'll celebrate finishing the wash. Hand me the soap there, *chica.*" Nana gestured with her chin, attacking another shapeless garment.

"Here. You can celebrate that if you want, but the rest of us are celebrating my engagement to Miguel," Mariah said, joy coloring her voice.

"Bah. Celebrate the engagement with a wedding and leave me less work until then."

Mariah caught the good-natured smile that Nana attempted to hide. The girl beside Nana gave her a horrified look, and Mariah winked at her. The girl blushed and ducked her head, focusing intently on her work.

"What do you think I should do for my dress?" Mariah continued, undeterred.

"Black," Nana said flatly, "with black lace."

"You're no help at all! Of course it will be black. It should be silk, though." Mariah babbled on about what cut it would have and how many layers of petticoats, while Nana grunted her approval or made suggestions.

As they talked, a cloud entered Mariah's mind, muting her joy. "To tell the truth, though—"

"You should always tell the truth." Nana turned to the girl who watched their conversation in open shock. "Ana, we can finish without you. I'm sure Cook needs help. Go on."

Ana nodded and dried her hands before running back to the house.

"Of course. As I was saying, the Díaz family is coming to dinner tonight—"

"What of it? They're good friends of your father's."

"They're coming to dinner tonight, and I worry about how Elisa will take it." Mariah rushed through her sentence before Nana could cut her off again.

"Why should she be a bother to you?"

"I don't know," Mariah sighed. "She's just always jealous if I have something she doesn't, and I am worried she will not take the news well."

"She's a spoiled girl. It would do her some good to learn that not everything is about her."

"I suppose." Mariah shrugged, but she couldn't help worrying. What could Elisa possibly do to mess this up for her? She couldn't imagine, but knowing Elisa, the girl would find a way.

Once they had finished hanging the laundry, Mariah returned to her father's study but was informed that her help would not be needed for the afternoon.

With nothing better to do, Mariah found her copy of Robinson Crusoe and set out for the garden to read. The rain had cleared up, but the clouds overhead promised its return. The humidity stuck her dress to her skin, but she didn't mind all that much. She preferred the chance to be outside when she could.

Mariah settled down on a bench beneath a massive *roble de sabana*, its green branches shading the path, stark against the white stucco of the garden wall. Birds chattered and chirped in the foliage, unconcerned with her presence as Mariah opened her well-worn book to a random page and began reading. After a time, the disconcerting feeling of being watched by unfriendly eyes pulled her from the pages. Looking up, she found Elisa, standing proud and arrogant, her blond hair pinned high on her head, glaring at her from across the garden.

They looked at each other for a long moment, a breeze whispering through the *roble*'s leaves.

"It's been a long time since you were here last," Mariah said, finally breaking the silence.

"It hasn't changed much." Elisa's voice held a hint of disgust as she glanced across the garden.

Mariah marked her place and closed the book. "I like it well enough."

"I'm sure you do, wrapped nice and snug in your little haven." Elisa walked around, feigning interest in the various plants and finding them horribly lacking.

Mariah watched her quietly, noting that Elisa had dressed herself in the latest fashion, far too elegantly for the occasion, her dress cut almost to the point of impropriety.

"If it is so distasteful to you, why do you remain?" Mariah said when Elisa snorted at her fourth plant. "Really, this aloof attitude does not become you."

"What does not become me," Elisa said, continuing her poised perusal of the flora, "is being forced into bad company."

"I do not see anyone holding a knife to your neck." Mariah leaned to the side as though to look for a person behind Elisa. "Perhaps he is invisible?"

Elisa turned and looked down her nose at Mariah, who remained on her bench, unruffled.

"What does not become me," Elisa said serenely, "is coming to congratulate a mestizo bastard girl on her engagement to some sea mongrel." She gave a small laugh as though she couldn't believe what she was about to say. "I am here for my father, who, for some absurd reason, feels an obligation to your father."

How dare she! Mariah stood, grateful that she had the advantage in height. Schooling her face to calmness, she leveled her gaze at the girl before her.

"I know how highly you prize your standing in society, so I will not tell anyone of your gross breach of etiquette, not to mention your slanderous tongue." Mariah allowed a note of disdain to enter her polite tone. "Perhaps you ought to go run to your father. I'm sure his presence will help to quell your childish impulses, and if his will not, no doubt your mother's can." She gave Elisa one last hard look and strode away.

The rich, wet scent of rain followed Mariah to the house, along with the sound of the first heavy drops of rain hitting the orange tiles of the covered walkway. *Good,* she thought. *Let that wisp of a girl ruin her fine dress.* Elisa's words sat like a rock in her belly. What had she meant by it, calling Mariah a mestizo? Mariah knew she wasn't a bastard; it had been made clear to her at various times in her life that her parents had been married, but was it possible that she could, in fact, be of mixed blood?

Mariah rubbed her hand against her dress, the cloth still damp in a spot from a moment of carelessness helping Nana. In an unexpected rush, she recalled all the times that servants seemed to have been extra-kind to her, treating her so much less formally than everyone else. She ran to her room, shut the door, and peered into the mirror to scrutinize her features.

Her eyes were still the same dark, rich brown they had always been, a color so deep that it was difficult to tell where the iris ended and the pupil began. Her hair, even darker than her eyes, waved gently down her back. Her high cheekbones gave a soft definition to her somewhat wide face, but nothing so different from any other Spaniard. Even her skin was rich olive color, darker certainly than Elisa and Betania's, but not unusually so for a Spaniard. She shook her head at her silliness and stepped back from her reflection.

"She was just trying to ruffle your feathers," Mariah consoled herself.

"It looks like she succeeded." Mariah spun around to see Nana standing quietly in the doorway.

"What did she say to get you so upset?"

"Nothing worth repeating."

Nana snorted.

Mariah gave a dismissive gesture. "She is upset about not getting Miguel and so she flung insults. She called me a mestizo and Miguel a sea mongrel. Calling Miguel a dog I'd expect, she's done that from the beginning, but calling me a mestizo is a new low for her." She busied her hands in the silence that followed by straightening her dress and adjusting her mother's necklace.

"I see," was all the answer she got from the old woman.

After composing herself, Mariah left the room, determined to finish her role as hostess as well as she could for the evening. The meal went smoothly, though Elisa remained cold and aloof. Mariah noted with satisfaction the stains from the rain on Elisa's elaborate dress. Señor and Señora de la Cuesta were lively guests and spoke a great deal with their hosts about a range of topics, from past escapades of Sergio's and Ciro's lives as young traders to the current political climate and the growing tension with the natives. Mariah found it fascinating, invigorating, and a little strange, since Doña Olivia had never spoken with her as an adult before.

As the guests prepared to leave, there were more congratulations, and even Elisa condescended to offer terse felicitations. When the Diaz family had finally driven away and the doors were shut, Mariah, Miguel, and Ciro sagged with exhaustion.

"I thought they'd never leave," Miguel joked, rubbing the back of his head. "My face hurts from smiling so much."

"You'd better work on those muscles, then," Mariah laughed, nudging him. "I expect you to smile all the time."

"You're a hard taskmistress. Have mercy on me." Miguel pulled her close, and heat filled her face as he kissed her jaw.

"Shall we go to my study?" Ciro cut in, unperturbed.

Mariah pushed away from Miguel but held his hand, following her father to his study.

"Well, it certainly was a pleasant evening," her father said as they passed through the study's door.

"Except for Elisa." Miguel shook his head, letting go of Mariah and taking a seat on the couch. "She acted like she had mold in her dress or something."

"It would serve her right if she did," Mariah said irritably, leaning against a mantle displaying several old revolvers.

"What do you mean?" Ciro settled himself into his favorite chair.

"She sought me out when they first got here so that she could tell me that the marriage of a mestizo girl and a sea mongrel was a waste of her time. She's changed lately, and I don't think it is for the better." Mariah pushed away from the mantle and took a seat in a nearby chair.

Miguel snorted at the comment, but Ciro went very still, and Mariah looked over at him curiously.

"What is it, Ciro?" Miguel asked quietly.

Her father heaved a sigh and walked to Mariah.

"I should have told you about this long ago, *mi querida*," Ciro said sadly, kneeling next to Mariah's chair. He touched the stone on her necklace, seeing things from long ago.

"Tell me what, Papa?" Mariah asked softly, smoothing the wrinkles of his shirt across his shoulders.

"I loved your mother dearly. I first met her shortly after I'd broken with my first business partner."

"Gonza?" Miguel asked, and Ciro nodded.

"Our partnership failed over differing moral stances. I had a need to leave Maracaibo for a time, and a fellow, the son of a Spanish merchant himself, offered to take me along on his trading route. We stopped at his home, a Wayuu village, far to the north of here."

The knot in Mariah's stomach tightened.

"And there, like an angel, was your mother. I loved her from the first time I saw her. She was very kind to me, helping me more than perhaps I deserved. As soon as we could, we married. Ayelen was an amazing woman. I'd always hoped to return there someday…"

"Why didn't you tell me?" Mariah whispered, shaking her head in disbelief. "You let me believe…" *a lie.* How could he have lied to her for so long?

"What good would it have done?" Ciro hung his head and sat back on his heels. "The way the wealthy Spanish colonists treated Ayelen before I met her wounded her deeply, though she was far too proud to admit it. She had almost entirely given up her Spanish heritage by the time we met. She never wanted that for you, Mariah, and I agreed. At best, you would have been treated no better by Society than they treat servants, but more likely they would have treated you worse for being my daughter. People are cruel, especially when they feel afraid."

"What would they have to be afraid of from me?"

Miguel gave her a thoughtful nod. "They feel they have dominance here by right of their birth. You would fly in the face of that. They would feel threatened, because if you could be in the upper circles of society, then why not their servants? They would see that their position is not as secure as they want to believe."

"You still should have told me." Bitterness constricting Mariah's throat. "What else have you kept from me? Is my mother still alive somewhere?"

"Nothing, *mi querida,* nothing, I promise," Ciro said quickly. "As for your mother, I dearly wish she was—" His voice broke, and he returned to his chair, staring despondently into the fire.

"And what secrets do you keep from me that I ought to have known?" Mariah turned her pain toward Miguel.

"I will tell you anything you ask." Miguel took her hand. She threw herself into his embrace, taking comfort in his strong arms. He spoke quietly to her while she rested her head against his chest. "I'm sure it was hard for your father to never openly speak of your mother. I think that if I ever lost you, I would do everything I could to keep your memory alive. However, I believe Ciro has been wise to keep this secret."

Mariah pulled away a little to look at Miguel. "How could you think lying to me is a good thing?"

"You are to inherit all that he has, *mi morena*, and if it is found out that you are mestizo, not a full Spaniard, people will fight to rob you of what is yours. All that he has done, he has done for you."

Ciro roused from his reflections and looked at his daughter. "It is true, *hija*. After your mother died, you were my only direction, my only reason not to return to the sea and lose myself as quickly as I could. Perhaps, sometimes, I have even envied Vasco the ease of his escape after his wife died in childbirth, but I loved your mother too much. I loved *you* too much to run away like he did."

"I think it would be prudent to continue to keep this quiet," Miguel added. "I think so long as we don't make a fuss of it, any rumors Elisa starts will come across as nothing more than spite."

Mariah looked into the fire. Perhaps they were right. It all felt too big for her to handle. She nodded her agreement. They understood better the intricacies of politics, and she didn't want to try to understand it all right now. They spent the rest of the evening quietly making plans for the wedding along with how to handle any further accusations. It was past midnight before they separated to go to their own rooms.

Mariah flopped down onto her bed with a sigh, and Nana materialized out of the darkness.

"What a long day." Mariah dragged herself to her feet and began undressing.

"Indeed," Nana said softly.

"I can't believe I never figured it out. Why couldn't you at least have told me?"

"I would have, but Ayelen asked me not to," Nana said, her voice unusually subdued.

"And you loved Ayelen more than me?"

Nana shook her head. "I have served the women of your family for a long time. Asking which I loved best would be like asking a mother which of her children she cherished more."

Mariah thought a moment as she pulled off her dress. "Was it she who told you not to talk of her?"

"No, that was your father's request." Nana took the dress and handed Mariah her night dress. "I only obeyed because it served Ayelen's wishes as well."

"Wishes? Besides hiding my heritage from me?"

"Ayelen was also of both worlds. Her mother was Wayuu and her father a Spaniard. He stayed with us in the village. He taught her and her twin brother the ways of the Spaniards, and to speak Castilian, alongside her mother, who taught them how to live as her people, the Wayuu. When they were old enough, she and her brother went with him to see the towns and live for a time among her father's people."

Mariah sat on the side of the bed, her irritation forgotten, enraptured to hear the tale of her mother and grandparents.

"She was beautiful, talented, smart. Well-spoken and well-mannered. But whenever her or her father's peers learned she was mestizo, they would turn on her. She used to tell me that she could see it in their eyes the moment it happened, when their thoughts turned to disdain. She learned to rise above it, of course, but it always bothered her.

"There was one man, though, whose eyes never hardened against her. Despite many of the young men who sought her out among her mother's people, it was this Spanish merchant with whom she fell in love."

"My father!" Mariah perked up in excitement.

"Your father, Ciro Álvarez Bosque." Nana nodded, sitting on the bed beside her. "His eyes would follow her everywhere. At first, she rebuffed him as insincere, but his persistence eventually won her over. 'It was his eyes,' she told me once. In his eyes, she could see that he never cared that she was anyone but Ayelen Zyanya."

"Zyanya?" Mariah asked. "Not Cordova?"

"Your grandfather's name was Cordova. But by right, you are Mariah Álvarez Zyanya."

"Zyanya," Mariah repeated, trying the unfamiliar name on her tongue. "Does it mean anything?"

Nana gave Mariah an appraising look. Just as Mariah began to squirm under the scrutiny, Nana answered. "It means forever, or eternal. The women of your line have continued, unbroken, for a very long time. You are the firstborn daughter of a firstborn daughter whose mother, too, was a firstborn daughter, back generation upon generation."

Nana hesitated, took a deep breath, and continued. "Do you remember the story I told you, *hija*? The Wayuu legend of the Slaver and the Noble One?"

"Of course. I told it to Miguel and the girls once. He told us a story of a murderous, blood-sucking vampire called Arnold Paule in Europe. They dug up his grave and stabbed him with a stake, and then burned him for good measure." Mariah smiled at the memory of the way Miguel had used the light of the bonfire to frighten and delight the girls as he'd told his gruesome tale.

"What do you remember of the Slaver and Noble One?" Nana prompted.

"It's the one where a strange, pale-skinned man appeared on the Wayuu shores centuries ago, with unnatural speed and strength. The Wayuu had been a peaceful people, and so they welcomed him, but he, in return, used his magic and enslaved the youth, hence the name of the Slaver."

"And the Noble One?"

Mariah wondered what this had to do with anything, but her curiosity demanded she go along with it. "Some time later, another one of these creatures showed up, and this time the Wayuu were cautious, despite this man's claim of noble intentions."

"He claimed to be able to free us from the Slaver who had stolen so very much from our people already. When the elders had tried everything else they could think of and still failed to free themselves from the power of the Slaver, they turned to the noble one. He did as he said they would, but he was as they had originally feared, a trickster. The price he extracted from the Wayuu was even higher than the Slaver, but he kept his promise to help the Wayuu. To this day, they maintain their independence from all foreign invaders. This is why there have been two major rebellions against the colonists already." Mariah picked at a bit of lint on her skirt. "Does Papa believe that tale? Is that why he thinks there will be another war?"

"That is the one, but I don't know if your father knows of it or not." Nana shook her head. "There is more to that tale than I have told you. Your mother knew, of course, but asked that I not say anything until you were ready."

"You think I'm old enough now?" Mariah tried to swallow down the bitterness in the back of her throat. Even Nana kept things from her.

"I think there is no reason not to tell you, now that you know about your mother's family."

"Well, late though it is, today seems to be the day for telling me things." Mariah tried to make light of the knowledge that, once again, important information had been hidden from her. *That's just the way it is. Everyone lie to Mariah, she won't mind.*

Nana took both of Mariah's hands into hers. "There is a prophecy connected to that tale."

Mariah raised an eyebrow but didn't interrupt.

"It is said that one day a woman will arise who will free us from the continued servitude of the Noble One and the Slaver. One who will destroy those bloodsucking vipers who prey upon the hearts of our most vulnerable."

Irritation rose up in Mariah. She was exhausted, and while being kept up later for tales of her mother was one thing, foolish ghost stories were quite another. "Why is this so important to tell me now? Why could it not have waited until the morning?"

"I'm telling you because you deserve to know. I'm telling you because the woman in the prophecy will be one of the Zyanya. She will be the last of the unbroken line. We will know her by her firstborn being a son."

Mariah had had enough and pulled her hands gently from Nana's grasp. "And you believe this?"

"I'm certain of it."

"Nana." Mariah shook her head. "I'm tired, and I've had a lot thrown at me today. Don't try to saddle me with some native ghost story that you think I'm part of and expect me to believe it."

Sighing, Nana stood to leave. She stopped at the door on her way out and looked back at Mariah, sitting on her bed in the lamplight.

"Your mother believed it."

"Not tonight, Nana."

"Do you ever have strange dreams?" Nana tried one last time, but Mariah had had enough.

"Good night, old woman." Mariah blew out the lamp, dropping the room into starlit darkness. She heard her door close without another word. Relieved, she dropped onto her pillows and was asleep within seconds.

Chapter 3

DECEMBER 1740

THE BROAD, DEEP green leaves of the roble trees, half again as long and nearly wide as Miguel's hand, swayed in the gentle wind. The trees that lined the road ahead of him moved in the dark night like dancers to music. Miguel shifted his heavy blue greatcoat on his shoulders, ignoring itching sweat that had formed on his back. Mariah had given him the coat shortly before they'd begun courting, and though it was uncomfortably warm, it excelled at keeping out the unending rain, protecting the powder of his flintlocks.

His horse snorted, shaking his head and prancing, much to Miguel's irritation. The scar on his ribs still pulled, and, despite the months since the attack at Betania's wedding, nights like tonight still made his skull ache. But that was no reason to not keep his wits about him. Miguel touched the hilt of his cutlass, confident that it remained loose in the scabbard. He ran a mental checklist of his other weapons—two pistols and three knives—as he scanned the shadowy buildings.

Exhaustion pressed on him as thickly as the humidity. He, Dom, and Ciro had already had a full day of work inspecting the ships and cargoes before they'd gone off to find Gonza. The man had escaped, and rumors of his sudden ill health had passed through the community. Miguel wasn't certain, but it was likely close enough to midnight that Mariah would be worried despite the messenger they'd sent back several hours ago. *Or perhaps because of it.* Miguel's horse snorted again, snapping at the tall grass beside the road.

"Keep your head up, mate," he said quietly, pulling up the gelding's head and patting his neck. "There'll be plenty of hay for you when we're safely home."

"You all right there, *amigo*?" Dom asked, looking back at Miguel. Ciro's steward and unofficial bodyguard rode beside his employer, their horses walking further ahead and at a more energetic pace than Miguel's.

"Fine." Miguel urged his horse forward, but the gelding ignored the signal. What was it that made horses hate him? "It's just quiet. I'm not sure I dare to trust that Gonza is really no longer a threat. We should pick up the pace."

Dom turned and spoke in a low voice to Ciro, who hadn't spoken since he'd seen Gonza, or what was left of him, with his own eyes. Ciro nodded and kicked his horse to a trot with Dom following suit.

"You better pick up the pace," Miguel said to his horse. Before he could adjust his seat, the gelding started off in a swift and uncomfortable gait to catch his stablemates as the walls of the *hacienda* came into view.

The three horses came to a clattering stop in the courtyard beside the stable, where Mariah stood waiting, wrapped in a dark shawl with a lamp at her feet. Almost before Miguel's feet had touched the ground, Mariah threw herself into his arms. He pulled her close, savoring the softness of her body and the warm, floral scent she wore. Someday, he would have to ask her the name of the flower, he decided, kissing the top of her head.

"I see how it is," Ciro said, dismounting, a playfulness in his voice that Miguel knew was forced. "Now that you are getting married, you don't even have a hug for your old Papa."

Miguel let her go, and she gave her father a grin. "I'd have hugged you first, but you're so slow to get off your horse, I might have died of old age if I'd waited."

"You're impossible, *chica.*" Her father pulled her into a hug, and Miguel smiled as the last of her tension melted away in her father's embrace. *How would it have been to have a father like that?* Though Ciro treated him increasingly like family, Miguel knew no one would ever love him as unconditionally as Ciro loved his daughter. Miguel handed a sleepy young stablehand his horse's reins.

"What happened? Why have you been gone all day?" Mariah nodded a greeting to Dom and led them across the courtyard to the main house.

"Can't it wait until we had some food?" Ciro asked with a sigh, removing his coat and draping it over his arm.

"There's food for you in the study and has been for hours. Now, what happened?"

"Antonio Gonza is as good as dead." Miguel took Mariah's hand as they entered the house. "He is refusing to tell the authorities who shot him, but word is his wound has gone septic. I hope, for his own sake, it kills him quickly."

Miguel gave her hand a quick squeeze before letting it go and removing his own coat as they entered the cool study. The gentle glow of the lamps against the pale stucco walls gave it the feel of sanctuary as the weary men entered, and Mariah took their coats, setting them across the back of a chair. Miguel's eyes were drawn immediately to the food set out on the side table. Though his stomach growled, he held back, allowing Ciro to go first. Mariah stood beside her father, who merely stared down at the food.

"He was your friend once, wasn't he?" She touched her father's arm lightly.

"Once," Ciro responded gruffly, turning away from her. Her hand fell away, coming to rest on the table. "Have something brought to my room. I'll see you two in the morning."

She watched, hurt and confusion on her face, as Ciro stormed away. This, at least, was something Miguel understood. He stepped closer, taking her hand,

and she leaned in to him with a sigh. He ran his thumb across the back of her hand, organizing his thoughts.

"It is hard for him. Seeing Gonza was like looking at a living skeleton." Miguel rubbed absently the long-healed stab wound on his ribs.

"That could have just as easily been you," she said softly, pulling her hand away and handing him a plate.

Miguel took the plate and set the cold food onto it, ignoring the dull ache in his head. "You have to understand that if it weren't for Gonza trying to have your father killed, he never would have met your mother. So while that man is responsible for some of the hardest parts of Ciro's life, he's also the cause of some of the best. And, as you pointed out, they were once friends."

"Seems strange to credit him for happiness when he's been trying to kill us," Mariah said dryly.

Miguel shrugged and tossed a grape into his mouth, the glorious, juicy sweetness of it exploding on his tongue. When had he last eaten anyway? He took a seat on the couch by the empty fireplace, watching her.

"What of his business? The rumors in town are that Gonza was ruined when the ships were delayed." Mariah's concern for her father was written across her face as she looked, unseeing, at the food before her. Setting her empty plate back on the table, she turned instead to sit on the couch across from Miguel.

Miguel shook his head. "When his latest planned shipment didn't show up, it ruined him. It seemed he owed considerable amounts of money to the wrong people, and they have picked him dry, unwilling to wait longer for his ships. Naturally, he blames your father for this."

Mariah nodded. "Because this was the one that Papa refused to take. I remember hearing about that early on. Papa said that if he took Gonza's entire shipment and any of the ships went down or were delayed, it would ruin his client."

"But all your father's ships have returned and departed again since then." Miguel shrugged, taking a bite from his empanada. He savored the spiciness of the perfectly tender meat as he chewed. "The only positive side to all this is that Gonza can no longer cause us problems. Your father even set up a trust for the man's son, though Gonza tried to spit in his face when he told him."

"How did things go with Sergio today?" Mariah asked after a pause to let Miguel swallow.

"About the same. I think Sergio remains in awe of your father, but Ciro has been a little more cool to him. Overall, the crop should be good this year, though, so there's little to worry about on that front. How about you? How were things with Betania today?"

Mariah grinned, her entire demeanor lightening. "You'll never believe it, but Selena has a beau. She's been downright chipper the last couple of weeks."

Mariah loved spending time with Betania and Betania's cousin, Selena. When he'd been employed as Mariah's bodyguard, Miguel had spent many hours listening to them chatter from the other side of the walled garden at the de la Cuesta plantation. He still laughed at some of the strange things they'd come up with, though, more often than not, the conversations had turned to discussing boys.

Mariah continued while he ate another empanada, this one just as delicious as the first.

"I think being married suits Betania, though. She's still terribly enamored with Benito, always going on about his accomplishments or giggling of his endearing inadequacies."

"Endearing inadequacies?" Miguel wiggled his eyebrows at her, and she rolled her eyes.

"Just because she finds them sweet doesn't mean I would." Mariah ran her long fingers over the upholstery of the couch, picking at a loose thread. "As lovey, idyllic, and carefree as their futures look, I don't envy them. They'll run a home, but I'll run a business with you in addition to our home. Their children will grow up with hardly a care in the world beyond wearing the latest fashions, but ours—" Mariah blushed, a subtle rose spreading across the gentle, tawny bronze of her skin "—will always have the stigma of being mestizo lurking in their shadows. Their families will be able to proudly show pedigrees going back generations, and ours will show only one line in four."

"And that bothers you." Miguel had thought little of the legacy he might pass on to his children someday, but he would never regret his choice to start with a blank slate. *Blanco del Mar, indeed.*

Mariah smiled and moved to sit next to him, taking his hand. "Just the opposite. Don't you see? Our children will know the satisfaction of earning what they have and of marrying for love's sake and not because it is good for business. Betania has been fortunate in that respect with Benito."

Miguel nodded. "I suppose that's true. As much as Elisa likes to pout about it, had I tried to court her, Betania, or even Selena instead of you, the match would have been rejected outright. There is far too much of a class difference between us."

"But I'm just a wealthy merchant's daughter, free to accept whomever I choose."

Miguel laughed and squeezed her hand. "Even some stray puppy the ocean saw fit to deposit at your feet?"

"Even then." Mariah stood, took his empty plate, and returned to the side table.

Leaning back, Miguel stretched out against the couch with a yawn. "What's been going on with Elisa these days anyhow? I haven't heard much about her lately."

Mariah returned to Miguel, his empty plate now laden with food. "All I know is what Betania tells me. She says Elisa has moved on from our circle of acquaintances. She doesn't talk to a single one."

"I'm afraid I just can't see that as a loss. Thank you." Miguel took the refilled plate from Mariah and immediately started in on it, as though he hadn't eaten in days instead of minutes. The moonlight that fell through the open window disappeared, and within moments, the whisper of the coming storm pushed its way through the trees.

Mariah rushed to shut the window before the rain began, and the first heavy drops pinged the glass as she returned to Miguel's side. "What did you hear today about the trouble with the Wayuu?"

Miguel had wondered when she'd bring that up. Ciro refused to talk to her about it, a policy Miguel heartily disagreed with. "I think major fighting is going to be inevitable. The upper class still tries to ignore the unrest, or believes it will pass and die out. Many think that if it comes to open rebellion that they will be able to put out any spark of trouble quickly, like they did back in '27."

"But Papa doesn't believe that." Mariah took Miguel's hand as he set down his plate and she gently traced the lines of his veins down the back of his hand with her fingers, sending a pleasant shiver through his body. She turned his hand over as the blue line made its way up the inside of his arm to his elbow, pushing his sleeve out of the way, then followed another back down to his palm. He sighed and leaned back, relaxing at her touch.

"No. And there are many like him, hidden in the corners of society who sympathize with the Wayuu." Miguel caught her hand with his before she could trace another vein up his arm. "He feels it is wrong to oppress them, and that the Spanish who came before us were wrong in stealing their lands, their riches, and their very lives. And I can't say I disagree."

Certainly the house staff knew where Don Ciro stood on the issue. Mariah still took an escort with her whenever she went out, but more and more often, it was one of the household staff rather than Miguel. He'd reluctantly turned over his duties as her bodyguard as Ciro had brought him more fully into the business. Having Ciro's trust had long been a point of pride for Miguel, but some days he longed for the simpler days when protecting her was his primary concern. But Don Ciro had a way of gathering loyalty from people, and Miguel trusted his men. They often treated Mariah as though they were protecting one of her own.

The demeanor of the town had changed along with the weather. It seemed that even the ever-present street music had begun to carry a tension.

"Nana thinks that Papa might try to go adventuring, and that will turn out badly for him." Mariah leaned her head on Miguel's shoulder. "I only hope Papa will do no more than talk. I couldn't bear it if he left to join the fighting. Do you think we could convince him that trying to help here will be enough?"

Miguel put his arm around her shoulder and held her tight, brushing his fingers over her arm. "I seriously doubt that, *mi morena*, but we can try."

Chapter 4

FEBRUARY 1741 - MARACAIBO

"**P**APA!" MARIAH cried out, watching her father stuff clothes into a saddlebag. "You can't do this!"

"Why not?" Ciro asked without pausing. "You don't need me to run the business anymore; you and Miguel have that well under control. You don't need me to protect you; Miguel and the staff do that without my help, and I'll be back before your wedding. As far as I can see, all matters here are settled, and I am a mere ornament."

"You're not!" Mariah took clothes out of the bag as quickly as he shoved them in. "I need you, Papa!"

Ciro stopped and looked at his daughter. His grey eyes, flanked by lines as much from laughter as from care, were full of both pain and longing.

"You're all grown up now, *mi querida*. It is time you learned to stand on your own, to trust in Miguel to support you when you feel you should fall, and to pick you up when you are down. That is the role of a husband," her father said gently, caressing Mariah's face.

She didn't feel grown just then. She felt like a young child standing on a ledge with nothing to hold on to.

"But why must *you* go? There are plenty of other men who will fight—"

"There are indeed, but they will be on the other side. I go to help your mother's people. You know how I feel about what is being done." Ciro returned to his packing.

Asking clearly wasn't going to work. She needed a different strategy. "You're not as young as you used to be," she said tentatively, moving him aside to repack his clothes, refolding them neatly inside the bag. "What if you get hurt and can't return?"

"Then I die for the cause that burns within me," he said fiercely. "It is a better choice than growing old and musty in a house, growing useless, becoming a burden."

Realizing that she had only furthered his resolve, Mariah closed her eyes, pushing back the tears that threatened to form.

"If you die there, who will I have for family at my wedding?" she said softly, gently placing the last of the clothes in his bag.

For the first time that morning, Ciro paused. A spark of hope lit within Mariah's heart.

"You are right," he said reluctantly, sitting down heavily on a chair.

"Of course she is," Miguel said cheerily, walking briskly into the room. He stopped abruptly at the sight of Ciro on the chair with his head in his hands. "What are you right about, *mi morena*?" he asked softly.

Mariah turned to Miguel, who pulled her into his arms. Perhaps he could talk some sense into her father. Pulling back, she spoke softly to him. "Papa has decided to leave for the rebellion. We've got to stop him. I've tried everything I can think of, but he won't listen to me. Maybe he'll listen to you. Please make him stay, Miguel. Please?"

"I think," Miguel said slowly, "that if a man feels strongly that he must do something, if he feels that he is morally bound to do that thing, then he must do it."

Mariah pulled away from Miguel in disbelief. How could he? He'd said he would help her convince her father to stay. She looked over to her father. Ciro met Miguel's steady gaze and nodded, standing slowly and returning to his packing.

"I must do this, *hija*. They are your mother's people, her family, and so they are mine. I stayed out of it last time they were slaughtered, for the sake of my infant daughter. But I cannot do it again," Ciro said. "As for your wedding, I do not like the idea of you marrying so young. I had hoped you could wait another year. You're still only eighteen. When you're as old as I am, eighteen seems so incredibly young. However, I think it would be best if you were married before I leave. If you will agree to it."

Mariah was speechless. Could she get her father to stay this way? Would Miguel be upset at having their engagement used this way?

"And if I don't?" she finally asked.

"Then I will leave tomorrow and try my best to return to you and finish my responsibility as your father."

"Miguel?" she asked, looking up at her fiancé with pleading eyes.

He looked back at her, his eyes kind, but the disappointment that lay beneath it was clear. In that moment, she knew she couldn't use him to manipulate her father. Miguel would see it as betrayal.

"I agree with your father," Miguel said, and Mariah dropped her hand from his arm, her fingers sliding down the soft cloth. "He needs to go. I would go, were I in his place. I would go with him now, except we both agree my place is here with you."

Mariah turned from him and dropped into a chair. Emotions warred within her, and she tried to sort through them. She dropped her head into her hands, the pressure building up again behind her eyes. How could Miguel betray her like this? He was supposed to side with her!

Her chest tightened, and she tried to steady herself through deep breaths. How could her father leave her to go and most likely die for people he hadn't seen in decades? How could he choose them over her?

She sat up, turning her head away from the talking men so that they wouldn't see, her hands clenched into fists. Didn't they know how much they were needed here? How much she needed them both?

How could her father, the only family she had, leave her all alone? Why, if he loved her, was he leaving her?

Something broke in Mariah, and she squeezed her eyes shut, pushing out the tears that had formed despite her efforts. Why, if she loved him, wasn't she letting him go?

Mariah swallowed and discreetly wiped her cheeks. Her father felt that she could do this. And she wouldn't be alone. She'd still have Nana and Miguel to help her. With a deep steadying breath, Mariah braced herself for what would come next.

"We will move the wedding," she said quietly. "We can get married tonight, if you think it can be arranged so quickly."

Ciro and Miguel both looked at her, startled.

"Are you sure, *mi querida*?" Ciro asked, walking toward her.

"Yes, Papa. If you feel you must go, then I must not stand in your way."

"Oh, Mariah, my little girl!" Ciro exclaimed, hugging her. "I will miss you. I'm glad to have lived to see you become such a woman."

"I love you, Papa," was all Mariah could say through her tears, feeling more like a child than ever as she clung to her father.

"I will see what can be arranged," Miguel said. Ciro nodded to him, and he left. Before long, Nana came in and led Mariah to her own room to wait.

Events swirled around Mariah as though she wasn't really a part of them. Nana produced a black silk dress from somewhere, and, after a quick fitting, started making the necessary adjustments for Mariah.

Mariah pulled out a shirt she had been working on for Miguel. She rubbed her fingers over the tight, decorative stitching. This shirt was not meant to have been the one she made for Miguel to wear on their wedding, but it would have to do. Spreading the shirt over her bed, she began planning what it would need to be fit for a groom. Gathering her sewing basket and the shirt, she sat beneath the sunny window in her bedroom. The memory of Miguel's sleeping face in the sunlight in that same chair made her smile as she picked loose the pattern.

The sun had moved enough to put her in shadow and her fingers ached by the time Miguel returned. "The priest was busy today, but he is prepared to marry us tomorrow evening."

Mariah nodded soberly and continued her needlework, listening to Miguel's soft footsteps as he left.

When her back and neck ached, her father appeared with black lace for her veil, all wrapped up in paper. She thanked him warmly, rolled her shoulders and stretched her neck, and returned to Miguel's shirt.

Mariah reached for the next color in her pattern, and with a start realized the light had faded enough that she could no longer tell the colors apart. She looked up, hoping to light a lamp, and her stomach growled. Setting the shirt aside, she stood and stretched. The movement felt as though she'd breathed for the first time in hours, and it cleared her mind. Had she really not eaten all day? What smelled so good? A tray of food sat on her side table along with an unlit lamp, and Mariah smiled, grateful for Nana's foresight.

Stifling a yawn, she lit the lamp and changed into her nightdress. Her mind churning, she sat down to her food. What was left to prepare for the wedding tomorrow night? Miguel's shirt was nearly finished. Putting together a mental list, she allowed her eyes to wander while she ate, and they stopped on a parcel. Pulling it nearer, she inspected it in the quiet lamp light. It was the lace her father had brought earlier, the paper wrapping fresh and crisp. Had she even thanked him for it? Unable to remember, she carefully unfolded the packaging and found a letter on old, yellowed paper on top of the lace. Opening it carefully, she read the strong, unfamiliar handwriting:

My Dearest Child,
There is so much that I would tell you, so much I would like to see. Old Nana says that you'll be a girl, and she is never wrong. I feel so strongly that I will not

be there for you, though I dearly wish to be. Who will teach you how to be a woman? Who will give you the love that you will need the first time your heart is broken? Who will show you your way?

It breaks my heart, knowing I will miss so much, but I trust my dear Ciro to take care of you the best that he knows how. Old Nana will be with you, too, to watch and guide you. Trust them, for I know they will never lead you wrong.

My heart is so full with love for you, though for me, you are still unborn. You move around inside me, kicking me restlessly, but I love you all the more. Know that when you read this, I will still be loving you.

I hope, too, that someday you will find a man worthy of your love. When you find that man, if he is worthy of you, he will cherish you as I know your father cherishes me. You must remember to love him with all of your heart. Your father and I have known such love. It is a force that overcomes all opposition, all obstacles, and even death will not long hinder it. I know my dearest Ciro will find me when his turn comes. I shan't be far from him, either. Or from you.

A lifetime of experiences I would impart to you, my daughter, a lifetime and more of hard-earned wisdom. But that would take longer than I have, and more pages and ink than there are. Old Nana and an old letter are poor substitutes, I know, but they are the best that I can give you.

I love you so!
Your loving mother,

Ayelen Cordova Zyanya

Mariah set the letter down with tears in her eyes and looked back to the dark lace, running her fingers over it. She pulled it out to try it on, and another, smaller bit of paper fell out. Setting the lace mantilla carefully across the table, Mariah picked the paper up. Her mother's handwriting flowed across it, this time weaker, crooked, and painstakingly written.

My dear Mariah,
I had hoped to last longer than this, a few years at least. You are such a beautiful baby, and you amaze me so.
This lace is for your veil when you are wedded to the man aforementioned. I have instructed my dear Ciro to buy the finest veil he could find, holding nothing back, as soon as he approved of your choice. I believe in his judgment; so, since you are reading this, know that you have my approval and best wishes, too.
Your loving mother,
Ayelen Cordova Zyanya

Mariah touched the lace again, hardly able to believe these letters had been waiting for her. They had been somewhere in this house her entire life, waiting, like a held breath, to speak to her. She again lifted the lace, folding it carefully and draping it over the back of her chair. Then, taking both letters and moving the lamp to her bedside, she slid to the floor beside her bed.

She read and reread her mother's last words, memorizing them and trying to soak in whatever of Ayelen's essence they held.

***

Nana came late in the night to clear away the food, hoping the fool girl had had enough sense to stop and eat at least. The lamp on the nightstand illuminated the sleeping Mariah, sweet Ayelen's letters clutched to the girl's chest. The gaping pain of loss tried to push its way wider in Nana's chest as she took the letters from Mariah and lifted the fool girl into her bed. Mariah stirred, and Nana hummed the quiet lullaby she'd sung to Mariah as a child, and the girl stilled. Gently, Nana moved Mariah's hair from her face, an echoing pain of all the children who'd come and gone before, bearing those same eyes, those same lips…

Nana drew back. She'd loved each of those children as dearly as she loved Mariah. Snorting, she shook her mind from its pensiveness. She had work still to do. Fold and put away the veil, clean up the dishes, blow out the lamp. She shook her head, and her wordless song stopped. Weddings were harbingers for the life to come and deserved great celebrations. Such dark events would bring nothing but trouble.

***

Mariah walked through a field of grass. Before her the distant mountains loomed, a silent sentinel over the noisy jungle that spread from their feet. Behind her, just as distant, lay Lake Maracaibo and home. A warm breeze flowed over her and brought with it the scent of roses and water. The wind playing with her hair, Mariah turned her face toward the sunny sky. It would rain soon, but it always rained here.

The jungle noises intensified, and a sound she'd never heard before seemed to thread its way beneath it all. Curious, she turned toward the distant dark foliage. A familiar growl made her turn and she threw herself at her dog, wrapping her arms around Alistair's strong body.

Everything is changing, she sobbed to him, spilling her emotions as he pressed against her as though trying to knock her to the ground. She only held him tighter, the feelings of being left behind by those she loved flowed around her, forming into waves of deep blue. The water had carried away her mother. It had carried away her beloved Alistair. Now her father was leaving her, and each one had been her fault.

Alistair pulled away and cocked his head as if to disagree. Mariah settled herself onto the ground, and Alistair flopped across her lap, his tail making a dull thump on the ground as he wagged it. She leaned back, bracing herself with one hand and running the other across the large dog's head.

It's true, though, she said, scratching him behind his ear. *My mother died because she had me. I lost you because of my own foolishness, demanding you come, though you knew better.* Alistair huffed at that and nipped at her hand. Mariah gave a sad smile and gave his shoulder a voracious rub until he flopped over again. *Now Papa is leaving because I couldn't stop him.* She leaned forward again and gathered him up in her arms, burying her face in his warm fur. *Everyone leaves me, and it's my own fault.*

The noise from the jungle reached out for her again and Alistair stiffened, growling. Mariah stood, looking toward it, but her dog pushed against her legs, pushing her back toward the lake. Toward home. With one more glance back at the jungle, she let her dog guide her away.

Chapter 5

SUNLIGHT SPILLED into Mariah's room, waking her. An unease lingered in her mind, but she washed it away with the water she splashed across her face. She smiled into the mirror. Today she was getting married. For this one day, perhaps, she would set aside her worries. It didn't matter now that they'd had to rush. Nana swept in with her breakfast, and the morning moved past in a blur. Throughout the commotion, Mariah swung from giddy to nervous to nearly breaking down in tears over her father, and back again.

When a servant brought up a tray of fruit in the early afternoon, Mariah was more emotionally drained than she'd ever experienced. Her stomach fluttered as she looked at the food, and she opted for a drink instead, afraid anything she ate would find its way back up. She sent the now-finished shirt to Miguel, and still her mind gnawed at the many possible outcomes for the day.

Nana cackled from the doorway, joking with the servant about young brides. Mariah glared at her blatantly good mood and paced the room.

"I know better than to tell you to eat." Nana grinned as she turned from the now empty doorway. "But I am going to anyway."

"What if he changes his mind? What if I'm making the wrong decision? What if he decides I'm not... to his liking?" Mariah said in a rush, her hand pressed against her rebellious stomach.

"What if, what if, what if!" Nana huffed. "The future will take care of itself. Do you love the boy or not?"

"Yes. Well, I think I do. I mean—I don't know!" What if she only *thought* she loved him? "How do you know you're in love?"

"You're asking the wrong person, *chica,* I'll tell you that." Nana moved to the table and looked thoughtfully at the food. "But I do know how to see if someone else is in love, and if you're not, then I'm a frog."

"Well, you do kind of look like a toad from certain angles...." Mariah grinned.

"Also, he won't change his mind. You've caught that boy so securely, he couldn't not love you if he tried."

"Do you really think so?" Mariah looked skeptically at the fruit, poking at it.

"Why must you always second-guess me?" Nana asked, waving her green chirimoya at Mariah. "I hardly know why I bother telling you anything. You always ask if I'm sure, or if I really think what I'm saying. Of *course* I do, girl!"

"Well, what about that other...."

Nana heaved a sigh and took Mariah by her shoulders. "You have nothing to worry about, *chica*; now stop fretting. Since you won't let an old woman eat in peace, I suppose we'd better get back to getting you ready. Go, sit!" She waved in the general direction of Mariah's dressing table.

Mariah's nerves calmed a little as they set her hair. They were just settling her black silk dress on her shoulders when her father knocked on the door.

"Come in," Mariah said while Nana worked the laces closed.

"Ah, you're looking beautiful," Ciro said as he entered. "Miguel insisted that I give these to you." He held out a small bouquet of beautiful orange and white flowers that filled the room with their fragrance.

"Oh, they're lovely!" Mariah took the flowers. "Are there many guests here?"

"Not as many as you deserve, *mi querida*."

"Would you help me with this, please?" Mariah asked, holding the necklace with her mother's stone to her father.

"Certainly, child."

When he finished tying the necklace, Mariah turned around to show him her entire ensemble with a face-splitting grin.

"You are a vision," he said to her, gesturing for her to look in the mirror.

Mariah's face practically glowed, framed by her long dark hair that blended with the black of her wedding dress. The red and silver of her necklace was the only color she wore. Nana placed the elaborate black veil over Mariah's face, and Mariah watched the tears form in her father's eyes.

"What is it, Papa?" She turned back to him, laying a hand on his arm.

"I can hardly believe you've gotten so old. When did that happen?" He smiled down at her, his face full of love, and took her hand. "I remember holding my newborn little girl in my arms as though it were yesterday. You were so very small."

Mariah smiled up at her father through the veil. Dom knocked on the doorway to let them know it was time before dashing off again. With her hand on her father's elbow, she followed him out. A small jolt of surprise stopped Mariah at the top of the stairs. The open, tiled foyer before them stood empty. Miguel was not there. It seemed that in every important part of her life he had been there, waiting for her. Smiling up at her.

"What is it, my dear?" Ciro asked at her hesitation.

"It's silly." She tried to wave him away. He refused to move forward until she spoke. "It's just that..." Mariah gave him a sheepish grin. "Just that it seems like Miguel has always been there, waiting for me at the bottom of the stairs."

Ciro squeezed her hand, tucked it more firmly into his arm, and started down the steps. "Today, he will be waiting for you at the chapel. A better place, perhaps, to wait for one's bride than the foot of her stairs."

With a discreet look at her father, she caught the sad smile on his face. Had there been a place like that for him and her mother? "Miguel has some strange notions, being English. Did you know that Doña Olivia offered to escort him down the aisle, as he did not have a mother to do so?"

Ciro nodded and helped her into the carriage. "He asked me about it, saying he preferred to wait at the chapel with the priest, and wanted to make sure there were no hurt feelings."

Mariah shook her head at the unconventional behavior of the man who would soon become her husband. But she'd come to expect that sort of thing.

Before Mariah knew it, they had arrived at the church. Then she walked beside her father down the aisle. Miguel broke into a brilliant smile as she reached him. She smiled back, heat in her cheeks as her father placed her hand in his. She hardly heard the words spoken by the priest, caught up in Miguel's intense gaze. He wore the shirt she had embroidered. Was it only yesterday? Surely an eternity had passed between then and now. Her hands should be sore from sewing the day before, but she felt only joy.

She soaked in the vision of Miguel, unable to look away. Every small detail seemed to fill her mind. His dark hair was pulled back neatly, for once, none of it falling into his eyes. The dimple when he smiled. His beautiful green eyes that she always lost herself in.

It seemed like a dream when Miguel handed her the small bag with the thirteen *arras*, when she said the words in the right places, as she slipped the ring onto his right hand and he did the same for her. The moment seemed to stretch out forever, filling Mariah with a sense of all being right in the world, while the entire world was comprised of only her and Miguel. All else was insignificant and merely existed around them as Miguel led her back down the aisle, through a shower of rice, and into the coach.

She leaned contentedly against him, and the coach started forward, taking them home. He stroked her hair, his fingers trailing over her ear and down her neck. Warmth flowed through her as he reached her collar bone and traced it across her shoulder. She shivered and took his hand, setting it in her lap, and ran her fingers up his arm. The muscles in his arm tensed under her fingertips as she pushed back the sleeves of his shirt and dress coat.

With a small groan, he kissed the top of her head and moved his hands up to her shoulders, moving her away from his chest. "I have something for you," he said before she could protest.

Seemingly from nowhere, Miguel revealed a long strand of deep red flowers and held them out to her.

"Amaranth." She smiled, taking the posy and repositioning herself more properly in the seat beside him, the flowers easing the sting of his rejection. "It is said that they never die."

"Did you know they're found around the world? Different varieties and colors, for sure, but the same flower."

Mariah laughed and shoved at him playfully. "Of course they are. You wouldn't have the slightest interest in them if you hadn't seen them everywhere."

"On the contrary." He caught her hand and pulled her back to him. "Nothing is as unique as my dark angel, and she interests me most of all."

Mariah blushed and looked down at the flowers in her hand. "And what do you know of these?"

"'We that with like hearts love, we lovers twain,'" Miguel began in English, pulling Mariah onto his lap, his words whispered into her ear. "'New wedded in the village by thy fane. Lady of all chaste love, to thee it is we bring these amaranths, these white lilies, a sign, and sacrifice.'"

He slid one hand around her waist and the other trailed down her arm toward the flowers.

"'May Love, we pray, like amaranthine flowers, feel no decay. Like these cool lilies may our loves remain, perfect and pure, and know not any stain. And be our hearts, from this thy holy hour, bound each to each, like flower to wedded flower.'"

As he finished the poem he touched her jaw, turned her face toward him, and kissed her. The flowers fell from her hand, and with them the world around them.

When they parted and Mariah opened her eyes to find the world still there, she smiled. "And just how long have you been preparing that one?"

He returned to her a rakish grin. "I can't take too much credit for the poem. I found it in a book many years ago. By a fellow named du Bellay, as I recall. As for the rest, you'll never know."

Miguel picked the flowers back up and set them into her hair as she pulled out the bag of *arras* he'd given her.

"And will I find anything half so romantic in here?"

"Open it." His grin grew even wider.

Mariah opened the bag expectantly and spilled the coins onto her lap. They were not the traditional gold coins, and not even all of them were gold. She spread them across her lap, the metal brilliant against the black cloth of her wedding dress. Not a single one was like another, varying as much in size as in design. She grinned. They were exactly the sort of thing she expected from Miguel.

"What are they?" she asked.

"Coins from around the world," Miguel said proudly, moving the coins on her skirt so that each lay separate from the others, his arm around her waist to steady her on his lap. "Your father offered to lend me some money, saying I'd earned it, but I refused. I didn't want it to be an empty gesture, giving you something that was already yours. He laughed and said he understood *that*."

"That sounds like him." Mariah ran her fingers through the coins, enjoying their variety. "Tell me about them."

"They're from my travels, the most valuable of each country's coin that I had. This one here is from China," Miguel pointed to one with odd symbols on it, "and this one is from India—"

Abruptly the carriage pulled to a halt and the door opened.

"Ah, there you are!" Ciro bellowed merrily at them, holding the door. "We'd worried that you two lovebirds had run off already, and we couldn't have that, now could we?"

Mariah blushed, hurriedly setting the coins back in the bag before she could get off Miguel's lap. Miguel simply waited, grinning at his new father-in-law.

After Mariah put the precious coins back into the bag, Ciro helped his daughter from the carriage and walked between her and her new husband. As they entered the *hacienda's* small ballroom, already full of guests, Ciro shoved them in gently and whispered, "Good luck!"

The crowd pushed them to the center of the room, and the musicians started the traditional wedding dance. For a moment, she froze. Did Miguel even know how to do this dance? She'd forgotten about it entirely, or she'd have made sure it wasn't done. Too late now; the music had begun. They would be the center of gossip by the end of the night. They'd be—

Miguel reached for her hand and led her through the dance. Her surprise immediately quieted her thoughts as they moved through the steps. He was graceful, as though he'd been practicing all his life.

"When did you learn this?" she asked as she relaxed into enjoying the dance.

"The moment I decided that all I wanted was to make you happy." Miguel smiled down at her. "Or, that is when I would have started learning, but I didn't know it would be required until Betania's wedding, and by then I had a lot of lost time to make up for."

Once again, time slowed and the world disappeared as she danced with her husband. For a moment, she wondered why that was, followed quickly by the wish that it would never end. But, like all things that begin, it also ended. They applauded the musicians and moved off the floor to allow others to dance.

They made the rounds about the room, enjoying the company and general good cheer, though there was not even half the number of guests as there had been for Betania.

"I can't say I mind the smaller wedding party," Mariah whispered to Miguel in between well-wishers.

"Why is that? You deserve something much grander." He smiled again as an elderly couple approached them.

"It'll cost less," Mariah said once the couple had moved on. "And there will be less work all around for the staff."

Miguel chuckled at her as a boisterous group of young men approached.

As he talked with them Mariah looked around, relieved to realize they'd spoken with almost everyone at this point. As the men spoke, she mentally added "getting off my feet sooner" to the list of benefits of a smaller wedding party. Despite the engaging conversations, she could not help but note the absence of a certain disdainful personality. Elisa had made an appearance shortly after Ciro had abandoned them near the door, looking haughty and indignant, and Mariah had not seen her since. *Good riddance,* Mariah thought, drinking from a glass she didn't remember picking up.

"Here, you drink this." Mariah handed the glass to Miguel when the men moved on. "It's *sangria.* I've never cared for it."

Miguel sipped it. "I've had better," he said with a shrug.

"Miguel, have you seen my father?" Mariah asked, suddenly realizing she hadn't seen him.

"No. Now that you mention it, I haven't seen him since right after the dance…." Miguel looked around the room and set the glass on a table.

Mariah clutched at Miguel's sleeve. "We must find him. I can't have him leave like this."

Miguel nodded. "I'll see if I can find him. I'll check the stables first and work my way back. It'll be easier for me to slip out than you, *mi morena.*" Miguel kissed the top of her head and strode off.

She watched him go, frustrated by the sudden press of well-wishers. Mariah spoke with each of them as briskly and politely as possible as she made her way to the nearest door, which seemed miles away. An extremely old lady waylaid her three feet from the door, the only person between her and escape. Mariah managed to catch the attention of Rosia Garcia, Betania's sister-in-law, who foolishly came over. Mariah introduced them and turned the old lady's conversation over to Rosia. Insisting that she felt faint and needed a little air, Mariah finally slipped out.

She practically ran to her father's study. The room, which had always seemed warm and inviting, felt unusually barren. The weapons she'd always thought merely decorative were missing. With a deepening feeling of dread, she rushed from room to room, hoping to find her father. With no other reasonable places to search inside the house full of guests, she headed to the courtyard.

The sound of Miguel's angry voice around the corner stopped her abruptly, and she crept closer to listen.

"... realize how this will affect Mariah?" Miguel demanded.

"I have thought it through and think this will be easiest for all of us. No drawn-out goodbyes, no more fretting about what will come, no more seeing her tears," Ciro said quietly.

"Easier for you, perhaps. Ciro, the whispers have already started. They're claiming scandal. What else would they think of a rushed wedding? Then a strange disappearance from you the same night and your entire estate left to us? You may be a distinguished person here, but there are *rumors* already about Mariah's lineage, and I have *no* past here."

Mariah peeked around the corner to see Miguel facing Ciro. Her father was dressed for travel with a pack over one shoulder, bulging saddlebags on the other, and two rifles under his arm. His horse pranced nervously behind him.

"I have full faith that you two will manage. Ignore rumors, and they will die down." Ciro tossed the saddlebags onto his horse and tied them on deftly.

"There will be questions," Miguel hissed, grabbing Ciro's arm.

"You mustn't tell them where I have gone, or we all will lose everything." Ciro shook his arm free and strapped the rifles down across the saddlebags. "Tell them I have gone on a journey to give you two some time to yourselves. That my feet have been itching to go, and that if I wait any longer, I'll be too old. Tell Sergio it is the journey I have talked about taking for nearly twenty years. He'll understand."

"Papa," Mariah said softly, stepping into view.

Both men turned toward her.

"Mariah, I'm sorry. I wanted to leave quietly without further heartache." Ciro looked miserable.

She walked over to him and hugged him. "It's all right Papa, I understand that you must go. I just wish it weren't so soon." Tears filled Mariah's vision, threatening to overflow as she blinked.

"As do I. I had always hoped that an end had been made the last time, but people can't seem to live in peace. I shall miss you, *mi querida*."

"I will miss you, Papa." Mariah buried her head in his shoulder. "Come home to us when it's done."

"I will try my best." Ciro held Mariah out at arms' length.

She felt that he looked at her as though trying to memorize each feature. She tried to commit his face to memory, too.

Ciro turned to Miguel. "You're a fine man, Miguel. Take care of her."

"I will do my best." He drew Mariah from her father and into his own arms.

Mariah watched her father mount the horse and walked him out of the rear gates without a backward glance. He rode tall and confident, guiding his horse expertly.

"I fear that is the last time I will ever see him," she whispered, feeling Miguel's arms tighten around her waist.

"So do I, Mariah. So do I."

***

The speculation immediately flared up around the young couple before all the guests had left for the evening. Neither Miguel nor Mariah could find it within themselves to put on happy faces and return to the party, so they retreated to Ciro's study to talk. Sergio found them there looking for Ciro himself.

"What are you two lovebirds doing, hiding in here? You have guests!" Sergio gestured expansively, his speech somewhat slurred. "Have you seen your father?"

"He has gone," Mariah said.

"Whatever do you mean, girl?" Sergio picked up a decanter of brandy sitting on the sideboard.

"He left earlier tonight." Miguel stood, pulling Mariah up with him. "He wanted to give us time alone and decided that it was the perfect time to take that journey he's always talked to you about."

"Ah, I see." Sergio's voice turned serious as he returned the bottle unopened. He stood there, looking at the bottle a moment longer before muttering to himself. "You've finally gone and done it, have you, you old scoundrel?"

"Señor?" Miguel asked.

Sergio took a deep breath and turned back to the couple, a devious grin on his face. "Well, in that case, I suppose the party is over, eh? As I'm sure neither of you wants to disband the guests, I shall do it for you!" He puffed up his chest and swaggered out of the room.

Miguel and Mariah looked at each other, trying not to laugh, and snuck after him to see what he would do.

Sergio barged through the doorway to the ballroom acting more drunk than he was, and bellowed, "*Felicitaciones* to the new couple!"

Cheers rose from the guests, who all raised their glasses and drank.

"It would appear that our dear host Don Álvarez has decided that his old bones have one last adventure in them, so he has gone and run off to have a little fun, leaving our guests of honor to themselves. Now they've gone and run off, too!" There were chuckles and a general buzz, and Sergio motioned them to quiet down before continuing. "So, let us all have one last drink and make our ways home before we are all too drunk to stand!" He made a performance of doing just that and staggered down into the crowd toward an extremely disapproving Doña Olivia.

"Well, he certainly has a flair for the dramatic, eh?" Miguel said to Mariah, who giggled.

"I'll say. Doña Olivia seems none too pleased. We'd better go before anyone sees us; we'd be in danger of being here all night."

"In that case, my Lady, please allow me to lead you from such a danger," he whispered into her ear.

"Where shall we go, my Lord?" she replied, hoping she'd used the correct English term.

"Anywhere you wish, *mi morena*," he replied, his voice turning husky.

"Anywhere you lead," she said quietly, caressing his face.

Miguel took her hand and they snuck away to their own world.

Chapter 6

THE ENTIRE FIRST week of their marriage, neither Miguel nor Mariah saw anyone else. The household staff seemed to make a game of it. Meals were always fresh and ready for them on the dining room table, their rooms clean and orderly no matter how short a time they were gone from them, fresh flowers in all the vases.

The first letter from Ciro came during that time, cheery and full of false information, for which Mariah and Miguel were grateful. They found it sitting prominently on a table where they would be sure to find it, but with a poorly disguised broken seal. The letter had been read. They returned a letter equally cheery, with their sincere hopes that Ciro was well and that he wouldn't get himself into trouble, and included some of the relevant news. When they couldn't find anyone to give the return letter to, they simply left it on the table, and it wasn't seen again.

Nana was the first to let herself be seen, and the rest slowly followed suit. Sergio visited a few days later to help them catch up on business affairs. At first,

Mariah thought it was mere kindness that Sergio came to help, but as she and Miguel worked with him, they began to see how deeply enmeshed in Sergio's assets her father truly was. When they asked about it, Sergio indicated that Ciro had far more interests in various things than even Miguel had been made aware of. It was as much to Sergio's benefit to keep Ciro's affairs in order as it was to the Álvarez family's.

Ciro's letters continued to arrive every week or two, much like the first one, and Miguel and Mariah always promptly replied. The days turned to weeks, and the weeks into months. Mariah's anxiety for her father lessened as she became used to his absence, though he was rarely far from her mind. She tried to keep herself occupied and found it easy to fill her days with meaningful work and her nights with Miguel.

Life in Maracaibo continued at its regular pace, and even the third Wayuu rebellion could do little to stop it. The fighting took place far to the north, and though supplies were diverted to the troops, and skirmishes broke out in the streets, it seemed little else changed. Crops were planted. Ships came in, traded, and sailed. Betania came more and more often to visit, and it was to Mariah that she first confided when she became pregnant. Mariah found new depths in her friendship with Betania, who had blossomed with marriage. Elisa, on the other hand, showed herself less and less in Mariah's circles. Mariah commented on it once to her friend.

"You know, I hardly ever see her anymore either." Betania did not look up from the tiny dress she was embroidering. "She used to come calling almost daily. Now if I want to see her, I have to go back to the Casa de la Cuesta. Not that I mind, of course; it is always so relaxing going home, but then it isn't really my home anymore. I can't imagine home anymore without my Benito. You're so lucky to have inherited your childhood home. I'm not really sure who will inherit ours. My father never talks about it, though I'm certain Elisa will never get it."

"Why is that?" Mariah asked, though Betania would have told her even if she hadn't.

"Well, if it were me, I wouldn't give it to her because she thinks she is so high and mighty, thinking she knows everything about the world there is to know."

"And this is a new trait?"

Betania shook her head and continued. "She imposes herself on all the upper-class circles—not that she shouldn't be there, my family is perfectly qualified for them—but she goes as if she *deserves* to be there, and I never could stand people who think they deserve what they have in life, unless they earn it, of course."

"As if Elisa has ever earned anything in her life short of a slap in the face," Mariah said dryly before Betania could start again about how wonderful her husband was.

Betania snorted, trying not to laugh. "You know, I don't think she ever really got over Miguel choosing you over her. I remember she would pine about him all the night long until I'd hit her with my pillow and tell her to hush up and go to sleep. Of course, I only did that so that I could dream of my own Benito...."

Mariah smiled down at her own stitching as Betania went on and on. Betania would continue until stopped, once she started talking about her husband. Nevertheless, Mariah always enjoyed Betania's company; it was a welcome relief from helping Miguel with her father's business. Her family's business, Mariah corrected herself.

Not long after Betania revealed her pregnancy, Mariah woke feeling strange. Not wanting to worry anyone, she ignored it. It was nearly seven months since her father left. They had been seven wonderful months and Mariah was happy, content, and finally feeling comfortable in the new pattern of her life. But the odd feeling didn't go away.

"Are you sure you're all right?" Miguel asked, sitting on the bed beside her and gently rubbing the small of her back when she insisted he go to breakfast without her for the third day in a row.

"I'm fine, just tired still." She gave him a smile and a quick kiss. "Just have Nana bring up some food later. I've got some work here to do, so I'll see you this evening."

With reluctance, Miguel stood and put on his coat. He paused at the door, turning back to her again. "You're sure you're not hungry?"

"Yes, go!" She snatched a pillow off the bed and threw it at him, and he ducked out of the way. With a sigh of relief to have him gone, Mariah lay back in the bed. She was actually hungry, but the thought of food made her nauseous. She must have eaten something bad. *Every day for the last week?* Well, it was possible. Except that she'd eaten pretty much everything Miguel had up until a few days ago, and he wasn't sick. Mariah sighed and put her arm over her eyes to block out the bright morning light. Really, she just wanted to sleep.

"I could be wrong, but hiding from him won't stop him from worrying," Nana said, waking Mariah abruptly.

She sat up, trying to get her bearings. The shadows had moved considerably since she'd closed her eyes. How long had she slept? The older woman set a tray of food down and brought over a bit of bread, which Mariah ate.

"And it certainly won't change anything."

"What do you mean?" Mariah tried desperately to keep down the small bit she'd just swallowed.

"Really, *chica*, I thought we'd taught you more about life than this." Nana shook her head and helped Mariah over to the table. "But I suppose since you've never been around other pregnant women, and Betania has had such an easy pregnancy thus far, you can't have been expected to put it together on your own."

"I thought being pregnant was supposed to be this great and wonderful experience. Are you sure I didn't just eat some bad fruit?" Mariah tried to be defensive and succeeded only in rushing over to a pail into which she could vomit.

"I wouldn't know, having never been myself," Nana said calmly, holding back Mariah's hair. "But all the women I've ever talked to insist that it was. It seems they all forget, after a year or so, how miserable it made them."

"Right. So am I going to have to fast until the baby comes?" Mariah asked irritably as Nana helped her shakily back to her seat. The wonder that she now carried a baby, Miguel's baby, slowly blossomed across her mind, subdued by the rebellion of her stomach.

"Goodness, no!" Nana laughed. "The worst of it will pass within a month or so. Then you won't be able to stop eating. Miguel will be running to the kitchen at all hours of the night to find food for you, and when he brings it to you, you will turn it down because it doesn't look good anymore."

"I'm not that picky." Mariah looked at the tray of food with loathing and longing.

"It's not you who is rejecting it, but the little one. As I recall, Ayelen had every bit as much trouble with you," Nana said with a warm smile.

The knowledge didn't make Mariah feel any better. She lay back down on the bed, Nana rubbed her back, and the conversation turned to ideas on when the baby would come, if it would be a boy or a girl, and how best to tell Miguel.

***

Miguel sat at Ciro's desk staring at a ship's manifest in one hand and a ledger beneath another. Dutifully he penned in the appropriate numbers, but his mind wandered.

I ought to quit for the night. He looked at the remaining pile waiting for him to get through it. His head ached, as it always did lately after reading for too long. Mariah sat on the other side of the room, intent on some domestic project. Perhaps she'd want a break?

But if you keep going, you can finish that stack and not have it looming there. Miguel finished with the manifest and ledger and dutifully reached for the next item awaiting his attention. He stretched his neck and rolled his shoulders, settling in for another boring document. Mariah had been acting strange with him lately. It was unlike her to let him handle the paperwork alone. He'd only made it a couple lines in before he realized he wasn't paying attention.

It is late, you should stop, he tried to convince himself.

I can finish this, he growled back.

You've read that line three times now, at least. And you're talking to yourself.

Miguel sighed and set down the pen, glancing at his wife in the corner quietly sewing. *Or embroidering. Tatting?* He rubbed his forehead; he'd never gotten it straight. She was beautiful, though, whatever it was she was doing in the soft candlelight. Working hard. *Like you're supposed to be doing.*

Miguel picked up his pen again, but still couldn't focus. Why had she been so off the last couple of weeks? She even refused to eat with him, though she smiled and seemed friendly otherwise. Maybe she was angry at him, and there had been that time she hadn't spoken with him for weeks. But she seemed beyond such a degree of pettiness now. Then again, she was female, and if there was one thing he knew about women it was that they were unpredictable.

She glanced up and caught him staring. A grin lit up her face for a moment before she blushed and looked away. No, certainly she wasn't angry at him. Maybe it was just the custom here that married couples didn't eat together for a month out of the year? The Spanish had such odd customs, and he certainly hadn't figured them all out. Miguel shook his head with a smile and looked back to his ledger. That, at least, was something he understood. If he could manage to focus.

"Miguel, I have something to tell you," Mariah said, breaking their comfortable silence

"And what would that be, *mi morena*?" he asked without looking up from his books.

"In about seven months, you're going to be a father."

Miguel's heart stopped, and his mind went completely blank.

A father? His numb fingers dropped the pen as the world seemed to lurch beneath him, shifting beneath his feet like a deck in a squall. He stood, gripping the desk for balance. *A father. Me...?* Waves of emotion crashed down on him, each vying for space. Fear and betrayal, the ghosts of a past that he refused to remember taunted him. *How could you be ready? How could you do better? How could you possibly be enough?* He looked at Mariah, his beautiful, brave wife and was nearly brought down again by a new wave of emotion. Joy. Complete and utter joy. He could be better, he would be better than those who had come before. He was going to be *a father!*

Mariah just grinned as she watched him work through his emotions.

"Are you sure?" he asked when he was able to speak again.

"Not so much about the timing, but yes, pretty sure that we'll be enjoying an addition."

Miguel dropped back into his chair, running his hand through his hair. Mariah laughed lightly as she came over to him and kissed the top of his head.

"I'm not sure I'm ready for this." He pulled her around and set her on his lap.

"I would doubt that anyone ever is. Besides, you still have a few months to get ready. The baby's not coming tonight."

"Do you think it will be a boy or a girl?" he asked, setting his hand on her belly, wondering if he'd be able to feel the child move.

"I'm sure I have no idea!" Mariah laughed again.

"Well, what should we name him, if it is a boy? Or a girl?"

"Ciro Miguel Álvarez del Mar for a boy?" Mariah suggested, leaning against him.

"I like it, but I thought the father's surname is supposed to go first?"

"Well, I figure that since you took surnames that meant nothing, we should give our children a family name that has a history." Mariah ran her fingers through his hair.

"What is wrong with my surnames?" Miguel pulled back, looking her in the eye.

"Well, both Blanco and del Mar are generic names given to children who don't have parents."

"Then they are appropriate for me."

"What is your real name, Miguel?" Mariah leaned against him again, toying with his hair. "If you tell me, we'll put your surname first."

"I don't mind your family name first."

"Someday you will tell me what your real family name is, Michael." The English version of his name sounded harsh and foreign on her tongue.

"Someday," he agreed, and kissed her.

***

Mariah couldn't wait to tell her own father the good news, hoping that perhaps it would convince him to come home. The expected letter didn't arrive, and without a carrier who knew where to find her father, they could not send one. *Things happen,* she told herself. Horses lose shoes, riders lose their way or get sick, letters get misplaced. There would be another letter soon, no doubt filled with her father's concern that they hadn't responded to his last. She was certain of it. So she waited. Two months passed without news and slowly the morning sickness ceased, but in its place, the dreams began in earnest.

Chapter 7

AUTUMN 1741 - MARACAIBO

MARIAH WALKED ALONE near the edge of the jungle, waiting for her canine companion. A warm breeze flowed over her, and she looked at the sunny sky. It would rain soon, but it always rained here. The jungle had always fascinated her with its dark colors and the strange sounds. Even the smells were different from home. She had not been so far from Maracaibo for many years, but the jungle didn't worry her, despite its many dangers.

She walked peacefully along the loose treeline for a time, the trees sliding out of her path as she moved forward. A rustling from within the green depths gave her pause. Curious, Mariah turned toward the sound. The breeze, carrying on it the smells of hibiscus, roses, and fresh rain, flowed around her, whispering its nonsense to her soul. Pushing her way through the undergrowth, Mariah stepped into the cold jungle, leaving behind the safety of the fields.

A branch snapped back into place behind her, and Mariah looked back. For a moment, fear stilled her heart as she searched the dark entanglement of foliage for sight of the field. A glimmer of light caught her eye, and she stepped to the side for a better view. Before her, in the distance, through an opening in the trees, shone the warm, clear daylight, and the fields beyond. Mariah rubbed her numb, damp hand on her skirt. Surely she could go a little further and still find her way back.

Mariah turned back to the darkness of the jungle. She needed to know what had made the noise. She stepped forward, only to find her way blocked by a large dog. A wave of warmth and joy washed over her at the sight of her Alistair. She dropped to her knees, throwing her arms around his neck.

Where have you been, you scoundrel? she asked him as she rubbed his ears. His only response was a whine and a wag of his tail.

The rustling came again and she looked up at it, standing.

What do you suppose that is? Mariah asked, taking a step forward.

Alistair growled and pushed her back.

Alistair! Move! She tried to get around him, pushing his head away, but he wouldn't let her go. Step by step, he herded her back out of the jungle. Peering back into the dark foliage from the warm sunny fields, she tried to glimpse at what had been making the noise. She realized with a shudder how cold and full of dread she had been.

A loud scream pierced the air around her. An all-too-human scream, coming from the jungle. Perhaps it ought to have filled her with fear, but instead she felt only a deep sense of sorrow. Alistair growled, and Mariah mounted the horse that had not been there before. Looking back for Alistair, she saw him bristling at the foliage. He charged in on the attack as Mariah's horse carried her away.

***

Miguel woke abruptly to find Mariah sitting up, her head in her hands.

"What's wrong?" Miguel mumbled, trying to clear the fog from his brain.

"Nothing. I had a bad dream; that's all."

"You sure? Want to tell me about it?" Miguel asked, sitting up.

"It was about Alistair. You know, my old dog?"

"Mmmmhmmm." He rubbed his eyes and stretched. It was still hours until dawn.

"It's strange. I've dreamed of him so often, but never like this. I was out near the jungle, and he stopped me from following a strange sound. As I left, he went in after it." Mariah paused and shuddered.

"And?" He put his arm gently around her shoulder.

"And then I woke. It was just a silly dream. Go back to sleep, *mi amor*."

"Are you sure you don't want to talk about it?"

Mariah shook her head and lay back down with her back to him, her head pillowed on his shoulder. Miguel draped his arm over her, resting his hand on her gently rounded belly, and wondered if she could feel their child move yet.

He felt her slowly relax in his arms and finally her breath evened out into the pattern of sleep, but sleep did not yet come for him. He traced her curves with his fingers and watched her in the gentle moonlight that spilled into their room. He loved the scent of her, the shine of her silky hair across the pillow, and the weight of her in his arms.

As his hand returned to her belly, he wondered about the life they had created there. The thought of a son whom he would teach to ride horses and to sail thrilled him. Or perhaps a daughter he would spoil and dance with. Of course, if they had a girl, she'd be as beautiful and amazing as her mother, so naturally she'd learn to shoot and ride, too. He would carve them wooden toys and carry them on his shoulders.

Would he be a good father? Would he know what to do and say to teach his child the right things? The responsibility for so much of a life terrified him. Would he be able to teach them respect without cruelty, manners without meanness, loyalty without loss? He had learned life's lessons from a cruel master and from the unforgiving mistress of the sea. He barely remembered his mother, just the memory of love, really, in the shape of a woman. His own father had been a good man, but after his death….

Angrily Miguel turned from the thought. *There's nothing but pain there. Leave it.* But what if? What if he, too, was taken from his child? How could he possibly allow them to bear the pain of being alone? Mariah was a capable woman, and if it came to it, he had no doubts she could manage well enough without him. But growing up without that person who should have been there yet wasn't—that was something he knew too well. When the person who was supposed to teach you, guide you, protect you, comfort you, work with you, and love you was simply gone.

"I won't do that to you," he whispered, pulling Mariah tighter against him until she fidgeted in her sleep and pulled away, murmuring.

But what if you can't stop it?

***

Mariah stood in a field near the edge of the jungle, waiting for her canine companion.

This is a dream, a distant voice whispered in the back of her mind. A warm breeze tugged at her hair, whispering that it would rain soon despite the sunny skies. Mariah smiled. It always rained here.

The same dream for weeks now, the voice sighed.

She walked along enjoying the deep colors and the exotic sounds from within the trees. A strange rustling, unlike anything that could be made from leaves or fur, beckoned to her from within the dark depths of the trees. Curious, she followed it in, unconcerned as all sense of warmth and security drained away. She paused beside the tall roots of a Ceiba tree, touching its smooth, cool wood. She turned back through the darkness, looking for the path back to the light. She knew that was important.

This is getting predictable, the voice said, bored. Ignoring the voice, Mariah turned back toward the unknown depth of the jungle, only to find a large dog blocking her path. A wave of warmth and joy washed over her at seeing her Alistair.

Why didn't you meet me sooner, you scoundrel? she asked. She dropped to her knees to hug him but he bristled, growling. Shocked at his alarm, Mariah stood, backing into the root of the Ceiba. *What is going on?*

The leaves rustled again, drawing all her attention. As she moved to step around Alistair, he growled at her and blocked her path. In a moment of lucidity Mariah knew what would happen next. *There will be a scream, and someone I love dearly will die*, the voice whispered.

Mariah glanced behind her, looking for the way back out of the jungle, her heart in her throat. Perhaps she could change things, prevent the inevitable. The warm light from the field slanted into the forest, showing her the path back. She could make it out, back to safety. Pointing back toward the depths of the jungle, Mariah ordered Alistair to attack. With a growl, he leapt past her, deeper into the darkness, and she ran toward the light. The sounds of fighting followed her through the trees. Alistair's growls were cut short by a chilling impact and a heart-rending whimper. She nearly turned back, but the trees seemed to push her forward into the field and onto the waiting horse. Together, they fled.

The world passed Mariah in a blur, and she found herself standing on the docks of Maracaibo late in the night. *Strange,* the ethereal voice echoed in her head, *I've always woken up before....*

The lights from the *palafitosi*, the floating villages on Lake Maracaibo, danced on the water's surface while the nightly Catatumbo lightning worked itself into a frenzy in the distance. Below her, Mariah saw Alistair as she had last seen him in her waking life: laid out on a makeshift barge, wreathed in flowers, and entirely lifeless. Pain seared through her chest, a sharp emptiness that threatened to consume her, a missing piece that had once been the source of all the joy in her life along with a tearing of guilt at knowing it was her fault it was gone. Mariah looked away and found her father standing beside her, his arms resting pensively on a stanchion. A vague sense that someone was missing nagged at her, but they stood alone and watched as the funeral barge drifted slowly toward the ocean.

Mariah woke with tears on her cheeks and an ache in her heart. *Someone was missing.* She glanced to her side and found Miguel asleep. She touched his outstretched hand, desperate for the tactile reassurance. He was there; he was alive. But it was not enough to release the tension inside her. Trying not to panic, Mariah lay back, rested her hand on her belly. Forcing her breathing to be deep and even she waited. The gentle flutter of feeling pushed within her, and she nearly let out a sob at the release of tension. She still had her child.

It was only a dream. Mariah wiped the tears away and stared at the canopy above their bed, unable to fall asleep again. Thoughts about what the dream with its new ending could mean tumbled about her skull. She remained in bed, thinking until the baby began dancing on her bladder. Sighing, she threw back the covers and got ready for the day.

***

"Betania, do you find you have strange dreams?" Mariah asked her friend a few days later, the new version of the dream reprising itself nightly. She had thought of asking Nana, but found that between her morning sickness and managing the business, she had little interest or energy for Nana's tales.

"No, not particularly. I certainly dream more often now, and more vividly, but the dreams are not unusual. Why?" They walked slowly through Betania's small garden that lay beside her modest home.

"Oh, I've just been having this dream every night for the past few weeks. It's usually the exact same thing over and over." Mariah tried to make it sound uninteresting.

"Is it about your baby?" Betania asked hopefully as she leaned over to cut a flower for the bouquet she was building. "I've heard that when you dream about your child, you'll know things, like if it will be a boy or a girl, or what temperament it'll have."

"No, actually it's about my old dog, Alistair. Do you remember him?"

"Oh, yes." Betania laughed as she straightened, setting the flower in the basket Mariah carried. "I remember that time we went swimming and Elisa refused to get in the water, so he pushed her in. It ruined her dress, and she was furious!"

Mariah couldn't help smiling as she remembered the incident.

"Oddly, the dream seems to center around him. We're out for a walk near the jungle—"

"Oh, how brave!" Betania grinned at Mariah, then reached for another flower.

"—and there is a rustling in the trees. He doesn't let me near it. Then, as I ride away, he attacks it. After that, I am standing with my father on the shores of Lake Maracaibo and he, Alistair that is, is dead. It's just like the funeral we had for him, except that you, Elisa, and Selena are not there."

"That is odd, but I don't seem to remember that being the way that he died." Betania reached for a rose, then shook her head, moving on.

"That is what is so bizarre about it. That isn't how he died. He was run over by a carriage in town." Mariah leaned against the trunk of a rain tree, reluctant to share the details about the scream that sounded far too human. "It's so peculiar. It feels so real, especially when I'm watching Alistair go out to sea. When I wake up, I still feel like I'm there and it's just happened. Even with dreaming it every night, I still wake up confused for a minute...."

"Well, I'm sure it is just a dream and will pass in time," Betania said cheerily and changed the subject.

Mariah let her, but the dream and the feelings it evoked were never far from her mind. The feelings it evoked had started to affect her waking hours, too. She looked out toward the distant hills with their carpet of green jungle, and a dread cold enough to chill on even the hottest day crept down her spine.

***

Twelve long weeks had passed since the last letter from her father. Mariah stood on the jungle's edge, acutely aware of the silence, the total lack of sound from any of the fauna, the stillness of the flora. Its darkness beckoned her, more beautiful and entrancing than ever. A warm wind rustled the grass at her feet, and she could taste the rain that would come. The sunny skies didn't fool her; it always rained here. A rumble of thunder rolled through the dream. The strange rustling pulled her attention back to the silent trees. She walked in, following the sound, stepping around fallen logs and thick undergrowth.

Mariah looked back to ensure she had not gone too far to return to safety. The window of sunlight waited for her at the edge of the trees. Between her and the depth of the jungle stood Alistair, larger than life and bristling with warning. Her heart filled with love for her friend and she stepped back, prepared to run when the rustling came closer. Alistair growled, and she drew a breath to send him in to save whoever was going to scream, even at the cost of his own life. Out of the corner of her eye, she noticed the low branches of the roble beside her were perfect for climbing.

The world seemed to pause as she hesitated. She could run for safety, or she could finally see what had been haunting her dreams for so long. Perhaps if she knew, she would be free of them. Mariah ran to the tree and scrambled up to watch, hiding in the oak's broad leaves.

The trees rustled, their leaves moving slowly, as though reluctant to give up their secret. With a grunt of effort, the leaves finally parted, and out stumbled a man, emaciated, old, and hardly recognizable. Mariah gasped, and realization washed over her. It was her father. She'd always known it was her father. He locked eyes with her.

Run! he croaked, falling to the ground. Without waiting for her command, Alistair leapt over her father's body and into the dense foliage. Without consciously moving, Mariah was on the horse, racing for town. She stood on the lake's edge in the darkness. Her father strong, whole, and sad stood beside her, as the martyred Alistair floated out to the sea.

"No!" Mariah shouted, bolting up in bed.

"What, what is it?!" Miguel jumped out of the bed wielding a knife, immediately dropping into a defensive stance. He looked over at a very startled Mariah, the sound of the rain on the window filling the silence.

Where does he keep those knives? He's not even wearing anything! Mariah smiled through her tears despite herself.

"What? What is it, *mi morena*?" The knife disappeared. He crawled over the bed and wrapped his arms around her. She sank into the calming comfort of his embrace as the wind rattled the shutters.

"My dream. My father is in terrible danger, I just know it, Miguel!" She looked up at him through her still-wet eyes. "I can't go to him. I can't help him; I can't save him. It's one thing to worry about what might happen, but it's so much worse to *know*!" Mariah buried her head into his chest and sobbed as a great feeling of helplessness washed over her. He held her until she began to quiet, feeling helpless himself.

A knock on the door made them both look up.

"Don Miguel? Doña Mariah?" Nana's voice came through the door.

"Yes, come in," Mariah said in a choked voice, dread weighing on her chest as Miguel quickly covered them with the blankets.

"There is a letter just arrived for you." Nana entered, shutting the door behind her. "The messenger said it was urgent that you receive it as soon as possible. I did not think you would want to wait until morning." She set the letter on the bed in front of Mariah and lit a lamp. Nana turned to go, but hesitated in the doorway. "If you need anything, I'll be waiting in the hall."

Mariah did not wait until the door was shut before tearing open the letter. It was from her father, as she had hoped, but the message did nothing to relieve her fears.

Mariah,
I am well. Do not seek me out, I am content with my lot. Know that I will always love you.
Don Ciro Álvarez Bosque

"He sounds like he means to die out there," Mariah said, her voice thick.

"There is certainly something strange about that letter." Miguel held the lamp closer to get a better look. "The writing is Ciro's, of that I'm certain, but everything else is so odd. To send such a short note such a long way, then to sign it so formally, without any ado."

"Miguel," Mariah said, her voice tense, "there's a stain on it...."

A dark, splattering stain marked the bottom half of the page. Miguel took the paper from her to get a closer look.

"It's blood, isn't it?" Mariah watched his reaction. His silence, the way he tightened his mouth, confirmed that he thought so too. "What will we do?"

"What can we do?" Miguel asked, shaking his head. "He told us not to go looking for him and that he is content. We should let him be."

"I *know* he is in danger, Miguel," she said. When he started to protest again, she told him about the dreams.

"Mariah—"

"Miguel, listen to me. Those dreams I've been having, for months now... I haven't told you everything." She searched his eyes, trying to convey her urgency. He nodded, and she told him all the details rather than the vague non-answers she'd always given before. *But still...* Guilt and fear washed over her as she told only the first half of the dream. She shied away from the second half, fearful of what it might mean. *They were only silly dreams*, she told herself, *and that wasn't what had happened anyway....* When she finished, a silence fell between them and Miguel looked her in the eye as though trying to gauge the veracity of the matter. She waited with baited breath, watching emotions war within him.

"If it is what you want, I will go find him," he said finally. He stood and pulled on his breeches.

"Not without me!" she said immediately, throwing on a robe of her own.

"Nana!" he called out. She was in the room in an instant. "I am going to retrieve Don Ciro. Please explain to Mariah why she cannot come with me."

"No," Nana whispered in shock. "No, you mustn't go."

"I will go!" Mariah argued, speaking over Nana.

"You will *not!*" Miguel shouted at her and she shrank back. Miguel had never raised his voice to her. He immediately softened when he saw her look of shock and hurt, and gathered her into his arms. "*Amor*, you are with child. I cannot risk it; *you* cannot risk it. I will go and find your father for you, but if I were to lose you on the way, I would have nothing to live for. If your dream was true, then your father is in danger, and you would be, too, if you came. If it is not, then I will bring your father back, kicking and screaming and tied to a mule if I have to." He drew her closer, holding her tight. "I care about him, too. He's been like a father to me since the day I arrived."

When they broke apart, he began packing, telling Nana to have supplies and two horses readied.

"You are going now?" Mariah asked softly.

"Do you really believe the danger is as imminent as you say?" Miguel asked.

She nodded reluctantly.

"Then why would I wait?"

"It is just so sudden." Mariah shook her head and sat down on the edge of their bed. She picked up her mother's necklace from the nightstand and gently spun the red stone in its setting. She felt as though she were falling slowly off a cliff, as though something had started and she had no way to stop it or slow it. Sighing, she worked the stone and its setting off the necklace and held it out to Miguel.

"Take this," she said. Miguel shifted his gaze from the stone to her and back again. "Please. I don't know why, but I feel that you should have it with you."

"Then I will take it, *mi amor*." He took the pendant from her outstretched hand and set it into one of his pouches.

She watched quietly from her seat while he put together the things from their room. He armed himself amply; she had been surprised when they were first married and had realized just how many weapons he carried. She was still amazed at how easily he concealed them all. When he finished, he looked over the room slowly, checking that he hadn't forgotten anything. There was nothing to do now but wait until everything else was ready.

His eyes came to rest on his wife, who looked forlorn. Miguel led her from the bed to the window seat and pulled her down onto his lap. He rubbed his hand over the bump of her belly, wondering at the life that was growing there.

"Can you feel him move yet?" he asked, hopeful.

"Sometimes I think I do, it's like a fluttering. It's hard to describe, but Nana says it should become more certain within the next few weeks." They fell again to silence while they sat, holding each other.

"I'm so sorry, Miguel." Mariah started sobbing again, turning her head into his shoulder. "I don't want you to leave. I want you to be here to feel him move, to see your son born…."

"So you think it will be a boy?" Miguel said softly, trying to cheer her up.

"I don't care! I just want you here with us." Mariah held him tighter.

Carefully, Miguel raised her face to his as her crying subsided. "I will do everything I can to be here for that. With any luck, I won't be gone more than a few weeks. One way or another, I will return for you. For you both. I won't leave you alone, I promise."

They stayed together, soaking up the feel of each other, memorizing every detail of the other that they could, both sensing that it would be a long time before they were together again. All too soon, a knock came at the door, telling them that Don Miguel's horses and supplies were ready. While he finished dressing, Mariah wrapped the robe more tightly around her night dress, a weight pressing on her shoulders at the future that lay before them. Without a word, she helped Miguel into a greatcoat he'd been given at their wedding and walked with him to the stables. The warm rain fell onto her hair and face, and she wiped it from her eyes, watching silently as the last bags were tied onto the horses.

Miguel mounted the tall steed and nudged him forward. Mariah walked beside them through the courtyard, barefoot and ignoring the rain that plastered her dress and hair to her body. They reached the edge of the main house, and Miguel reined his horse to a stop. He reached down, caressed her hair, and touched her face gently.

"You look like a drowned rat, *mi morena*."

"And you, a mangy dog." She held his hand to her face. He leaned down and kissed her one last time, tucking her hair behind her ear.

"I love you," he whispered.

"And I love you," she whispered back as he straightened in his saddle, unwilling to release his hand. She kissed his palm and he pulled away.

Then, reluctantly, she let him go.

Miguel started the horses forward, the pack horse behind him tugging at its lead. As he reached the *hacienda's* gate, he stopped and looked back at his wife. Even barefoot, soaked to the bone, and pregnant, he thought she had never looked so beautiful. Then, to escape the feeling of his heart being torn from his chest, he kicked his horse firmly and galloped into the rainy dawn with the messenger trailing closely behind him.

Mariah stood in the rain watching out the gate. She reached up to touch her face where he had laid his hand and felt something in her hair. She pulled on it and found a long sprig of amaranth in her hand. She stood in the rain holding the flower, her tears mixing with the rain, until long after the gates had shut and someone had thrown a heavy blanket over her shoulders.

Chapter 8

DECEMBER 1741 - MARACAIBO

THE DISTANT CACOPHONY of unidentifiable jungle sounds drifted across the still night and filled the dark halls of Mariah's home. Ghostly moonlight illuminated the hall she walked through, bright enough that she felt no need for a candle. Sounds that had for the more part of her life brought her a sense of comfort, tonight seemed only to underscore the tension that had filled the *hacienda* since she had sent Miguel to find her father.

Mariah ran her fingers along the cool, polished wood of a hall table as she walked, her other hand on her belly, waiting for the baby to kick. The grain of the wood stood out to her in the dim light, running along the line of the table until the top dropped off, abruptly redirecting the line, forced by an unseen hand into a shape the tree had never intended to be. A shudder ran through Mariah and she jerked her hand from the wood.

At first, the pain of missing Miguel had tried to consume her. She felt his absence everywhere and constantly berated herself for so foolishly sending him off. But she came to accept that what was done was done, and short of going after him herself, there was nothing more she could do. In the moments she felt most honest with herself, Mariah knew the only thing that stopped her from actually leaving was that she had no idea where he had gone. And what if he returned while she was away? So she stayed.

"At least the dreams have stopped," she said to the baby in her belly who had begun to grow in earnest the last few weeks. "Who knew growing a child could be so exhausting?"

And yet she wandered the large, empty house in the darkest hours of the morning, restless and unable to sleep. With a resigned sigh, she turned toward the stairs. She may as well get an early start on the day's work, and perhaps she'd be able to nap later.

The morning sunlight slanted across the room, illuminating glittering bits of dust when Mariah woke, her neck stiff from sleeping in her father's chair. She rubbed her neck, groggy, trying to think of what had woken her. Hoofbeats clattered in the courtyard and Mariah's heart jumped at the sound. A commotion outside the house jerked her further into wakefulness, and she rose to see what was going on.

"Probably some merchant discontent with his shipment," Mariah mumbled to herself as she reached the front door. Then, louder, as she stepped outside, "What is going on?"

"Doña Mariah! Come quickly and see! Your father is returned!" a nearby servant exclaimed.

"What?! Papa!" Joy lifted the lingering haze from her mind as she ran forward, moving through the press of servants. She scanned the horses that had come in, led by a native man she didn't know, but none carried her father. Then, with a wave of understanding, she dropped her eyes lower to the cart that rumbled behind them. She rushed to it with her heart pounding. Within, lying pale and unmoving, was her father.

"Papa? What happened?" she asked, momentarily relieved to see him turn toward her voice. A chill stole through her stomach. "Where is Miguel?!"

"One thing at a time," he said weakly, trying to wave her away.

"Doña Mariah, get out of the way," Nana ordered. Mariah held her ground stubbornly, holding her father's hand. Nana turned to a group of servants standing nearby. "You, take her inside. You and you, go get some hot water. You three, help me get him inside."

Mariah fought to stay by her father's side, but somehow her hand was removed and she found herself sitting outside her father's room while servants bustled in and out. She looked up, her stomach in knots, when the doctor passed by, then again when he left. And what about Miguel?

Finally, Nana emerged and motioned for her to go in. "He is asleep. Don't wake him and don't worry him with questions if he does wake," she admonished, then swept away down the hall before Mariah could ask about her husband.

Mariah went in and sat by her father's side. His shallow, noisy breathing belied the deathly pallor on his gaunt, pale face. He looked as though he had aged twenty years in the single one he had been gone, a mere husk of the man he had been. The similarities to the version of her father she'd seen in her dream wrenched her gut. She took his hand gently and he stirred.

"*Mi querida*," he whispered hoarsely.

"Shhhh." She swallowed back the questions that fought their way up her throat. "Nana says you must sleep."

"I didn't think I'd make it back, but I'm glad I did," he said, nodding. When she said nothing more, his breathing evened out again as he fell to sleep.

She waited by his side, insisting on doing as much of the nursing as they would let her. Nana maintained that Mariah must at least sleep in her own bed, and it wasn't until she cited the baby's health that Mariah acquiesced. When the fourth day dawned, Mariah rushed to her father's bedside, fearful that he would be gone, remembering clearly that Alistair had died after three.

"Ah, there you are, *mi querida*." Ciro smiled, his voice still weak, but his eyes wide open and lucid. Mariah paused, shocked to see him so improved.

"I have hardly left your side, Papa." She smiled for the first time in days and took his hand.

"I see you have news for me." He gestured toward her belly. "When will you make me a grandfather, do you think?"

"Not for four more months, at least." She smiled broadly. Then, as quickly as it came, the smile disappeared. "Where is Miguel, Papa? What happened? Why did he not come back with you?"

"I told you not to come for me." Ciro's face darkened. "I was dropped from my horse during the fighting, and one thing led to another, and I never really recovered. I stayed in your mother's village for a while. It was good to see so many old friends...."

Mariah waited impatiently for Ciro to continue, and when he didn't she prodded him on. "Miguel, Papa. What happened to my husband?"

"Your what? Oh, yes, Miguel. That's right; you two were married before I left. *Felicitaciones.*" Ciro fumbled back into silence.

Mariah looked at him in despair, for the first time realizing that it was not just his body that had been damaged. "But where is Miguel?" she whispered as her father slipped back into unconsciousness.

***

Ciro's body began to heal, but his mind continued to slip away. Sergio often came to visit his old friend. Ciro usually remembered him but talked like it were years ago. After one such visit Sergio, sat down heavily beside Mariah, who had been waiting in the hall.

"It is getting worse, isn't it?" he asked her, pulling a small flask from a pocket.

"Most of the time, in the beginning, he knew that I was his daughter, but after a while, he began to call me Ayelen." Mariah waved away the flask when he offered.

"Ah, his wife. I never met her but I've never seen a man so deeply in love with a woman as your father is with her. After nearly twenty years, he still holds true." Sergio nodded thoughtfully and took a quick sip.

"One good thing about this, I suppose. I've come to appreciate a little better how proud he is of me." Mariah smiled. "He'll often talk to me like I am her, telling me his version of all my adventures. Sometimes he talks as though I haven't been born. I suppose my pregnancy is to blame for that."

"I hope you humor him." Sergio leaned back. "I'm sure it does him good."

"I do." She nodded again. "At least once every day I ask about Miguel, but I've found that talking about him, or anything related to what happened, sends him into a deeper confusion."

"Have you learned anything about him yet?"

"I am not entirely sure, but it does seem that Miguel found him and sent him home to us." She hung her head fighting for control of her voice. "But I still don't know why he didn't return."

***

As the days passed, Ciro's body seemed to decide that if the mind wasn't going to heal, it would not either. The turn was gradual but quickly apparent. Mariah sat at his bedside late one night, trying to keep her hands and mind busy as she adorned a tiny dress. She couldn't believe that a child would ever be small enough for such a thing, but all the women she talked to assured her that it was the right size.

Beside her, her father twitched, caught in a bad dream. She waited a minute, hoping it would pass, but he only tossed worse, as though fighting off some evil. Setting her sewing aside, she reached for his frail arm, hoping to rouse him. At her gentle touch, he sat upright so quickly that she gasped, jumping back. The candlelight flickered across his face as he turned to her, his eyes staring at some distant thing only he could see.

"He took my place, but he was not prepared to die as I was." Ciro's voice remained weak and paper-thin. "He sent me away, but a replacement was demanded, and he foolishly volunteered. Do not go to him." Ciro exhaled heavily and lay back in his bed.

"Papa?" Mariah asked cautiously, creeping back to his bed. He smiled up at her, his eyes focused and clear, and touched her hair tenderly.

"Do not go to him," he said softly. "Stay here and raise your baby. Be happy." His breathing rattled and weakened, and his chest heaved. "Do not go."

Mariah's breath caught in her throat. He knew where Miguel was. He could tell her, and she could find him. She leaned closer as he struggled to draw breath.

With a final whispered breath he said the last thing she expected. "Run, Mariah. *Run….*"

She froze, looking at her father, hoping that she was wrong, that he had not just died. Her world waited, a breath away from shattering at the loss of her greatest pillar of strength and stability. She listened intently and watched desperately, hoping for anything. Stillness filled the room as the distant sounds of the jungle crept into the open window. Sorrow, hopelessness and the sense of being left utterly alone overwhelmed her and left her gasping for breath. Mariah dropped her head onto the edge of the bed and cried.

Nana appeared beside her and led Mariah to her own room, insisting that she sleep, but Mariah could not. She did not sleep again until her father was interred. When sleep finally came again it brought with it the dream.

Chapter 9

JANUARY 1742 – GUAJIRA PENINSULA

MIGUEL WIPED THE sweat from his brow. The heat rose from the barren ground; a more drastic change from the green jungles near Maracaibo, he couldn't imagine. He'd been away from home far too long, but soon he'd be headed back. Soon. If he pushed himself, he would be home in time to greet his son when he came into the world. Mariah seemed to think it would be a boy, so that was what he hoped for. But a girl would be fine, too. No doubt she'd be as lovely and sweet as her mother.

The horse plodded along the path Miguel's native guide had nervously set him on the day before. *What a silly thing*, Miguel thought as he rounded another hill. It had been a task to convince the dying Ciro and the village elders to send Ciro back home. His father-in-law had never actually agreed, and the village elders had only permitted the sick man to return home if Miguel would take his place on this absurd task. Miguel doubted they'd expected him to agree to it.

There was some native god or other who demanded a sacrifice of a man every month or so, or so the elders had explained through a translator. The only thing required was that a person enter a certain cave far to the northeast. The person didn't need to go all the way in, or stay, or even die if they could manage it. They only needed to go. Typically, older and already dying men were sent. *Seems like a good way to get rid of the burden of the old*, Miguel scoffed. If they didn't die on the way, they probably died on the return trip.

Once again, Miguel was tempted to just return home, certain there would be nothing there but an empty cave. But he had given the elders his word, and perhaps there would be some old shaman waiting to make sure he actually arrived. Miguel sighed as he resigned himself once again to completing his task. Dishonesty and cheating were not things he tolerated in himself.

A sudden drop in temperature surprised him as the sun sank below the desert hills behind him. A creeping sense of foreboding worked its way up his back and scalp, and Miguel stopped his horse for a moment to recheck his weapons—his pistols ready to shoot, his knives accessible, and his cutlass loose in its sheath. *Just because there are no people here doesn't mean there's no danger.* What kind of predators did this strange, lifeless land hold?

Moving forward again, Miguel's sable gelding rounded a turn, and there it was—a dark, yawning opening in the hill. There could be no mistaking it. A feeling of darkness and evil emanated from the cave. Miguel dismounted and tied his horse to a nearby bit of scrub. The gelding snorted and edged sideways, every bit as uncomfortable with the situation as Miguel felt.

"I know how you feel, mate." Miguel patted the horse's neck. "I'll only be a minute, then we can get on our way home."

The horse pawed at the ground, and Miguel stepped away. *Just to the entrance*, Miguel reminded himself, rechecking his weapons. *Then I can go home.*

Cautiously, Miguel approached the entrance. *One more step.* He moved into the darkness. He stood there for a moment, his eyes adjusting. He had fulfilled his promise. He could turn around and go home.

He should have felt relief, but instead his senses only heightened as though searching for an unseen predator. Miguel tried to turn, to step back, to leave, but he couldn't move. His body seemed rooted to the spot, and fear crept up on him, slowly overtaking his previous sense of foreboding.

Steeling himself, Miguel forced himself to take a step back, but found, instead, that he had taken a step forward. He froze, his heart beating faster. Something was definitely wrong. He thought of Mariah, of returning to her, and to their child. He focused his entire mind on it and took another step back, only to find himself again moving forward.

Come to me. A dark, silken voice caressed his mind, and Miguel took another, involuntary step in the wrong direction. Panicking, Miguel fought for control of his body and forced himself to stop once again.

Come to me, the voice repeated, stronger this time, compelling him forward.

Miguel fought it desperately, knowing with his whole soul that nothing good would come of following the voice. But, despite Miguel's strength, he could not overcome the power of the voice. The harder he fought it, his muscles straining against themselves, the stronger the voice became.

He fought each slow step until his muscles trembled with exhaustion, but he remained standing, as though an unseen force held him upright. Miguel found himself in a barren, dirty, moonlit chamber. Desperate, he drew his sword only to fling it away. He tried his knives to the same effect. Finally, he drew a pistol, determining that if he was to die, it would be by his own choice.

"I can't have you doing that, now." The voice tsked at him, and he lowered the unshot pistol. Miguel looked around the room, startled to hear an actual voice in the emptiness. In the shadows a form coalesced in his vision, a grotesque…thing that resembled a human torso and head, shrouded in the darkness. Miguel's hand dropped the pistol.

"Come to me," the thing said again, and against all will, Miguel approached the thing. He refused to give up hope, to stop fighting. He could not abandon Mariah; he would *not* abandon their child so long as his heart beat. Pain seared through him, and Miguel realized the thing had bitten him. He felt himself grow weak and realized with a surreal shock that the thing was sucking his blood. He wanted to laugh, but his body refused to respond.

Vampire...? Miguel's thoughts were blurred as fire spread through his limbs.

Why, yes, I am in fact, the voice responded gleefully in his mind.

Miguel was too far gone to feel surprised. Instead, he felt a tear fall hotly down his cheek. *I promised I'd come back to you,* he thought as he fell into a burning darkness, slumping to the floor, an image of his dark-haired angel appearing before his eyes. *I'm so sorry,* mi morena....

***

Mariah paced, anxious. The room was too small. The house was too small. The entire *hacienda* was too small. She wanted to get out, to go do something. Anything. But she'd just returned from her daily ride, and it was raining now. The rain was light, but the wind was strong and driving, howling through the courtyard and pulling against the doors.

The year had turned, and Mariah had to face it alone. Her father was in his grave, and Miguel had not yet returned.

As though in protest, the baby kicked her, turning in her belly.

"You're right, of course." Mariah rubbed her belly where he'd pushed. "I'm not alone, not with you here."

A knock on the door was followed by the small, timid voice of Ana, one of the newer servants. "Señora? Don Díaz has come to speak with you."

"Yes. See him to my father's office. I will be right down." Mariah paused and took a couple of deep breaths, trying to calm the growing nervousness inside her. "Well," she said, addressing her baby, "I wanted something to distract me. It may as well be this."

She held her head high and walked confidently down the hall, trying to push away the unease that had begun the day before and had only increased with the passage of time. She entered her father's office to see Sergio helping himself to a drink.

"Sergio!" She smiled and gestured to the decanter he held. "I hear that is a good vintage. From a wonderful local plantation I know of." She winked at him as he drank.

"You'd better believe it. I always save the best for the Álvarez family."

Mariah noted that his smile seemed forced as he downed the entire glass at once. She placed her hand on his arm and looked up at him.

"Sergio, what is wrong?"

"Bah, it is nothing." He gently shook her hand off and sat in one of the overstuffed chairs, and she followed suit. "Betania's time has come, and I never could stand to be around such things. Men only get in the way."

Mariah raised an eyebrow at him. "Surely there are better places to wait than here?"

"Nothing like business to keep your mind occupied, I always say. Keeps a man out of trouble."

"So you've come on business then?"

Sergio stood and helped himself to more wine while Mariah waited patiently for him to speak. She wondered if Miguel would be so distracted when her time came to have their baby. She didn't think she'd want him gone on business; she'd want him there with her, to support her and to see their baby come into the world. Surely her father would have been with her mother.... The baby kicked again and she hid her discomfort.

Heaving a sigh, Sergio set his glass down and Mariah looked up at him. "Truth is, girl, your father was a good and generous man. A much better man than myself, of that there is no doubt."

Mariah watched curiously as Sergio searched through the older records. He pulled out a couple of dusty tomes and set them heavily on her father's desk. *My desk now*, she reminded herself as she went over to inspect them. They were from a couple years after her birth.

Sergio pulled a large folded document from his jacket and laid it out above the books. Mariah peered at it.

"This is the subject of one of your father's wills. As you know, we were partners for a long time, and the fact is that your father holds considerable interests on my plantation."

Mariah opened the parchment and scanned through it, shocked at what she found. "But, this... this is most of your property. How did...?"

"Ciro was a good man, honorable and excellent with finances. And he had the wiliest brain I've ever seen in a man. When I was a younger, more foolish man I... got into some trouble, made some poor decisions—" he waved at the accounts on the desk "—and your father bailed me out of my quickly sinking ship. The terms resulted in this. His interests are now yours. We agreed to keep it a private matter between us. Livvy doesn't even know how much..." Sergio cleared his throat. "Ciro asked that on his death you be made aware of our situation."

"So, what is it that I need to know?" Mariah asked.

"The way I see it, there are two options for you. You can either pull out of my plantation—that is I pay you your share and you will no longer have any hold on the Casa de la Cuesta or its associated lands and incomes—or we can continue as before."

Mariah glanced through the paper as Sergio waited, tense. She didn't know much about Sergio's assets, but considering his current distress, buying her out was not something he hoped to do.

"I see no reason to change what seems to be working," Mariah said slowly as she read through the paper again, pushing back against a bump in her belly.

Sergio let out a breath, his face relaxing. "I am glad to hear it."

"Tell me, how is Elisa doing?" Mariah asked, handing the document back. "She's avoided me this last year, and I haven't seen her at all lately."

"Hmph. That childish girl." The papers disappeared into Sergio's coat, and he poured himself another glass of wine. "For as much animosity as she had for you and Miguel, she sure is mopey about his leaving. When he left to find Ciro, she railed on about you for a while. She spends most of her time now sulking in her garden, lamenting to anyone within earshot about Miguel not being hers."

"She needs to move on. You should send her to Spain for a few years; it would do her good."

"I've suggested it to Livvy, but she's having none of it. My wife's frightened out of her mind of the ocean passage. My only hope is to find Elisa a nice, sensible young man who can take her in hand. In the meantime, though, I've had her removed from direct inheritance from the plantation until she either comes to her senses or finds a sensible man."

"Which, aside from a dowry for Selena, leaves only Betania and Benito to inherit. Have you told them yet?"

"I just..." Sergio shook his head, sipping at the wine. "Everything is happening so quickly. Ciro was always better at handling these things than me. Besides, it was always my hope, and Ciro's too, that one day our children would unite this little business venture. However, as we both only had girls, it did not seem likely. Now, though, with some luck between your child and Betania's, perhaps that can one day be a reality."

"I hope so, but know that I do not want to force my children to marry because of a business deal." Mariah moved toward the door.

"Of course not." Sergio raised his glass to her and downed the remaining drink before bowing and turning to leave. He passed Nana on his way out the door.

"Did you want any supper tonight, Mariah?" Nana asked as Mariah looked out the door after Sergio.

"Did you know that my father owns the majority of the de la Cuesta plantation?" Mariah asked absently, rubbing her belly where the baby continued to kick against it.

"I'm not surprised." Nana crossed her arms and leaned against the door jam.

"You are being a downright nuisance, child," Mariah muttered as the baby rubbed disconcertingly across her abdomen.

Nana cocked her head as she looked at Mariah. "Are you all right, *chica*?"

"Hmm?" Mariah started and looked back at Nana. The anxiety she'd felt before pushed back into her chest. "I'm just a bit distracted. Sergio surprised me with this, and the baby is restless. I'm not sleeping well, and I've felt so anxious all day. As though I need to *go*, but I don't know where. Like something is pulling at me to leave."

"Is it Miguel you are worried about? Or the baby perhaps?" Mariah sat and leaned back, closing her eyes. "I don't know. The baby seems as anxious as I am, but aside from driving me to distraction he seems fine. Perhaps it is Miguel." Mariah looked over at Nana. "If I just knew what was going on, if I knew that he was well, I think I should be content."

The older woman hesitated a moment, then knelt beside the chair. "Do you trust me, child?"

"Of course I do, you crazy old bat. You've always been there for me, as long as I can remember. You're family."

"Then perhaps there is a way I could help you."

Mariah raised a skeptical eyebrow. "How is that?"

"You have been having recurring dreams?" Nana stood and walked around to stand behind Mariah's armchair.

"How did you know about those?" She turned to look back at her duenna.

"I listen, silly girl." Nana smiled and chucked Mariah's chin, before turning her head back to face forward. Nana's hands were cool as they rested on Mariah's temples. "Close your eyes, child. There is someone you meet when you dream, is there not?"

"Alistair. He is always there in the beginning." Mariah closed her eyes and leaned back in her chair. "Alistair and the wind."

Mariah felt Nana's surprise in her hands, but the older woman's voice was calm and steady as she continued. "I want you to think of them, then. Concentrate on how he looks, how it feels in the dream."

Mariah thought of the way Alistair had jumped on her in that first dream, so long ago. She tried to picture it in her mind: Alistair sitting patiently for her in a field that danced in the breeze. The image came to her, dim and fuzzy, as she sat, fully aware of her surroundings. Nana's cool hands on her head, the weight of her hair on her neck, the chair at her back, the cushions' support, her uncomfortably tight shoes.

But, there, too, was the breeze. She could feel the grass beneath her fingertips.

"I see it," she said.

Good, Nana's voice was there. *Now, picture your husband. Can you feel where he is?*

Mariah thought for a moment, the feel of her father's office solidifying around her, but also a pull. A sense of urgency that spun off to the north. She grabbed hold of it. Urgency. Anxiety. Fear. *Pain!*

Mariah gasped and opened her eyes, jerking from Nana's hands. "What was that?" she cried, as the echo of fire running down her limbs faded.

Nana stood with her eyes downcast. "That is what you seek."

"That was Miguel? What is going on? What if he's hurt or dying?" Mariah grabbed Nana's hands and looked up into her eyes.

"There is nothing you can do, child."

"I have to know. I have to help! Please, Nana!" Mariah searched the older woman's eyes. "Please."

Nana's shoulders slumped. "I would there were another way, child. Sit, and think of your dream."

Mariah obeyed. The cool hands calmed her worried mind as again she found the shadow of her dream world waiting behind her eyelids. She grabbed the rope of pain and pulled it towards her. She pulled and pulled, and with each effort the scorching heat grew more intense until she looked down and found it was an outstretched hand that she grasped.

Miguel! She could almost see him, through the clouded shadows in her mind and the mists of distance.

Mariah! His anguished cry, distant and weak, pulled at her, and for a moment, she could see him clearer. He lay curled in agony, a breeze rustling his hair. Mariah could feel his searing pain wash over her. She could feel his muscles tense, burning, threatening to crack the bones they pulled against as the fire within him licked and scorched his mind. She felt his heartbeat race as he thrashed and twisted and screamed, fighting back the inferno that was destined to consume it.

She cried out, reaching toward him, fighting the grey mist that lay between them. If only she could reach him, she could help! Together they could stand against the flames! But even as she strained forward, Nana's cool hands held her back, pulling her away.

NO! Let me GO! She strained against the hands that thickened the mist, shielded her from the flames, and pulled him from her view. She twisted and strained and could still feel his heart, desperately beating.

I can help him! She pulled, but Nana was unrelenting. Mariah felt his heart begin to slow, to falter.

MIGUEL!!

Nana pulled her back, and his hand slipped from hers. Mariah's heart raced, trying to remind his how to keep beating, to fight. She felt his heartbeat fading.

Faltering.

Stopping.

Nothing.

Mariah screamed and pulled herself from Nana's grip, falling to the floor as pain like a searing knife stabbed through her heart. She couldn't breathe. She couldn't think.

That was not his death.

Miguel could not be dead.

If she could find him, pull him back, surely he would be there. Anything to prove it wasn't real.

Mariah pulled herself up and ran blindly to their room. She threw open the closet and dug frantically until she found it. His greatcoat. The one she'd given him before they'd begun courting. She held it to herself and breathed in the smell of him. There was a moment of bliss in the scent, a wave of memory filled her. He couldn't be gone, it simply was not possible.

"Mariah...?" Nana's voice came from the doorway, breaking her reverie and laying bare the fresh, burning wound in her heart.

"Leave me alone!" she cried, and fell, sobbing, onto the bed, clinging to her husband's coat.

***

Mariah woke from a dreamless sleep, feeling drained. She reached out to the deep blue coat and pulled it to her, inhaling the smell of it. She curled up on the bed around her growing belly and the folds of cloth, certain that if she held it close enough, she would feel him there with her. All she felt was a hole in her chest as though her heart had been ripped out, leaving her ragged, bleeding, and empty.

The baby kicked restlessly, forcing Mariah to get up. After relieving herself, she wrapped herself in the long coat and sat in the chair to stare out the window. Her mind and heart were at war. Her mind insisted that Miguel was gone. She had felt it, felt the fire that had consumed him, felt the moment that death had arrived and stopped his heart. Her heart rebelled, knowing that he couldn't be gone; she'd know he was gone, she would feel it in her soul. But wasn't that the emptiness she felt? But shouldn't it feel worse?

But she had been there, hadn't she? Had she? How could such a thing have been real? So perhaps she was working herself up over nothing. Around and around her mind chased her heart, both swinging from hope to despair and back again as she watched out the window.

"Child?" A hand on her shoulder startled Mariah from her reverie. She wiped her tears onto the soft, stained sleeve of his great coat, which nearly set her to sobbing again. She wiped her nose on a handkerchief she found in her hands and looked back out the window.

"Was it real?" she whispered.

Nana stood at her side. "Yes."

The word was like the banging shut of a door that could never again be opened. Mariah struggled with her warring emotions. She swallowed down the fear, the pain, the disbelief, and the tears. She swallowed again for the sobs that filled her throat, making even breathing a struggle.

"Then he is dead," she said, unsure if it was a statement or a question, but she was alone in the room.

***

Mariah sat in her parlor, lost in memories. Teaching Miguel to play chess on the table over there. His triumphant smile when he thought he'd done something clever. The feel of his hand over hers and his breath on her cheek when he'd taught her to shoot. A bright morning walk in the garden. The feel of his scruff at the end of the day rubbing against her neck. Miguel spinning her while they danced until she became dizzy and fell into his arms as they laughed. The feel of his palm on her face in the rain, the last touch they'd shared before she watched him ride to his death.

"... I just know you'll feel the same way, Mariah," Betania said.

"Hmm?" Mariah startled back to the present. "I'm sorry, Betania. I'm afraid my mind had wandered."

"Oh, I'm so sorry. I've spent this entire time talking about my little Emilia and haven't even given you space to talk." Betania looked a little ashamed as she drank her chocolate.

"Don't worry about it. I'm afraid I'm not very good company right now." Mariah looked down to the cup she'd been holding since Betania arrived but that remained otherwise untouched. The idea of sweetness made her stomach roll, and she set it back onto the table.

"Yes, I heard that you'd received bad news about Miguel, but not the specifics of it. You know how I don't like to put any stock in rumors, but the word is that he's..." Betania looked suddenly abashed and whispered, "... that he's died?"

Mariah braced herself against the wave of pain that came with hearing someone else suggest it, and Betania gasped at her silence.

"Oh, my dear! I am so sorry! Here I have been going on and on about my baby while you're trying to deal with... with...."

"It's all right. It is only a rumor; we don't know anything for certain." Mariah's voice choked on the lie as tears ran down her cheeks.

Betania sat beside her friend and Mariah leaned onto her shoulder, letting the tears come again.

Chapter 10

MARIAH WALKED NEAR the jungle, admiring its deep, dark beauty. She was so tired of crying. Here there was a semblance of peace; here there were no tears. A warm wind blew her dress around her legs, and she knew it would rain soon. The sunny skies didn't fool her; it always rained here.

Something warm bumped against her hand, and she looked down to see her faithful canine companion at her side. Dropping, she hugged his neck and felt his love wash over her. They sat and looked up at the sky, so profoundly full of stars shining through the blue expanse. Alistair nudged her belly, and Mariah looked down.

Her baby bump was gone, but in its place shone a ball of light, about the size of her fists together, and pulsing with life. It twisted and twitched for a moment, and Mariah could feel the corresponding movement in her distant, sleeping body.

Hello there, little one. She rested her hand on the ball of light. She felt love return up her arm.

He's a sweet little thing, isn't he? she asked Alistair, as she rubbed the dog's ears. He whined and laid his head on her lap. *What do you think about Álvaro, for a name?* The dog said nothing but the baby kicked out again, and she laughed for the first time in days. *Álvaro then.*

They sat there and waited. She was expecting something, but she also wanted to ask about Miguel. Alistair raised his head and looked into her eyes. *I'm afraid to ask,* she explained. *I'm afraid because I know I will believe, and I don't know which answer would be harder to bear.*

She stared into the dog's soulful brown eyes until he jerked his head away, looking toward the sound they'd been waiting for. She strained to hear it, too. A strange rustling coming from a place just out of sight. This was familiar, and Mariah knew what to do. She stood and followed the sound in, careful to mark the way back to the light.

They paused, and she rubbed the dog's ears absently, waiting for the strange noise to come again. Alistair wagged his tail happily, thumping it against her leg as he waited with her. When the rustling came again, it was closer than it ever had been. Mariah's mouth filled with the taste of fear as she bolted back out of the trees, hearing the sounds of brave Alistair protecting her and dying for it.

She was on the horse, practically flying over the ground and felt the familiar stinging behind her eyes. He died because of her. Her throat constricted, and her heart ached. Next time, she wouldn't be enticed by the sound! She wouldn't!

She stood on the docks in the night, and her father, whole, healthy and sad, stood beside her as they watched the funeral barge float off into the darkness through the dancing lights reflecting off the water. *He is dead, and it is my fault*, she thought. *I am all alone, and it is my own doing.* Mariah looked off into the darkness, entranced by the jumping lights, wishing she could follow. She would wake up soon. She could feel herself sliding back toward consciousness.

Then, floating back to her over the water came a sound that chilled her to the bone. A long, plaintive howl, a cry that seemed to echo her own feelings of loss, loneliness and longing. She knew that voice, knew it so deeply. It was the voice of Alistair. If he was alive when she'd thought him dead...

Mariah's eyes flew open. Miguel was still alive! Somehow, she knew that was what Alistair's howl meant! He was telling her that Miguel still lived, and that she could still save her husband, could still go to him. Mariah had no choice; she *had* to go find Miguel. Her mind raced through preparations that would need to be made before she could leave.

Suffused with excitement, Mariah flung back her bedding and leapt up from the bed, only to crumble to the cold floor as a spasm of pain shot through her abdomen. She doubled over with the sudden pain and eased herself back onto the bed.

"Fool girl," she muttered as she waited for the pain to subside. There was a knock at the door.

"Come in," she called, standing up again, but slowly this time.

Nana walked in with a breakfast tray. "Are you all right?"

"I'm fine. I just tried to stand up too quickly." Mariah took a deep breath and held her back, finally upright. "You never used to knock," she teased.

"You never used to be married," Nana shot back. Mariah sat to eat her breakfast as Nana bustled about the room. "You are in surprisingly good spirits this morning."

"Indeed." Mariah set down her napkin and went to her closet to dress. "I have decided to leave."

"And just what has brought you to that decision?" Nana asked, helping her with her underpinnings.

"You say the dreams are real, but do they show the truth?"

"They are real and the truth can be… subject to interpretation. As can any dream," Nana answered cautiously.

"The babe is kicking!" Mariah smiled and grabbed Nana's hand to feel the movement. "Do you think my baby will be a good person someday?"

"If he has good and loving people to care for him and guide him, I have little doubt that he will be a good man." Nana smiled down at her hand as it was kicked and prodded.

"A boy, then." Mariah nodded to herself, content with Nana's confirmation of her suspicion. "I saw him last night when I dreamed. He was a small ball of light, but I knew him."

"So I have heard it described before." Nana pulled away and set to work folding Mariah's night clothes.

"His name will be Álvaro," Mariah said as she brushed her hair, "and Miguel will be here to meet him."

Nana snatched the brush from her and turned Mariah to look directly at her. "What are you thinking of, child?"

"He is alive, Nana. I know he is." Mariah stood and held Nana's hands in her own. "The dream. It told me that he lives, and if he lives, I can go to him. It's my fault that he went. I have to fix this. I can still save him!"

"Oh, Mariah, please understand. Where he is gone, there is no returning from."

Tears of joy filled Mariah's eyes. It was even better than she'd hoped. Nana knew where he was! "See! You know where he is! You can take me there, and I can save him. You know what is there. Surely together we can find a way to rescue him!"

"And what of your little Álvaro?" Nana folded her arms, her voice angry. "Do you think you can go adventuring without any concern for his well-being?"

"You are absolutely right, Nana." Mariah smiled in a way she knew Nana would not like. "That is why you will guide me to where I need to be, lest I be caught out adventuring by myself. You know where he is, you know how to get there, and I do not. So, you will take me there or risk breaking the trust my mother placed in you."

Nana's eyes narrowed, and Mariah recoiled a bit at the harshest look she'd ever seen from the older woman.

"You are a foolish child. Be it as you say." Nana stormed from the room, leaving Mariah startled and alone.

***

The clock ticked, each second compounding upon its predecessor. Mariah paced the parlor at Casa de la Cuesta, waiting for Betania and Benito. At long last, the door opened, and Mariah looked up to Betania rushing into the room.

"I am so glad to see you!" Betania wrapped Mariah in a hug. "I was so worried before. You were so very upset that I feared for the health of you and your baby. You look much better now."

"I feel better." Mariah pulled back, taking Betania's hands.

"Did you see?" Betania held up her right hand, flashing her wedding ring. "I've finally been able to put it back on. I felt so bare without my ring those last few months, but my hand was far too swollen to wear it."

Mariah laughed, rubbing the warm metal of her own ring with her thumb. "I hadn't even noticed, but I'm glad you're wearing it again." A servant carrying a bundle entered the room, and Mariah gestured to it before her friend could speak again. "You brought your little Emelia?"

Betania beamed as Mariah took the baby into her arms. "Isn't she beautiful?"

Mariah swayed and rocked the newborn, looking at her fresh little face, her calm, closed eyes and surprisingly red lips. "Yes, she certainly is. I'm sure they will be perfect playmates."

"Wouldn't it be wonderful if yours was a boy? Perhaps they would marry someday, and then we would be sisters in truth." Betania reached back for her daughter, and Mariah reluctantly let her go.

"He likes her already. He kicked me when you took her back." Mariah laughed as she sat down, rubbing at her sore belly.

"You're hoping for a boy then? What will you name him?"

"Álvaro Michael Álvarez del Mar."

"Oh, that's a beautiful name." Betania handed the infant back to Mariah as she took a seat beside her friend. "A little strange, using an English name and then your surname first instead of his, but I tell you, I've never thought that *was* his real name. Didn't we make up the surnames? Has he ever told you his real name?"

"Yes, we did, and Miguel - Michael - is his real name," Mariah answered, laughing and running her finger along Emelia's tiny, sleeping face.

"I think it is good to use unusual names from time to time, not unlike you yourself, Mariah. Why they didn't just give you a proper name like Maria, I'll never know. Anyway, that way they don't grow up with everyone else having the same name. Why, Benito and I had such a hard time finding a name for our little Emilia, it took us three days after she was born to settle on one." Betania smiled warmly as Benito entered the room. "But isn't this just wonderful? Our two little children will be born so close to each other and mine a girl and yours perhaps a boy. We could be family someday, Mariah. Wouldn't that be just the greatest thing?"

Mariah managed to concede that it would indeed be great to be related to her friend before Betania's mouth could take off again.

"Doña Mariah! Welcome! I'm glad you have come," Benito cut in giving Mariah a small bow. "To what do we owe the pleasure of your company today?"

Mariah took a deep breath and steeled her nerves. "Benito, Betania, as you both know, Miguel has been gone for some time. I sent him out to find my father, and, though he managed that, he did not return. Despite the rumors, I have reason to believe that he is both alive and in grave danger, and I can no longer do nothing. I must go after him."

"You're an amazing and capable woman, Mariah, but you are just a woman," Benito said hesitantly. "What can you do?"

"I can do anything a man can do, Benito. I have run my father's business for months and have learned to use a pistol and sword as well as any sailor." Her voice broke as the memories of hours spent training with Miguel flashed through her mind.

"What about your baby?" Betania asked. "You can't go adventuring off in the jungle in your condition."

"As for my baby—" Mariah's voice caught in her throat a moment as she rested her hand across her belly. "As for my son, I shall have Nana with me. I'm sure things will be fine; children come into the world all the time. But, given that my own mother died so soon after my own birth—"

"Mariah..." Betania started, but Mariah waved her away.

"Please, let me finish. I'm sure things will turn out fine, but if anything should happen to me once he's been born, even after I've returned, I would very much like you two to care for my son."

The couple looked at her in stunned silence, then at each other.

"We would need to discuss it," Betania said after a moment.

"I understand." Mariah stood, hesitating. "There is something else you should know. Most of Don Díaz's plantation belongs to me. If I do not return, and you have adopted Álvaro as your own, you will not need to worry about Emilia's future."

"I don't see what Emilia has to do with this," Benito started, but Betania put a hand on his arm and looked up at him.

"Papa has removed Elisa from the will. When he dies, we will inherit, but the truth of the matter is that the Álvarez family owns most of it anyway. Mariah would be doing us a great favor, and if perhaps they married, someday everything would be worked out."

"And if they don't?" Benito asked.

"I don't mean for this to sound like a threat," Mariah said, "but the fact is that I need to know my child will be cared for. To that end, I would need to pull my interests in Casa de la Cuesta now to find someone else to care for him and the business, and that will ruin Don Sergio. There are a hundred reasons that I don't want to have to take that route, but most of all, I trust you." Mariah stepped toward him, pleading. "I know that you are a good man, Benito, and I trust that you will be good to my son. I am certain that you will raise him to be a good man. Especially, if you hope that our children will marry, you will raise him to be a great man."

Mariah handed Emelia to her father. "I'm sure this arrangement will hardly be necessary, but if for whatever reason Miguel doesn't come back, and I... If I should die, like my mother did, I would like to know that he will be cared for."

Betania looked at her husband who nodded in acquiescence. "We will, Mariah. We will."

Mariah gripped Betania's hand in thanks, desperately fighting back the tears. "Please, come stay in my home while I am gone. The *hacienda* is spacious and beautiful, and you would have it all to yourselves. My staff will remain there and they will take good care of you. I already have a steward arranged for the business until I return, so between him and Sergio, you should be able to manage anything that comes up."

"Of course," Benito said.

With tears in her eyes, Mariah hugged Betania.

"I hope to see you again soon," Betania said through tears of her own.

"I hope so as well." Taking a deep breath and steeling herself, Mariah pulled away and brushed off her dress. "Well, then, I must be on my way. I still have some things to put in order before I leave."

"Good luck, Doña Mariah." Benito gave her an encouraging smile. "Things will be fine."

Mariah thanked them again and returned to her home, stopping at the office in town to finish things there. She trotted her horse part of the way home from the town, her mind full of the few loose ends that remained. Both she and the horse were sweating as she reined him in at the gates of the *hacienda*. Despite her caution, Nana was there to scold her.

"You foolish girl! Here you are preparing to leave on a long journey, and you go off trying to wind your steed. Get off and get him rubbed down, and be sure to do it yourself. You're going to be doing it every day for who knows how long, so you may as well start now."

Surprisingly tired from the day's efforts, Mariah didn't have the energy to protest. She did as she was told, as quickly as her changing body would allow, checking and rechecking in her mind that she had covered everything to allow for her absence. When she had finished and turned the horse into his box, she returned to her room to pack her personal items.

A glance at her reflection in her bedroom mirror gave her pause. There was hay in her hair and dirt smudged across her cheek. Her dress was even worse, with horsehair, dirt, and rain splatters across it. Irritated, she pulled it off and threw it into the corner. Her anger only grew as she rifled through her dresses, looking for something more suitable. Growling, she grabbed at the dress she'd thrown on the floor and tripped over her chemise, muttering an epithet she had unwittingly picked up from her husband.

She caught her balance on the chair that sat beside her bed, the very one Miguel had sat in, faithfully watching over her so long ago. Sorrow and love welled up inside her, but she crushed it back with her anger. Anger at everything. At the stupid dreams that had started all this, at Miguel for not refusing her, at her father for sending the note and not just dying in peace, at being thought less of for being a woman. At stupid dresses! She tore the chemise off and threw it into the fireplace, following it with the filthy dress on the floor. She watched them burn with a sick satisfaction.

"Well, now what will you wear?" she said, disgusted with herself. Sighing, she sat on the edge of the bed and leaned against the cool, tiled wall. Beside her lay Miguel's coat, and she pulled it to her, breathing deeply the scent of him that lingered in the cloth.

With a sudden realization, she threw open the wardrobe. Miguel had left plenty of clothes. She was smaller than he was, so it would all fit well enough, and she could roll the tops of his pants down to accommodate her ever-growing belly. Eagerly, she tried on each reasonable item. Each garment that fit comfortably, she threw on the bed, and the rest she returned the wardrobe. It was exhausting, but she pressed on.

Once she settled on the last outfit, Mariah did her best to conceal weapons the way she had seen Miguel do. In the end, however, she removed nearly half of the knives and kept only two pistols in addition to the two pistols her father had given her. As she returned the unused weaponry, a pair of boots hidden in the corner caught her eye. She pulled them on, and aside from being a bit snug in their newness, they fit perfectly. When had he thought to have boots made for her? Were they meant to be a surprise?

She sniffed back her emotion and, removing the boots for the time being, sat back to look over the room. Dressed in her husband's clothes with her commandeered clothing packed, there seemed to be nothing more for the moment than to wait. The kitchen would be preparing provisions, her horse was resting, and the business was in order for management by a steward. Mariah sighed and laid her head back to rest just as Álvaro decided that he was bored and began to stretch within her.

"Today has been an exciting day, hasn't it?" she asked him. Looking around the room again, her eyes came to rest on two papers sitting on the table. Her mother's letters. Reaching out to them, she patted her belly and asked, "Shall I read these to you?"

Her voice was soft and thoughtful as she read them aloud in the empty room. When she finished, the emptiness seemed to fill her, bringing with it the pangs of loneliness. Mariah let the sorrow wash over her. When she had cried herself out, she pulled out a fresh sheet of paper and penned her own letter to her child, just in case.

She wanted to believe that she and Miguel would return, but deep down, the fear that they wouldn't gnawed at Mariah. She wrote of how she and Miguel had met and of the circumstances that led to her decision to leave. Then she wrote of her parents and her hopes for her son. As she neared the end of the sheet, she paused and read over her mother's letters again, wondering if she'd forgotten anything important. Filling her quill with ink, she continued.

Álvaro, I hope and pray that you will be as good a man as your father. We love you so very much. I hope, too, that someday you will give your love to a woman worthy of it and be worthy of hers in return. When you find that woman, you must cherish her as I know your father cherishes me, and as my father cherished my mother. You must remember to love her with all of your heart. If she is worthy of you, she will do the same. Your father and I have known such love. It is a force that overcomes all opposition, all obstacles, and even death will not long hinder it. I will find your father again, in this life or the next.

A lifetime of experiences I would impart to you, my son, a lifetime and more of hard- earned wisdom. But that would take longer than I have, and more pages and ink than there are.

With all the love of a mother,
Mariah Álvarez Zyanya

Mariah dried and sealed it, addressed it to Álvaro, and set it on her dresser. She looked at it a moment, twisting her wedding ring around her finger. With some difficulty, she pulled off the gold band, the dark blue enamel and carved flowers warm and smooth beneath her fingers. She pulled out a fresh sheet of paper and wrote a simple note.

Álvaro,
Your father gave me this ring. I hope someday to reclaim it, but if I should not return, it is for you to give to the woman you would not only face down death

for, but who you would also live the rest of your life for. May you both have a long life of joy together.
   Mariah Álvarez Zyanya,
   Your loving mother.

Before she could lose her nerve, Mariah folded the note and slipped the ring into it, addressing it to her son on his eighteenth birthday. She pushed back from her table and looked again at the note on her dresser. *It will be fine. We'll all return home together. He'll never even read it.* She shook herself and strode to the office to spend a few hours writing directions for Dom, who would continue as steward, and Sergio.

She stretched her cramped hand and folded the last of the papers for the care of the *hacienda* in her absence, and set out in search of Dom to entrust the delivery of her ring to him. When she had finished tying up all the loose ends, she shouldered her gear and returned to the stables to load it onto one of the pack mules. Nana soon joined her, followed by a groom leading their horses.

"Are you sure you don't want to stay here?" Mariah teased her.

"You don't have a guide," Nana countered, her voice flat.

"I can get one in town."

"You don't even know where you are going."

"I will start at my mother's village." Mariah gathered her reins to mount up.

"Again, you don't even know where that is or what it is called. You can tell a guide you want to go to your mother's village, or even to a Wayuu village, but how would you tell him which one? You don't even know for yourself." Nana gathered the mules' lines as Mariah heaved herself up into the saddle.

Nana paused until Mariah was settled in her saddle. "You speak only rudimentary Wayuunaiki, and you have never in your life slept in a camp, out in the open. All you know are things you've heard or learned in books. My responsibility is to you, so with you, I will stay."

With a laugh, Mariah turned her horse to face Nana. "Well, either way, I'm leaving, if you're finally finished fiddling with your gear."

Nana snorted. "I have been waiting for you." She pulled herself onto her own horse with far more grace than a woman her age deserved.

"Sure you have, old woman." Mariah turned her horse back toward the gate and clicked it forward. Over her shoulder she asked, "How long have you been waiting?"

"All my life."

Shaking her head, Mariah led them out the gate of her home. As they rounded the first bend in the road, she looked back to see her home disappear from view and thought she heard Alistair's howl echo through her mind.

"I'm coming, Miguel. I'm coming," she said, turning back to the road before her.

Chapter 11

MARIAH'S HEAD DROOPED in the dark, suffocating heat of the jungle, her wet shirt clinging to her sweaty back. The large, dangling leaves of the canopy blocked out all direct sunlight, painting everything with a green tint. Progress through the thick, noisy jungle felt painfully slow, and she wondered how far they managed to travel each day. The claustrophobic closeness of the trees removed all sense of distance travelled, and occasionally she swore they were travelling in the wrong direction entirely. Time melted together as Nana had them on their way before sunrise and kept them going well into the night. Mariah slapped at a bug on her neck, and for a moment, her horse picked up its pace.

"Why don't they bother you?" Mariah called out, readjusting her kerchief that had slipped yet again.

Nana laughed. "Some people just taste better than others."

Annoyed, Mariah stood in her saddle, trying to stretch her weary legs. She hated to admit it, but by their first night she knew she'd have been completely lost without Nana. She'd been sore, hungry, and tired when Nana had finally pulled to a stop in a small clearing.

"This will be a good place to rest for the night," Nana had declared.

It was almost too dark to see anything. Mariah slid off her horse, her legs nearly buckling from the unaccustomed exercise. She held to the saddle for support as she dug around in the saddlebags for some food. Sitting down heavily on a log, she took a bite, not really caring what she had pulled out.

"What do you think you are doing?" Nana asked. Stung by the woman's tone, Mariah looked up. "Put that food back. Your horse has worked harder than you today. You must always take care of your mount first, or you will not long have one."

Mariah stood despite her protesting feet and aching back, returned the food, and cared for her horse while Nana gathered wood and built a small fire.

"Now, take care of the mules, too." Nana gave the order more gently this time, not allowing Mariah a chance to rest until they'd finished their small camp. Finally, Mariah dropped onto her blankets, too exhausted to eat.

"Here, eat this." Nana nudged her with some food.

"I don't want it," Mariah mumbled.

"There will not be anything warm for breakfast, and you will wish you had. Besides, you have a baby to take care of."

Mariah smiled at the memory. Little Álvaro, it seemed, had the power to make her do anything. She rubbed her belly as he stretched across it. The sounds she'd grown up hearing at a distance were far louder here. To actually be surrounded by the constant chatter and chirping sometimes unnerved her. When she'd asked Nana about the likelihood of being attacked by a jaguar, the old woman had laughed darkly but reassured her it wouldn't happen. Nevertheless, sudden noises in the dense foliage still made her heart skip a beat.

Well after dark, Nana stopped them for the night, and they fell into the now-familiar rhythm of setting up the camp under Nana's direction. The first two days, Mariah had been too tired and sore to be irritated by the change of roles, but as her body had adjusted to the new schedule, she'd realized that Nana was teaching her how to make a camp, and, in a way, how to survive. Now she looked on each new task as a chance to learn, no matter how she longed to collapse onto her blankets and sleep.

Mariah stirred a pot of dried meat and vegetables in water while Nana gathered enough wood to last the night. The heat beside the fire was still stifling, but it kept the relentless jungle insects at bay. What she wouldn't give to feel the breeze from across the lake. A gentle breeze flowed through the thinning trees, just enough to blow her hair into her face, as though it had heard her. Laughing at the thought, she moved the hair and sighed at the feel of the dirt and grease that clung to it. She'd always loved her long hair. Miguel had loved it, too. What she wouldn't give to give it a good washing.

The breeze stilled, and Mariah paused and cocked her head, half waiting for it to begin raining, the way it always threatened to do in her dreams following the breeze. When it didn't, she chuckled and continued stirring. Quiet singing made Mariah look up as Nana returned to the clearing. The older woman sang a song with hauntingly familiar melody, but the words were in Wayuunaiki, many of which Mariah didn't know.

"What are you singing?" she asked. "It sounds so familiar, but I know I don't know it."

Nana went quiet for a minute, kneeling to add the wood to the fire. "It is an old Wayuu lullaby," she finally said, not looking up from her work.

Mariah watched the old woman as they lapsed back into silence. "I'm glad you came with me. I certainly wouldn't have made it one night if I'd gone alone."

Nana grunted. "You're stubborn. You would have figured something out."

"I'm sure I would have." Mariah laughed, imagining herself cold, miserable, wet, and hugely pregnant, lying on the bare ground and getting swarmed with insects because she hadn't known the tricks to keep them away. That most certainly would have been the case without Nana's help. Nana was right, though. She wouldn't have given up.

Nana went back to her singing.

Mariah watched the old woman over the fire as the stew boiled and wondered just how old Nana was. There was something about her that spoke of age, but Mariah could not pick out exactly what. She didn't move like old women did. After a day on horseback, she walked well and moved surely. Mariah had shown more signs of soreness than old Nana ever had. But then again, Mariah was pregnant, which put her at a distinct disadvantage.

"Teach me," Mariah said suddenly.

"Isn't that what I've been doing?" Nana asked.

"Teach me to speak Wayuu." Mariah feigned exasperation. "Not just the smattering of words you've given me over the years, but how to really speak it."

"I thought you would never ask." Nana gave her an impish grin.

Nana started going over the words Mariah already knew. It surprised her to realize she knew far more than she'd thought. By that evening, Mariah had begun stringing them together into simple sentences. Mariah dutifully repeated everything Nana said and tentatively rephrased the words into responses until her head went fuzzy and she fell asleep despite herself, the foreign sounds of the language swirling through her mind.

Mariah woke with a start, the echo of a howl ringing in her ears, the way it did every morning. The colors of the world remained indistinct in the pre-dawn light as Mariah looked over to where Nana had slept.

The old woman was already up, sitting on a log near a neatly stowed pile of gear.

"You're awake. Good. Let's get moving," she said.

"Well, a good morning to you too," Mariah mumbled, climbing out of her blankets. They wasted little time breaking camp, while Nana kept up a constant stream of simple chatter in Wayuunaiki. As they traveled, Nana began working new words into their conversations, refusing to use Castilian to translate while Mariah worked on understanding, trying to use the new terms as often as possible.

"They Wayuu are matrilineal," Nana said when Mariah asked about the culture. "That is, the mother's name is the one that is passed to her children."

"So my mother's surname, Zyanya, was her mother's name?" Mariah clarified, relieved that she could make the entire sentence out of Wayuunaiki words.

"Yes, and her mother's before her, and her mother's, and so on." Nana nodded. "It is actually not inappropriate to name your son the way you've suggested, giving him your surname, since you also have the Wayuu heritage."

Mariah nodded, and her mind wandered to her child. Perhaps she, too, would have a daughter someday. It seemed a shame to let such an old name die out. She realized Nana had begun talking again and forced her attention back to the conversation.

***

They had traveled west at first, but once they'd entered the jungles and mountains, Mariah lost all sense of direction, trusting Nana to lead her true. The endless green of the jungle thinned, but instead of feeling reassured, the increasing openness left Mariah feeling exposed. The jungles gave way to low, rolling hills, and from there into arid desert, she wondered just how big the land was. Her father's maps had made it seem a very narrow stretch of land, traversable in a matter of a few days, but she and Nana had been travelling for over two weeks. Surely, they should have reached the shores of the Caribbean by now.

"We should reach your mother's village today," Nana said one morning as they broke camp.

Mariah smiled, her ears still ringing with the sound of Alistair's howl. It had seemed to grow louder and more urgent as she travelled, pulling her on. Mariah hadn't noticed the change at first, but it had made her edgy and increasingly impatient.

At the same time, each day was more wearying than the previous. Her hips ached with the weight of her child, her feet were often swollen at the end of the day, and her back never stopped aching. More than almost anything, Mariah wished they could just stop and rest, but the dreams spurred her forward. With luck, reaching the village would provide some relief from the feelings of unease as well as the increasing heat. However, as the small village came into view, the feeling of urgency only increased.

"So this is where my mother grew up?" Mariah fanned her face for a minute with her wide-brimmed hat before returning it to her head, grateful for its shade. Unusual buildings dotted the landscape, some with mud and wood walls and others merely thatched roofs with no walls at all, and many with brilliantly colored hammocks hanging within. Children ran around the open spaces, chasing goats and chickens, while the adults, dressed in beautifully patterned clothing, focused on their tasks. She wondered if a young Ayelen had played the same games and run about the same way. Would she, Mariah, have grown up here if her mother had lived?

"It is indeed," Nana said with satisfaction. "It was my home once, too. I've missed it."

The children noticed the visitors first and came running up to greet them, shouting and waving their arms. Mariah tensed up in the saddle, hoping that her horse wouldn't spook at the rushing children. She understood a little of the children's chattering before Nana sent them running back with a few stern words.

The adults were slower to look up at them, noticing the changed timbre of the children's near-constant noise. They glanced up at the two newcomers, and Mariah could swear she saw a look of recognition in their lingering gazes. Could they really remember her mother so well after nearly twenty years?

As they passed through the village, word spread ahead of them, and a crowd gathered, gazing at them in an almost reverential awe. It made Mariah uncomfortable until she realized that she wasn't the one they were watching. She peered over at Nana and tried to see her the way villagers saw her. There didn't seem to be anything special, just an old woman sitting proudly atop a horse. Mariah shook her head.

Nana stopped her horse before a building, larger and better put together than the others, and dropped smoothly to the ground. Mariah followed suit the that best she could. Three boys came to take the horses and mules. Nana didn't seem concerned about their ability to tend the horses so Mariah let them go. An old... person stepped out to greet them. Mariah couldn't tell if it was a man or a woman. He—or maybe she—was so old and bent that the body was practically shapeless and his—Mariah decided to consider him male for now— his long silver hair nearly touched the ground.

"Welcome home, old one," he said. Mariah was surprised and then disappointed; the voice wasn't as low as she expected, a perfect pitch to be either male or female. Perhaps a better look at the face would clue her in.

"It is good to be home." Nana swept the ancient into a familiar embrace.

"What news do you bring, *waré*?" the old... person—Mariah found she wasn't comfortable thinking of the elder as a he, either—asked. She recognized the traditional greeting, the word *waré* meaning 'friend.'

Inside the home, a pair of children rushed to hang two additional hammocks under the roof.

"Much is the same, but there is some troubling news that I would speak with you privately about," Nana said in a low voice to the silver-haired elder and gestured toward the doorway. They spoke quickly, and Mariah had to concentrate to translate the Wayuunaiki. She grinned ruefully. Nana had spoken slowly and distinctly to help her learn. But she'd done a good job; Mariah kept up well enough.

"Of course, of course, Old One. Come, let us go inside. You are tired from your journey, I am certain." The elder gestured them inside. "There is food and drink for you both, though we were not aware that you would be here so soon or we would have had… things prepared for you."

Though the hesitation before the word 'things' was very minor, Mariah had noticed it. She wondered, once again, who was Nana to these people?

"Do not worry about it too much, old friend. My patience is nearly endless," Nana said with a serene smile as she sat down.

Everyone in the room chuckled, and Mariah wondered if she had understood correctly. She sat next to Nana and smiled her thanks to the young girl who handed her a plate of food. It smelled warm and distantly familiar. She was both famished and exhausted from the travelling, and though her stomach rumbled, she watched Nana, waiting for her to eat first.

Nana took a bite, and the rest began to eat. The roasted meat nearly melted in Mariah's mouth, filling it with a warm, subtly spiced juice as she chewed, closing her eyes to better enjoy the flavor.

"Time has treated you well," the elder said approvingly.

"It has been far kinder to me than you," Nana said with a smile, and they all laughed again.

Mariah hid her confusion at their strange way of joking behind another careful mouthful of the delicious food.

"This, then, is the child of our dear Ayelen?" The elder gestured to Mariah, setting the plate of food to the side.

"She is indeed." Pride showed in Nana's voice.

"Well, well." The elder nodded thoughtfully, appraising her, and Mariah shifted under the scrutiny. "And the Zyanya line?"

"This is her first. It will be a son." Nana kept her eyes on her food, but Mariah could feel all the eyes in the room turn to her. A hush fell, and Mariah shifted once more, acutely uncomfortable at being the center of a conversation she didn't understand. She set her arm defensively over her belly. Whatever was going on, she did not want Álvaro to be a part of it.

"Then it is time." It was as much of a question as a statement and came from an elderly woman on the other side of the room. Nana said nothing, and Mariah concentrated furiously on her food. After a few minutes of silence that seemed to stretch forever, a buzz of quiet conversation started up.

Mariah remained wrapped in her own thoughts, trying to puzzle out the conversation that had passed between Nana and the elder. As the sun set, a group of giggling children, not older than seven or eight, led her outside. The smallest of the children took her by the hand, and a couple more pulled at her jacket, ushering her, into a central clearing already full of villagers. An elderly woman chased them away from her and Mariah smiled, amazed at the simple joy that surrounded her.

In the middle of the clearing, a large pile of wood smoked, just waiting to become a bonfire. With a pang of nostalgia, Mariah remembered the times her father had built such a large fire in the courtyard when she was little. She had sat on his lap while he'd told her stories and they sang together.

Nearby, the elders and Nana sat together. Nana motioned her over as the flames caught the dry wood. The sweet, tangy smell of the woodsmoke, along with the scents of dirt and goats, moved around her as she sat beside the elders, too tired to give them more than a polite smile as she did so. For the most part they ignored her, talking amongst themselves, and she ignored them in return, watching the dancing flames.

It reminded her of happier days. Mostly of days with Miguel. But then again, it seemed like every day with him had been a happy day. She thought of the sun on his dark hair, his mesmerizing green eyes that she often lost herself in, and the way time had seemed to slow whenever he'd been near. Snippets of conversations floated across her memory, along with times he'd laughed or smiled, or of the dark look in his eyes whenever he sensed danger.

Mariah smiled as she thought of the way he always left flowers for her on the bed when he rose before she woke. She reached a hand into her pocket and opened the pouch she always kept on her person. Mariah ran fingers through the thirteen coins he'd given her for their wedding; he never seemed quite so far away when she touched them.

A hand on her shoulder jolted her from her thoughts. A girl a few years younger than herself stood beside her, looking at her shyly.

"Old One says you sleep now," the girl said in halting Castilian.

"Thank you," Mariah replied in Wayuunaiki, hoping her accent wouldn't be too thick. The girl gave her a bright smile and said something Mariah could not catch. Heaving herself to her feet, Mariah allowed herself to be herded to a hammock hung under the elder's roof.

Despite her exhaustion, Mariah had difficulty falling asleep. Laying in a hammock felt so strange, so very different from anything she'd ever slept in. The world rocked and swayed gently beneath her as she stared into the darkness. Miguel had told her that sailors often slept in hammocks aboard their ships. Was it like this? The muffled foreign sounds of the village—goats, quiet chatter from the bonfire, the breeze over the arid land—wrapped themselves around her as she drifted to sleep.

In the early hours of the morning, when the sounds had finally settled for the night, Mariah thought she came to. Or perhaps she dreamed. From a distant place in her mind, she thought she saw Nana return with a small group, and a cup with a strangely salty and metallic smell. Nana accepted and drank, and seeming to lock eyes with Mariah for a moment before Mariah fell into a deeper and dreamless sleep.

Chapter 12

MARIAH WOKE BEFORE the sun rose, rested and anxious to be on her way. She tried to roll over, but the rocking of the hammock held her tight. She struggled a moment more before flopping back in momentary defeat. Closing her eyes, Mariah listened to the sounds of the village waking up around her, and another sound filled the back of her mind. Why, if they'd made it to the village, did the howl still echo so urgently through her mind? Wasn't this the place Alistair had been urging her to?

Her courage bolstered by the reassurance that Miguel still waited for her, Mariah stretched and yawned. Then, by carefully alternating her weight between her limbs, she scooted closer to the edge. With the relative solidity of the edge of the hammock beneath her, Mariah finally managed to roll to her side. She let out a breath, already exhausted from the effort. Who knew that hammocks could be such work?

Mariah dropped her hand over the side of the hammock and jerked back in surprise when it brushed against a dog's back. The movement upset her precarious balance, and she flapped around wildly for a moment as the hammock slowly, unstoppably, flipped over. Panicking, Mariah flung one arm back into the hammock, grabbing it desperately to keep herself upright as she landed hard on her knees beside the dog. Someone chuckled behind her. Mariah turned and glared at Nana while her hand sought freedom from the fabric. The old woman watched with humor in her eyes as she lounged on a nearby hammock.

"You've found a friend." Nana chortled as the dog flung himself onto Mariah, trying desperately to lick her face clean.

"I think he found me." Mariah shoved the dog off with one hand before he could knock her off balance.

"Are you hurt?" Nana asked as Mariah freed her hand and slowly stood.

"Just my pride, I think."

Nana grinned and settled back into her hammock. Mariah stood, looking at her again. She seemed different today, fresher somehow. *Perhaps it is sleeping in a familiar place*, Mariah thought as she wandered off to relieve herself.

When Mariah returned, she found Nana with what Mariah had come to assume were the village elders, eating breakfast and talking. She seated herself among them and ate in silence, wondering what the ever-present morning howl could mean. Obviously, Miguel wasn't here and, therefore, she could not stay here either. But where would she go next? Perhaps the elders would have a suggestion.

"Mariah!" Nana hissed, nudging her. She looked up, startled. Nana gestured to an old woman who was looking at her expectantly.

"I'm sorry. I guess my mind was elsewhere," Mariah said in her best Wayuunaiki. All the elders nodded as if her comment had a deep and important meaning.

"We were wondering what you plan to do now," the old woman said in a creaky voice. "The Old One has told us the events that have brought you here, but we believe that you have not told all, yes? We would give our assistance but cannot until we know in what form to give it." Again, all the elders nodded thoughtfully.

Mariah looked at her hands and collected her thoughts, hoping her grasp of the language was enough. "I hadn't really made any plans beyond coming here." She fiddled with the cuff of her sleeve. How was she supposed to know what to do next? She needed to find Miguel, but she had no idea where to go from here. "I was hoping that you might have some information that could help me, some direction on where to go next."

"So you are not staying." An old man spoke this time. His statement caused mixed responses from the other elders around the circle. Mariah looked toward Nana, who was concentrating on her food.

"As I said, I hadn't really thought about it, but no, I don't suppose I will be staying."

"What drives you forward?" the elder with an uncertain gender asked. Everyone around the circle looked at Mariah. "It is childish, I suppose." Mariah hesitated. What would they think of her following a dream? But Nana had taken it seriously, so perhaps they would as well. She swallowed, gathering her courage, and spoke. "I have been having a strange dream for a very long time."

"Listening to dreams is not childish," the first old woman said. "What happens in this dream?"

"I am standing at home, in Maracaibo, near the jungle." The words came out, almost without her thinking. "I hear a noise, but when I try to see what it is, I am stopped..." Mariah trailed off. The last time she'd told anyone about the dream, bad things had happened. She ought to have just forgotten about it and never mentioned it again.

"By what?" the woman prodded when Mariah didn't continue.

Mariah kept her gaze firmly on the cuff of her sleeve as she smoothed it over her arm. Best to just get it out quickly. Besides, what else could she lose? "By a dog I used to have. He protects me and dies doing so, but it isn't how he died in real life. Then I am by the lake, sending his body out to sea. Once he is out of sight, I hear him howling, and I know he is still alive. Then I wake up." Mariah finished with a shrug, moving her eyes to the floor.

The silence that followed was deafening. She gathered her courage and glanced up, certain that they'd be staring her down with disapproval. But not a single one was looking at her. They were all exchanging knowing looks with Nana.

"Thank you, Mariah, I think that is all we need from you for now." Nana gestured in a way that made Mariah feel that she was being sent out the door like a child who'd said too much. "Go amuse yourself or find something useful to do. I'll find you later."

Mariah stood without comment. Being sent away like a silly child stung, but then again, having someone else make decisions was a relief. Maybe they would send someone for Miguel for her, then she would not have to decide. Everything she did ended in disaster, anyhow. What would she even do? She wasn't even sure what direction to go. Obviously, there was much more going on between the elders and Nana than she had ever imagined.

Mariah wandered to the large corral that held their horses. Beside it, in an open shelter, lay her tack and saddle bags, and she rummaged through them for the horse brush. Its stiff bristles scraped and prickled her skin before she grasped the smooth wood handle. Grooming the horses had always had a soothing effect and let her focus her thoughts. With a whistle, she called her horse over and tied him to a picket line to begin the ritual of pulling the dirt from his coat.

What if they did make her decide? Or if they wanted to send her home?

Everything in her rebelled at the thought of turning back. She simply couldn't. There had to be a logical way to go about this. Perhaps the best thing to do would be to find out where her father had last been when Miguel found him. Hadn't he told her that he had spent time in the village here? She decided she would ask the elders.

When the horse's deep brown coat gleamed, Mariah stepped back to admire her work and sneezed. Stupid dust. She wiped her nose with a handkerchief and realized for the first time that she was still covered in grime from the trail.

"I've never been this dirty in my life," Mariah muttered as she returned to her packs to look for some clean things to wear. Everything was filthy, and she wrinkled her nose in disgust. They had not stopped long enough for anything as trivial as laundry.

Irritated, Mariah gathered up her clothes and followed the nearby sound of running water, determined to clean them, and if at all possible, herself. She wasn't surprised when she crested the small hill to find a group of women already there, washing clothing. They chatted amicably amongst themselves and only glanced at Mariah as she knelt at the water's edge and began her laundering, plunging the first of her shirts in the cool water. For the first time in her life, she was grateful for the times she had helped Nana with the wash back home.

The rhythmic, methodical pace of washing her clothes soothed her tumultuous thoughts. Before she was quite ready to be done, her pile of dirty clothes had disappeared, and she stood slowly, stretching her back. Her wet hands brushed over the still-filthy cloth of her shirt and she cringed. There was nothing for it though, all her other clothes were still wet. She'd just have to wait until they dried before she could change.

Lifting the pile of wet things, she straightened, wishing she'd thought to bring a basket. Well, she'd know better next time. As she situated the clothes in her arms, a shy-looking woman about her age and enormously pregnant approached, holding out a neatly folded bundle of native clothes.

"For me?" Mariah asked, reaching out tentatively. The woman nodded, painfully shy as Mariah took the deep red cloth. "Thank you. Do you know where I can bathe?"

The young woman nodded and pointed downstream, then returned to her own washing. Mariah tucked the clean clothes under her arm and went to bathe. The cool water that moved over her skin, rinsing the soap and dirt from it, felt glorious. Even managing to work some of the scented lye soap through her hair was calmingly straightforward. For a few minutes, life seemed simple.

When she was finished, she pulled on the loose tan pants and draped the long red dress with its lovely yellow geometric patterns over herself. The loose, relaxed cut of the clothing made her smile. It was so much more sensible than the corsets and layers of skirts she'd been raised in. She washed her last set of clothes, then draped her laundry across the scrubby trees that lined the river to dry in the warm sun.

Satisfied that they would be safe to dry there, Mariah made her way to a large rock to sit on, and brushed through her wet hair. With that out of the way, she set to work brushing the dirt and horsehair from the heavy cloth of Miguel's greatcoat, enjoying the warmth on her face and the rest for her travel-weary muscles. Álvaro did his typical little dance and Mariah laughed at his rambunctious nature. Wrapped in the warmth of the sunlight, her thoughts wandered.

Nana found her there later that afternoon, staring to the northeast.

"Have you been here all day?" Nana asked, pulling Mariah from her reverie.

"I suppose I have." Mariah reluctantly returned her attention to the present. She stretched and groaned as her stiff muscles complained of having not been moved for hours.

"I brought you something to eat." Nana sat down, handed Mariah a brilliantly patterned pouch, and set a basket at her feet. "And a basket for your clothes."

"*Gracias!*" Mariah pulled the bag open, her stomach growling with hunger, and immediately set to eating. She offered some up to Nana, who declined.

Mariah watched the older woman glare at the grass while she ate. "What's got you so upset?"

"What makes you think I'm upset?"

Mariah laughed, inadvertently spitting out a bit of her food. "Your teeth are clenched tight enough to crush rocks, and if you glare any harder at the grass you'll start a fire." She flicked the bread crumb onto the ground.

"Nana snorted and opened her mouth to speak.

"Oh no." Mariah cut her off. "You don't get to sit next to me with that sort of attitude, and then tell me it's none of my business. I'm betting you've had a disagreement with the elders' council."

"Have I ever told you what a nuisance you've become?" Nana asked wryly.

"I learned from the best." Mariah grinned and took another bite of food.

"Must have been your father," Nana grumbled. "It certainly wasn't me."

"Either give me something, or I'll have to start guessing."

"Have you decided on a course of action?" Nana asked.

"No." Mariah shook her head, her eyes flicking to the northeast. "I only know I can't go back, but I have no idea which way is forward."

"There is a legend among this people." Nana paused, but when Mariah did not say anything, she continued. "There is a place to the east, considered sacred to the Wayuu. It is said that the dead walk there. If your dream is any indication, perhaps you should begin your search there."

"Who are you here?" Mariah gave Nana a hard look.

"What do you mean?" Nana responded cautiously.

"I mean that you are revered here. Even the really old people seem to defer to you, and you haven't even been here for twenty years."

"Twenty years is but a passing breath for those my age, and our people have a long enough memory that what is a lifetime to you is negligible to us. And though I always have a spot in the council, they certainly don't defer to me."

"Is that what you're so grouchy about? That you're not getting your way?" Mariah's eyes glinted with amusement. How often had Nana lectured her about that same thing growing up?

"This is their home, their village, and their duty to serve their people." Nana gave a dismissive wave. "They must make decisions based on what they feel is best for those they are responsible for. I must do the same."

"And sometimes those things are at odds." Mariah rubbed her belly where the baby kicked against it. "I know the feeling."

Nana leaned back and turned her face to the sky, remaining silent.

"But you didn't answer my question," Mariah continued. "Who are you to the Wayuu? The only thing I've heard anyone here call you is 'Old One,' though you don't seem half as old as some of the elders."

"You notice much," Nana chuckled. "Let me tell you something that might help you on your search."

"You're avoiding my question," Mariah said in defeat.

Nana continued as though she hadn't heard. "There is a legend among us of two powerful, competing beings."

"You've told me this tale before." Mariah picked at the remaining food.

"There is much more to this tale than I have told you before," Nana said. "The first came among us a long, long time ago. He entranced many of our people, seduced many of them into following him without realizing that they had lost their individual wills. It was a dark time. The Slaver, we call him now.

"After many years of this, another creature with similar coloring and prowess came, offering to fight the Slaver on our behalf."

"The Noble One." Mariah leaned back and closed her eyes.

"Indeed." Nana sat forward, her elbows on her knees. "A cunning agreement was made with this Noble One, in which each side believed they got the better deal. In return for subduing the Slaver, the newcomer agreed to help us and protect us from all future threats. It was he who provided the knowledge of horses and guns when your father's people first landed here. It was he who protected us from the plagues that all but wiped out our cousins. Or so he likes to be credited with."

Mariah opened one eye and gave Nana a skeptical look. The woman spoke as if this Noble One was still around.

"Our continued freedom, however, was conditional," Nana continued before Mariah could interrupt. "A sacrifice is required each and every new moon. The sacrifice being that one of our people, only one, from any of the Wayuu, was to be sent north to die. But even that was to be conditional. Our sacrifice was to be one who was already weak and ready to die. One nearly dead already. He would go and die peacefully, and the body would be burned."

Nana turned to Mariah. "Not a traditional burial by any means, but the bones always made their way back to us. 'Hardly a sacrifice,' we thought."

"My father was to be one of these, wasn't he?" Mariah sat up, resting her weight on her arm.

"Yes."

"Is that what my father meant when he said that Miguel had taken his place?"

"Yes." Nana nodded again.

"I know he is still alive." Mariah stood and gathered her dry laundry. "I must go north and get him."

"No." Nana shook her head and silenced Mariah's protests with a gesture. "East is the only way for you to find him, the only chance for you to be with him if he still lives."

"Why east?" Mariah asked cautiously.

Nana sighed and looked up to the sky. "According to our tales, the powerful ones were friends once. The nobler of the two could not find it in himself to completely destroy our Slaver, his old friend. Those who go north go to serve the Slaver until they die. The Noble One can be found to the east." Contempt began to creep into Nana's voice as she spoke, drawing Mariah's attention. "The other concession from us, though we did not realize it a concession at the time, was that any woman who was discontent, who had lost her way, who had lost a loved one, who had lost her will to live, or for any other reason wanted a different life, was to go to the Noble One, and he would 'help her find her way.'"

Who had Nana lost to this tradition? Mariah didn't dare ask. "If you feel so strongly about it, why would you want me to go to him?"

"As I said, he is the more noble of the two. You have a better chance of obtaining his assistance than you have rescuing your husband from the Slaver on your own. Assuming he still lives."

"And if Miguel does not?"

Nana stood and smoothed out the folds of her dress. "Then, when you are ready, it is to the east that you will find what you seek."

Mariah set the last of her clothes into the basket. There was something Nana wasn't telling her, but she couldn't put her finger on it. "Have any ever returned?"

"Only one." Nana shrugged and walked away.

Mariah watched her go as lethargy from the meal and the warm sun settled on her. There was no need to haul her clothes back to the village yet, so she spread Miguel's greatcoat on the grass and lay down on it. It was too late to do anything useful today, anyhow.

Surely tomorrow would be soon enough for her to leave. The familiar smells of the coat surrounded her, and she drifted off to sleep.

***

Mariah awoke slowly, her mind full of the fuzz of sleep.

"*Majayülü*," a voice said.

"Mmmmhhhm?" Mariah responded, forcing her eyes to open.

"*Majayülü?*" she said again.

Mariah's brain slowly crunched the word. *Señora.*

"I'm awake," she mumbled, pushing herself up awkwardly off her side. The voice belonged to the shy, pregnant woman who had helped her earlier. Mariah repeated herself, this time in Wayuunaiki.

"It is good." The shy woman ducked her head from Mariah's gaze. "It will be dark soon, and you should not still be out here."

Mariah agreed and heaved herself up to her feet, picking up Miguel's dark coat from off the grass as she rose. When had standing become so difficult? No doubt it was still just soreness from traveling. They each took a side of the basket, and Mariah asked the woman her name.

"Muusa," she said as they began to walk back to the village.

"Cat?" Mariah asked in Castilian.

Muusa nodded and mumbled. "Because I am so nervous."

"When are you expecting?" Mariah gestured to the other woman's very large belly.

Muusa's smile lit up her face, and she looked at Mariah fully for the first time. "Soon. He doesn't move as much now, but I can tell it will be soon. And you?"

"Not for another couple turns of the moon." That would be enough time to find Miguel and return home, right?

"You look sad? Are you not happy to have this child?" Muusa asked.

"I can hardly wait." Mariah forced a smile back to her face. "I am only fearful that his father will not be here to see it."

"I understand that." Muusa's face fell, and she again hid her face. "My child's father will not return. He was lost in the fighting. I know it was a good thing, and we are proud of him, but the pain of his absence is great."

Mariah switched hands with the basket and wrapped her arm around the woman's shoulders. "I am so sorry for your loss."

Chapter 13

THE NEXT MORNING, Mariah woke with Alistair's usual howl in the back of her mind and a determination to not fall out of her hammock. She stretched slowly, careful of the precarious rocking with each movement. Ever so cautiously, she edged her leg over the side as the hammock tipped further and further. Relief washed over her as her foot planted firmly on the ground. Now she had only to work up the courage to get her other leg off.

After much careful maneuvering, she sat upright. Her triumph was short-lived, however, when she tried to actually stand and couldn't bring herself far enough forward to get out of the hammock. With a sigh, she lay back, rocking gently.

"Álvaro," she said with a hand on her belly, "you've got to help me out a little bit here, and not get any bigger."

"That's never a wise thing to ask," Nana said in her native tongue.

Mariah turned her head toward the other woman's hammock. "Do you just lie there, waiting for me to wake up?"

"You'll never truly learn your mother's language if you insist on speaking your own."

Mariah took Nana's suggestion and switched languages. "I think you delight in not answering my questions."

"You've at least another two moons before he comes, maybe even three. Now he begins to grow in earnest."

Mariah groaned and sank further into the hammock. "Don't tell me that."

"What would you like me to tell you? That you'll never fit into your dresses again? That your body will never be the same? That your world will shift when your son is born, so that everything is weighed against the wellbeing of your child? These are things you will not really understand until they come to be."

Curious, Mariah looked again at her mentor. "And have those things happened for you? Did you ever have children Nana?"

"No." The older woman laughed, but her voice was somewhere between wistful and bitter. "No, children of my own were never in my stars."

"Then, if you say that it cannot be understood until it is experienced, how do you know?"

"Child, there is a difference between knowing a thing and understanding it. I know it because I have seen it hundreds of times, but having never been through it, I cannot truly understand it."

"Surely not hundreds, unless you were a traveling midwife before you attached yourself to my mother."

"Oh yes." There was a smile in Nana's voice. "Hundreds. All the children here—before you were born, at any rate—and their parents, and theirs before them. Each one of them, completely enamored with their new little babes, as I'm sure you will be, the moment he is first laid in your arms."

"I think your memory is faulty, old woman. There are not nearly enough people here for you to have attended hundreds of births."

Nana laughed again. "Have you made a plan yet?"

"I suppose I will go east. However, if you think it is not imposing on their hospitality, I'd like to stay here and rest for a few more days. I'm so sore still that the thought of getting back into that saddle so soon almost makes me want to cry."

"You must stay," the voice of an elder cut in. A woman with hair as white as Nana's, and who stood just as proud despite her weathered face and gnarled hands, stood nearby. "We were not expecting you quite so soon. The other families won't be here for a few more days, and you will need to be here for that."

"The other families?" Mariah asked.

"Each community is mostly made up of family groups, so as to avoid mingling their herds. This one is one of the larger groups," Nana explained.

"We are blessed here with an unusually good water source and good grazing for our flocks," the elder added, "so it is natural that when we need to meet, it is here."

"The additional rest will be welcome." Mariah leaned forward to try to heave herself up again. "But for now, I think I am done resting. I need to...get...up." She flopped back into the hammock once more as her latest attempt at standing failed. She closed her eyes to the swaying world as the older women chuckled.

"Try walking backwards, *chica*," Nana suggested before turning to converse with the elder.

Backwards. Mariah's bladder informed her that it would burst if she didn't figure something out quickly. What could it hurt to try?

Leaning forward until her feet touched down, she carefully scooted her feet further and further back until she was standing, crouched over, with the hammock draped across her back.

"So undignified," she muttered as she slowly straightened herself, mindful of causing cramps in her abdomen.

Later, as she ate breakfast, Mariah called out to Mussa as she walked past with a bulging, beautifully colored bag under her arm and an elderly woman walking beside her.

"Good morning," Muusa returned with a smile. "Have you met my *maachon*?"

Grandmother, Mariah realized after a moment of searching for the translation.

The elderly woman gave Mariah a warm smile, and though her hands shook as they took Mariah's, they were strong. "You may call me Maachon, as the Old One tells me you have none of your own."

"*Gracias.*" Mariah's heart lifted at the offer. She nodded to the bags they carried. "What have you got there?"

"I am going to begin weaving another *mochilas.*" Muusa ducked her head from the attention.

"Did you make that bag, the *mochilas*? It is very beautiful."

Muusa nodded, blushing.

"Would you mind if I watched?" Mariah asked as she stood.

"We'd love the company, but why would you want to just watch? Did you not bring your own to make?" Maachon asked as they began walking and Mariah fell into step beside them.

"No, I didn't think my crochet needles would be something I'd need out here." She laughed. "Besides, I've never made anything as lovely as that before. Could you teach me?"

"You mean that you don't already know?" Muusa looked surprised.

Mariah shook her head. "No, not like that."

"Not even the Old One? Surely she would have taught you these things after your mother died." Muusa stopped beneath a tree, and Mariah helped her spread out a blanket on the grass.

"I never even knew my mother was one of the People until recently. The Old One helped raise me, but she never offered to teach me anything other than what any other Spanish girl might learn."

"So you were raised entirely as *alijuna*. You know nothing of Si'a, Pulowi and Juya, or Wale´kerü?" Muusa helped Maachon take a seat on the brightly woven blanket.

"Nana told me tales of Si'a as a child, stealing jewels from the sea goddess, and a few words here and there, but not much else." Mariah shrugged and took a seat beside them. "What is Wale´kerü?"

"Who," Muusa corrected. "Who is Wale´kerü. She is the one who taught us how to weave. She is a…." She trailed off, trying to think of a simple way to explain herself. Putting her hands on top of each other, Muusa wiggled her fingers, crawling them up Mariah's arm. "One who weaves?"

"*La araña!*" Mariah said, suddenly understanding. "The Greeks have a similar tale, of how Arachne angered the goddess Athena by being a better weaver, and Athena turned her into a spider as punishment."

"How terrible!" Muusa looked truly shocked. "No, Wale´kerü taught women to weave. She was a spider first, and she fell in love with a Wayuu man."

Mariah sat back, watching and listening as the other woman began her new bag and told the story of how weaving came to her people.

***

On the day of the celebration, Mariah found herself set to simple chores alongside the older children. Even the young women were doing more involved tasks than she. Not that she minded, though. Her attempts to assist with cooking or other preparatory work had only served to showcase her ineptitude at such things. The women had been gracious about it but clearly relieved when she asked how else she might help.

The last few days had been both relaxing and enlightening. Mariah felt she had picked up far more of the language as she spoke with and listened to the other women and the children who played about them. She had also felt a sense of inclusion and warmth that she'd never before known. She and her childhood friends had been close, but not like this.

Back aching, she took a seat on a stool beside a young tree to rest for a few minutes. She watched the boys on the outskirts of the village minding the livestock herds, and listened to the young girls giggling as they sang children's songs. The songs held a sense of familiarity about them, stirring in her a ghost of a memory. A distant echo of a song floated through Mariah's mind, and though she grasped at it, it eluded her like a wisp of smoke dancing around her hand.

Perhaps she would ask Nana about it the next time they spoke.

After a few minutes, Mariah's back began to ache horribly. Sitting on the stool was clearly doing it no favors, so she heaved herself to her feet. Her belly grew daily, and she could not imagine it getting any larger, yet somehow it did.

"How big are you planning to get in there?" she asked ruefully, rubbing her back with one hand and supporting her belly with the other. In response, Álvaro stretched and Mariah was treated to pain in both her rib and above her hip. "Enough of that!" she said with a smile. "We'd better go—"

A searing pain shot through her back and wrapped around her stomach, cutting off her breath. Gasping, she reached for the tree for support. The muscles in her belly felt as though they wanted to tear themselves from her body. The pain passed after only a few seconds, but Mariah stayed crouched over, leaning against the sturdy tree for a full minute. She breathed heavily, more from the shock of the experience than from the pain.

"Are you well?" a young voice asked, concerned.

Mariah looked up and saw a young woman with very short hair, fresh from childhood, looking at her.

"I think so." Slowly, she stood, straightening her back. "But I think I had better lie down. Would you help me to the *piichi*?"

"Of course."

Once in her hammock, Mariah's body finally relaxed, but her mind raced. She counted back in her head, and again, and a third time. At best, she was only seven months along. Ice clutched at her heart with realization—it was too soon!

"Mariah?" Mariah turned her head toward Nana as she entered the room.

"It's too soon," she whispered. "I can't have him yet."

"Was it only the one pain, or have you been having them often?" Nana's calm level voice did nothing to soothe Mariah. She'd heard that particular tone too many times.

"Only once. I stood up. Sometimes I get cramps when I stand, but not like this. This was… different. It was like a cramp over my entire belly."

"How long did it last?"

"Only a few seconds, I think." Mariah shuddered inwardly. *Only* a few seconds. A few torturous seconds.

Nana nodded. "I was afraid of this. Your mother had this problem, as had her mother and her aunts. The others, not so much. Perhaps, if we keep you rested, they will not start in earnest for at least another moon."

Mariah nodded and closed her eyes, hot tears forming in her eyes. The reality of her condition had not truly set in with her until the moment the pain began. Up until then, she had still harbored some foolish idea that she'd go gallivanting off on her horse tomorrow or the next day, dash in to some place, snatch her husband out of the hands of folklore demons, and be back to Maracaibo, safely in her home before the child came. And everything would be a lovely, happily ever after.

Reality dashed that dream like a boulder dropped in a still pond.

She would be here until her son was born. And then what? Hopelessness welled up inside her as she struggled to find her path forward. She couldn't just leave her infant son to go adventuring, yet nightly, her dreams reminded her forcefully that Miguel was alive. Alive and in need of her help. They both pulled at her, and she held them tight, for their lives depended on her strength. The howl that echoed through her mind each morning urged her forward, pushing her to go. Her son required that she stay.

I'm not meant for this! she cried out to whomever might be listening. *You never taught me how to hold people's lives in my hands!*

She opened her eyes to find herself alone in the room, the door left open. Through it stretched a sea of gentle grass, running straight from her heart into the unknown distance. She couldn't stay. But leaving her son was as impossible as taking him with her.

Despair washed over her and she turned to her side and wept.

***

Mariah stood in a field of gently waving grass. The jungle was nearby, dark, and green, and inviting. But today she did not care. Peace tried to wrap itself around her like a blanket, but her problems were too great and the peace too thin. She could still feel the bitter tears on her cheeks. A warm wind tried to stroke them away, lifting her hair, but she turned her face from it. She did not seek comfort tonight. The skies darkened, and she awaited the rain. It always rained here.

A warmth pressed itself against her hand, and she dropped down to her Alistair, hugging his neck tight.

What am I to do? she asked, feeling hollow inside.

As if he knew her inner turmoil, Alistair pressed himself against her, and she hugged him closer.

As they sat, she heard a tune from the distance. It was the elusive memory she'd had while the children were at play. She could hear it now and could tell that it was a lullaby, but it rose and faded as though carried away by a breeze.

When the inevitable rustling came from the jungle, Mariah simply turned her back on it and stepped out of her dream. Alistair's howl followed her to consciousness.

***

Mariah spent the next couple of weeks resting as much as she could. The thought of her son coming before he was ready terrified her. Occasionally, her pains would begin again if she exerted herself, and only immediate rest calmed them.

As she grew ever larger, Álvaro moved less and less. There were times when she'd suddenly realize that she couldn't remember the last time he'd moved that day. It felt as though the entire world held its breath as she stopped whatever she was doing and waited for him to move again, hoping desperately that he remained alive. He always did, eventually, flooding Mariah with relief.

Mariah passed the time with Muusa, *abuela* Maachon, and the other women, learning more of the language and listening to their legends. Often, she worked on crocheting a bag of her own as they patiently instructed her, but her mind seemed to refuse to retain their words.

Looking down at the mess of material she currently held in her lap, Mariah sighed. No doubt she would figure it out some day, but right now, she simply couldn't think.

She was just so tired, so uncomfortable, and so stressed. The dreams could not be stopped, and she tossed and turned in her hammock at night whenever she wasn't in the dream. The days crawled by in misery, alleviated somewhat by the company of the other women, but the nights ran even slower. Each night she was torn with the wish that she could just be finished with pregnancy, cursing her lot to be a woman and the terror of birthing him before he was ready. Each morning, she dreaded another day, but in the evening, felt blessed they had made it through another day.

The days became rainier and rainier, and one day Muusa and *abuela* Maachon were not with the other women.

"Her time has come," one of them told her when Mariah asked after her friend.

"I hope it all goes well," Mariah said.

"I'm sure it will be fine." The woman patted Mariah on the arm.

It was not until the next day that she received the news. Mariah was resting in her hammock, listening to the rain, when Nana came in with a smile.

"Your friend Muusa has been delivered."

"What did she have?" Mariah asked, sitting up carefully.

"A boy and a girl."

"Twins!" Mariah was astounded. Carrying one was bad enough; she could barely imagine carrying two at once. "Imagine that. Are they well? When can I see them?"

"So it seems for now. It will be a while before they are ready for visitors. The new ones can catch illness so easily the first few weeks."

"But her family at least is with her, aren't they? She's not alone?"

"Goodness, no!" Nana took a seat on the edge of Mariah's hammock. "Her immediate family is all gone, but she has cousins, aunts, and her grandmother here to care for her. When she and the children are strong enough, she will take them to her husband's mother so that they also may know his children."

Mariah lay back down and felt tears stinging her eyes. "I'm glad she has family to care for her."

"What is this, child?" Nana leaned forward to wipe the tears from Mariah's cheeks. "Do you think you have no family here?"

Mariah turned away. "There is only you."

The older woman sat back and folded her hands in her lap. "I am sorry, *chica,* I have been remiss in my responsibilities to you. May Ayelen forgive me of it; there has just been so much to do now that I am *home.*

"Did you forget that this was your mother's home as well? It's true that her brother and parents are long dead, but she had aunts and cousins. When your time comes, you will have family with you as well."

"Who? They are all at best my cousins. Yes, I eat with them and listen to their stories, but I still don't feel like I belong."

"That is because you don't. This is but a stop on your journey. You are not meant to stay here."

"Is that what the council has decided? Or you told them to decide? I'm to just do whatever they tell me?"

"The elders make decisions independently of me, and I of them." Nana touched Mariah's shoulder gently. "You must move forward from here. You can't go back."

Mariah turned back to look at Nana, her eyes narrowing as bitterness turned in her stomach. "You still believe that? That I'm supposed to somehow free this people from a supernatural force? Me, all alone with a baby slung across my back against an immortal—what did you call him? A blood-sucking viper? What does that even mean? That he's some snake you want me to stomp on? Or maybe some faerie-tale vampire? What other absurdities should I believe while I'm at it? The hydra, perhaps, or the *duende*?"

Nana's reply was sharp. "Well, he certainly isn't a snake, and whether or not you take your baby is entirely up to you, but I certainly wouldn't advise it."

"Then what would you advise, oh great and wise *Old One*?" Mariah's irritation flared up within her. "Do you actually believe he is real? You do, don't you? You think he's really out there, and that some ancient vampire feud exists. How do you know it's not just some other clan at this point who kills everyone you send? Have you ever been there? Ever seen him? Has anybody? You keep saying that no one ever returns. If that's so, how do you know this creature even still exists?"

"I have not seen him myself," Nana answered quietly. "But there was one who has."

"Who?'" Mariah demanded.

Nana stood and walked toward the door. For a moment, Mariah thought that she wouldn't answer, but Nana stopped and turned back.

"My mother," she said quietly, before slipping out of the room.

Mariah snorted and rolled over again, irritated, uncomfortable, and lonely.

Chapter 14

WHEN MARIAH'S PAINS finally came in earnest, she found she was unprepared for them. As each round of pain intensified, her anger and sense of loneliness grew. She gritted her teeth through the agony that doubled her over and cursed Miguel for not keeping his promise to return. As the vice-like grip loosened its hold on her body, she caught her breath and turned her anger toward her father.

She walked across the small room, aware in some small part of her mind that her anger was unjustified. As another contraction tightened her back, she cursed her father for leaving the first time, for getting sick, for returning, and then, finally, for dying. With each round of abdominal torture, she grabbed hold of something to be angry at. Her mother. Her father. Miguel. Mostly, though, Mariah berated herself for allowing any of this to happen. For causing any of this to happen. For being so stupid as to leave home while she was pregnant instead of just waiting.

When Nana came to prepare her to deliver the baby, Mariah was less than helpful. Mariah snarled at her through the pain and threw whatever came to hand at her until Nana retreated, shaking her head. Nana waited just outside the door until Mother Nature won the argument for her before returning to assist.

The labor continued, long and difficult, and Mariah lost track of everything beyond the next contraction and Nana's voice guiding her through them. Then, suddenly, it was over. Mariah held her beautiful, perfect, tiny son in her arms, and despite her exhaustion, she couldn't stop looking at him, full of wonder. He was the most perfect thing she'd ever seen. She marveled at his little features, his perfect, tiny hands and feet.

Eventually, she allowed Nana to take him to get cleaned, and she dozed off almost instantly.

She awoke to her son lying on her chest. His weight was so perfect, the way he breathed, the shape of his head, his beautiful dark hair. It all pulled her in. There was nothing in this world but her little Álvaro.

"Hello, little one. My little Álvaro Michael Álvarez del Mar. It is so nice to finally meet you." Mariah cooed and turned him over to admire his face with its exquisitely tiny eyes and lips. He squeaked, scrunched up his face, and started crying.

She looked helplessly up at Nana, who instructed her on how to nurse him.

"He's a good, strong boy," Nana said proudly as he settled to his task.

The little bundle in her arms entranced Mariah. "He's beautiful. So perfect."

"He looks just like you did when you were born, and you look so like your mother. I remember her looking at you the same way. It's that look all mothers get."

"Are they always this small?" Mariah asked as he fell asleep in her arms.

"No, not usually." Nana said. "He's a bit early. I worried at first that he would not breathe on his own, but he has a fine set of lungs and is eating well. It's too early to say anything for certain, but I wouldn't worry too much about it."

She patted Mariah's knee and took the sleeping bundle. "Get some rest, I will watch over him while you sleep."

Mariah wanted to protest, but the exhaustion overwhelmed her, and she slept.

***

The next few days passed in a haze for Mariah, an endless cycle of feeding Álvaro what seemed like every hour, and falling—exhausted—back to sleep. Occasionally, she ate and saw to her own needs, though it seemed that every hour of her day was shadowed by the nearly constant cramping of her womb. Nana assured her that the cramping was normal and would go away, but it made Mariah uneasy.

Álvaro, however, made every bit of the pain and sleeplessness worth it. She found she loved him more every time she nursed him, looked at him, or held him. There was nothing in the world she wouldn't give to keep him safe. She would learn to live with the ache that her dreams left her with each morning, begging her to find Miguel. Mariah smiled down at her sleeping son, and for a moment he smiled back, then relaxed again in sleep. She would even face Nana's disappointment. She would keep him safe no matter the consequences.

"I don't know what I'd do without you here to help me with him," she said to Nana one day after she had finished nursing Álvaro. "I can't imagine if I'd been left to manage this on my own."

"I don't think we were ever meant to do it on our own." Nana gazed at the little baby she held. "I know you've been preoccupied, but have you given any thought to where you will go from here?"

Mariah nodded, leaning back in the hammock. "As soon as we're both strong enough, I will go home. It is strange, the way the world changes when you have a child. It's like I never knew the meaning of love before. It's overwhelming and feels as though there is nothing in the world that I wouldn't do for this precious little one. Then I think about my parents and can hardly believe they felt so strongly about me, though I'm sure they did. I think I understand them a little better now."

"That sounds about right."

"Do you think that feeling ever goes away or lessens with time?" She watched the thatched roof sway above her as she thought about her father, seeing his actions across her childhood in a new light.

"I wouldn't know, never having had children of my own. But, from what I've seen, I don't think that it does. You just learn to live with it better. It's similar to pain in that regard, I think."

Álvaro began to cry, and Nana walked around the room, bouncing him on her shoulder until he let out a loud belch.

"I couldn't ever put him in harm's way, and Miguel wouldn't want me risking our son for his sake. We'll go home." Mariah gave a wry grin. "As soon as I can sit down without wincing, anyway."

Nana chuckled. "Give it time, *chica.*"

"I'm going to try to sleep." Mariah pulled her feet up onto the hammock with a shiver as a light rain began drumming on the roof. "Could you get me another blanket? It's a little chilly."

"Certainly," Nana said as she left.

Mariah was asleep before she returned.

***

Mariah slept fitfully. She was so cold. She tossed and turned in her bed, and something tangled about her, cocooning her legs and spinning the world beneath her. She tried to stand, but the rain beat down from an empty sky and the grass tripped her feet. Mariah clung to Alistair as he fed her warmth, but it wasn't enough, and still the world spun. Words whispered around her on the wind. Green eyes watched her from within her heart, and an infant cried for his mother. The world turned, and with it the bone-deep chill turned to heat, muggy and unbreathable. And finally, she slept.

***

Her lips hurt. Mariah tried to lick them, but her mouth was too dry. "Water," she tried to say, but her parched throat merely croaked. Nana was by her side instantly, sitting her up and pressing a cup to her lips.

"Slowly now," Nana said. "You've been ill with a childbirth fever for some time."

Glorious and cool, the water touched her lips, and Mariah let it sit, soaking into her mouth before swallowing. She tried to drink deeply next, but Nana allowed only sips. The next thing she knew, the light had changed and Nana offered broth. It, too, was wonderful. When she was finally able to stay awake for longer than it took to swallow a few bites she asked about her son.

"Don't worry about him for now, *chica*," Nana told her softly. "Get your strength back first."

At first Mariah was too weak to fight about it, but as her strength grew, so did her insistence about seeing her son. One day when she didn't fall immediately back to sleep after eating, Mariah drew her strength together and rolled from her hammock, dumping herself on the floor. Her arms and legs collapsed under her weight, and she lay stunned for a moment, shocked at her inability to catch herself. She gritted her teeth. That was not important right now. Finding Álvaro was.

Clutching onto the wall for support, she drew herself to a stand and hobbled to the door. Nana looked up at her from where she sat just outside the door and waited for Mariah to speak.

"Where is Álvaro?" Mariah asked, slow and concise.

"You'd best sit down, Mariah." Nana came and took her arm, helping her to a chair. "How are you feeling?"

Her limbs felt heavy and everything inside her said that lying on the floor and sliding into unconsciousness would be best. "Wrung out. Sore all over. I can't take a deep breath without pain. Where is my son?"

"You've improved quite a bit, but you're still ill. I was worried you might not make it for some time."

"I don't care about that. Where is my son?" Mariah tried to put force behind her words, but they were still weak.

Nana knelt down before her and took her hand. "Mariah, I am so very sorry—"

A chill stole through Mariah's chest, and she jerked her hand away, dropping it uselessly to her lap. Her heart sank beneath the fear that welled up inside her. "What are you saying?"

"I'm sorry, *mi querida*. Your son is dead."

Her heart seemed to stop, and she shook her head in disbelief, but Nana continued on.

"He died in his sleep. It happens, sometimes. No one really knows why."

"I don't believe you," she whispered as the chill in her chest turned to pain. Images of his tiny, perfect fingers curled around her own flashed through her mind. "Let me see him! I need to see my Álvaro."

"We've already buried him. He died while you were ill, and we couldn't wait for you to get better." Nana choked up. "There were a few times we thought we'd lose you, too."

"Then take me to his grave."

Nana stood and helped her to her feet. Darkness threatened to consume Mariah as she walked, but she held it at bay, concentrating on putting one foot in front of the other on the soggy ground.

They stopped before a mound of earth, still relatively fresh, and to Mariah's eyes, impossibly small. Too small to be a grave. No one should ever have to see a grave so small. She dropped to the ground beside it, her pain exploding out of her chest, and screamed in wordless agony. Never had she known pain like this, and she curled into herself on the cold ground, allowing the darkness to swallow her.

***

Time passed, and the season turned, but Mariah didn't care. She had nothing left. Death would have been a relief, but her body defied her. It wanted to live, and the people around her conspired to make it so. She ate. She drank. She slept. She grew stronger. She envied Selena's mother, who was said to have just turned her head to the wall and died after birthing a daughter instead of a son. Who knew that death was not so easy?

The spark of life was in her, banked but warm, as she lay in apathy and depression. Sometimes, when the wind touched it just so, it flared a little, and for a moment Mariah would awaken to the world around her. But then her arms would remember holding her baby, or another child in the village would cry, or her hands would brush her deflated belly, and the darkness would wash over her again.

***

One day that was no different from the ones before it, Mariah sat, staring out over the fields to the northeast, as she often did. A breeze sauntered past her, running its fingers through her hair. She closed her eyes and inhaled, half expecting to see ever faithful Alistair beside her when she opened them. But there was only Nana.

Mariah could hear the children playing in the distance around the village, and for the first time it didn't hurt. She didn't want it to not hurt, but it didn't care what she wanted. It never had.

"How could this have happened?" How had so much gone so wrong so quickly? Mariah stared into the distance, her mind running through the events that had brought her here, the path etched into her brain like ruts in the road, and just as inescapable. "A year ago, I had everything. I had Miguel, and my father. My home. Dreams and a future. Now I have nothing."

What had brought her to this? What a fool she had been, to risk Álvaro's life. "And what was it all for?" Mariah asked. *It was for Miguel.* She had told herself that a thousand times, and with each time the excuse wore thinner. And this time she saw through it. Mariah shook her head. "I did it for myself. My own selfishness."

Tears blurred Mariah's vision as the truth tumbled through her mind. Her own shortsightedness had brought her out here in the middle of a pregnancy. Her own arrogance had convinced her she would be fine. Sobs pushed their way up her chest and out her mouth. How could she have been so stupid? How could she have not taken five seconds to really think things through?

She dropped to the ground, breathless as though she'd been punched in the gut. She'd sent Miguel to his death. She could have stopped him. She could have simply held her tongue and not needed to stop him. Everything she had lost had been her own fault.

"Why couldn't you have let me die?" Mariah whispered.

"Because you are needed." Nana gently touched Mariah's hair.

"I don't care about your legends." Mariah's arms ached with their emptiness. She had nothing left to hold to. "I just want my son back."

Nana crouched down beside her and lifted Mariah's chin. "All things that begin must end. Your son is gone, *mi querida*. But you remain. You can make their sacrifices worth something."

Mariah looked away from Nana's intense brown eyes. It was selfishness that had brought her to this point. Perhaps it was justice that she let go of her own will and allowed herself to be swept along by fate. She snorted at the childish absurdity of the thought. No, it was responsibility Nana asked of her. Something she had avoided all her life.

Miguel still needed her help. And how would she tell him she had lost their child? The numbness within her spread. She had to find him, he deserved to know what had happened to their son. She couldn't undo what she'd done, but perhaps she could begin to pay for it. Taking a deep breath that served only to amplify the emptiness of her heart, Mariah stood.

"I'll go," she said in Wayuunaiki. "I'll leave tomorrow, if you will show me the way."

Nana nodded, and together they returned to the village.

***

The next morning, Mariah and Nana were on their way before the sun had risen.

"I'm glad you came," Mariah said after a few minutes.

Nana only grunted.

They rode in silence for most of the day and didn't speak much when they stopped for the night. As the sun neared its zenith the next day Nana pulled her horse to a sudden stop. Mariah pulled up and looked back at her.

Nana looked pale and her face taut. "This is as far as I dare go, child. I should not have come this far."

"You are a strange woman, Nana. Thank you for all you've done." Mariah leaned over to give her old nurse a hug, ignoring the moment of lightheadedness it caused. "Take care of yourself, old woman."

"And you, child. I shall miss you." Nana smiled a sad smile. "This will be the first time in many, many years that a Zyanya woman was not in my care. Things are in your hands now. Be wise, and follow your heart."

Mariah nodded and kicked her horse eastward. Behind her, a haunting Wayuu melody rose into the air. The music seemed to follow her longer than it should have. The song began with a sorrow that spoke to the pain in her heart, but it turned to a joy that Mariah did not want to understand. Then it was lost in the sound of her horses' hoof beats.

Chapter 15

RIDING ALONE FELT strange. Though she had not spoken often of late, Mariah missed knowing that she could talk, if she wanted. She tried talking to herself or the horse, but found that more often than not, she lapsed into silence, her mind as blank as the rolling desert before her. Exhaustion pulled at her constantly, and more than once, she fell asleep in her saddle.

The land dried out, and the vegetation became sparse as she traveled deeper into the arid land. She tried to keep her course due east but often found herself veering to the north. Mariah wasn't quite sure what she was looking for, though she felt certain she would know it when she found it. Her thoughts inevitably circled around to hopelessness, and she would close her eyes and simply try to breathe, trusting the horse to continue forward. Forward was the only direction that held anything for her. There was nothing to return to.

Perhaps she was foolish for holding to her husband so tightly. She paused near a stream as the sun sank against the distant hills to her back. Her horse dropped its head and drank noisily. Perhaps everyone would have been better off if she had stayed home. Perhaps Álvaro would have died anyhow. She drank from her canteen, the warm water unpalatable but better than nothing.

Perhaps, with time, the feeling that a part of her was elsewhere—to the northeast— would fade and she would no longer be drawn inexplicably toward it, compelled toward it. The pull that kept her alive and moving forward might finally weaken, and she might return to that life from before. She mounted the horse, nudging it away from the stream. If she went back... The idea that some other man might come and take Miguel's place, might try to replace her Álvaro with another child, filled her with fury. Kicking her horse into a gallop, they nearly flew across the landscape until they were both spent, as though she could outrun such haunting thoughts.

In the dark, starlit night, Mariah's horse stumbled to a stop, and she dismounted, clutching the saddle for support as she got her feet beneath her. This was as good a place to stay as any. Her horse grunted in relief as she unsaddled him. Mariah had felt no need to track the time since her son's passing; one day was like another to her, blending into a singular stretch of blurred actions and inescapable thoughts. The dreams had not stopped, either. She took comfort in the presence of her protector in her dream, often talking to him as she would have spoken to Miguel. In a way, the dreams had become more real to her than her waking

Amaranth Dawn

hours, for they filled her senses vividly in ways the desert could not.

Her fingers moved with a strange disconnect as she untied her saddlebags. She watched them as though they belonged to someone else. A bone-deep weariness filled her, but she looked forward to sleep with a mixed sense of relief and dread. Perhaps tonight, when she searched for Álvaro in the dreams, the way she had known him before he was born, she would at last find him. She had never caught anything more substantial than the sound of a cry lost in the breeze. But still she hoped.

She set her horses to grazing and stared over the land as the moon rose, illuminating the terrain. The soft chirping of crickets filled the desert landscape as she ate her meager dinner. She ate only because she knew she must. Taking stock, she looked across the landscape. To the south there were small mountains, and more to the distant northeast. To the west and north lay the desert she had come across. Mariah tried to picture one of the maps her father had hung in his office. She'd looked at them so often in her youth that she thought she knew them, but she'd never thought the land was so big. The maps had made everything seem small and close together.

Her eyes were drawn again to the mountains to the northeast. Was that where she would find Miguel? Was she going in the wrong direction? What if she had missed it, whatever it was that Nana and fate had directed her toward?

Mariah finished her food and stared into the darkness, absorbed in her thoughts. A woman stepped from the shadows and into the dim light of her fire, startling her.

Mariah leapt to her feet and pulled out her pistols, fully cocked almost before they were free. The stranger stopped abruptly and put their hands out slowly, empty palms up.

"Who are you?" Mariah demanded in Spanish. "What do you want?"

The shadowy figure—a woman—shook her head, so Mariah tried again in Wayuunaiki.

"I've been sent to collect you," the woman said.

Mariah peered over the fire, trying to make out details in the near darkness. "Come around so I can see you." She gestured to the side with one of the pistols.

The woman complied, moving slowly and deliberately. As she rounded the fire, her features and dark hair proclaimed her Wayuu. She wore strange clothes, unlike either the Spanish dress Mariah was used to or the native dress the people of the village had worn. Mariah guessed the woman to be about her father's age.

"Who are you?"

"My name is Iráma. I have been sent to bring you to your new home," the woman said, her voice calm and smooth.

"I am not searching for a new home." Mariah's pistols remained trained on Iráma, who smiled blandly.

"You seek something you cannot find. I wish only to take you to one who can help."

"The Noble One?" Mariah asked, hesitant.

"Yes. He'll be glad to know they still call him that." Iráma sounded amused. "Come now, we must get moving."

Mariah uncocked her pistols but put them at the ready before tucking them away, sending a grateful thought to Miguel for his lessons. She wished he could receive it. Mariah packed the camp as quickly as she could manage, her horse grunting with displeasure as she resaddled it. Iráma watched quietly, then led the way into the darkness.

At first, Mariah feared for the animal and herself, and led the tired horse behind her. What if one of them misstepped in the dark? But Iráma guided them without hesitation. Mariah watched the land pass by for a while before it occurred to her that they were headed south.

"We are going back south?" Mariah asked.

"Yes. You always seemed to turn toward the north, so the 'Noble One' decided to wait a little longer to retrieve you to make certain it was he you searched for."

"I see. Is that how you know who is looking for you?"

"Not me. No one is looking for me. They come for him and what help he might give," Iráma said.

Mariah gave her a curious look. Iráma did not volunteer any further information, and so they lapsed into silence.

As they walked through the night, the mountains loomed closer, and the moon traveled across the sky. Mariah felt she was going to collapse with each step when Iráma finally stopped.

"We will rest here for a little while. The land begins to climb soon, and I don't want to stop again." Iráma slung her pack off her back with an absurd amount of grace.

Mariah rubbed her eyes and exhaustedly followed suit, pulling the saddle from her horse and dropping it unceremoniously on the ground. She brushed, fed, and hobbled her horse, then lay her blanket on the ground.

Iráma, already in her own bedroll several feet away, gave her a warm smile. "Sleep soundly. We have a long walk tomorrow still."

Mariah mumbled a response and dropped onto the blanket. Once on the ground, she stayed awake only long enough to look up at the stars and wonder what Miguel was doing.

***

Mariah was home in Maracaibo. The day was warm and she stood alone in the fields. The clear sky, full of stars, shone above her, but it would rain soon. She missed the nearly constant rain of home. The wind blew the fresh, clean smell of the lake to her, and she inhaled it, savoring the taste. It washed away all the emotions that surrounded her, leaving peace in its wake. She looked around for Alistair but didn't see him. Shrugging, she took a seat on the long grass and started plaiting a few blades into a whimsical design. He would come when it was time.

As she braided the grass, she stretched her mind toward Álvaro, hoping to sense him, or perhaps call his spirit to her. As before, she found nothing. Mariah was disappointed but not surprised.

A rustling in the grass drew her attention, and she looked up to see Alistair standing over her. Mariah stood and threw her arms around the dog's neck, hugging him tightly. When she let go, he licked her face, and together they turned toward the jungle.

Tonight was different, somehow. The rustling didn't draw her. Instead, she found herself looking to the south, back toward the city. Curious, she started toward it and found herself riding her horse. They walked at first, but a sense of urgency overtook them and they broke into a gallop. It wasn't to her father's *hacienda* that the horse took her, but the Casa de la Cuesta. She reined the horse in when the large house came into sight. What in the world were they doing here?

She dismounted and ran up the front steps. Mariah stepped through the front door and onto the balcony that overlooked the gardens. Dancing music came from behind her—someone was having a party.

Was she dressed for a party? Looking down, she found she wore the red and black brocade gown from that night so long ago. It seemed like another lifetime. Couples walked in the gardens beneath her, oblivious to anything beyond each other.

Suddenly, a familiar shape in a familiar coat moved down the path. He had a familiar gait and a familiar cutlass swinging at his side. Mariah could hardly believe it.

Miguel! she shouted and waved her arm. *Miguel! Up here!*

But he did not seem to hear her. She lifted her skirts and charged down. When her feet touched the path, she looked for Miguel, but he was no longer there. She raced down the path she had seen him on. She turned the corner and came to an abrupt halt. She was back in the old dream, on the docks, sending her dead protector back to the sea.

Though neither her father nor Miguel stood beside her, Mariah knew she was not alone. Animosity surrounded her and she spun, looking for the source. A glint of gold in the shadows caught her eye; a figure stood there, just beyond her sight. Mariah turned back to the lake to wait for the howl that would relieve her fears and return her to the waking world.

The howl came and wrapped her in its embrace, depositing her back into her own body while urging her forward.

***

Mariah and Iráma woke before the sun rose and continued on, keeping up a brisk pace and resting only occasionally.

Mariah replayed her dream over and over in her mind, amazed and thrilled at the new turn of events. Perhaps next time, she could find a way to wait in the garden for Miguel, to follow him. Perhaps even stop him. She imagined his look of joy when he turned and saw her. It would be so good to see his face again, even if it was just in a dream. His dark hair, always so smooth to run her fingers through, his beautiful smile and his entrancing green eyes. She remembered all of it.

She remained lost in her daydreams until a turn around a switchback presented her with a sight she could not ignore.

The sun had touched the low horizon behind them. Before her stood a cliff face, with a large, central section smoothed and carved to resemble an ancient building around a dark entrance. Mariah was stunned. To think someone would have gone through all the trouble to cut such a likeness into the very stone!

Mariah rifled through her memories of her father's books, trying to place the ancient style. Greek, perhaps. Two multifaceted pillars stood on either side of the entrance. On either side of the pillars, several feet up, circles had also been cut into the stone— presumably to allow light into the cave. Above the pillars rested a triangular façade with figures worked into the edges. As they drew closer, even more extravagant details became clear.

"What is this place?" she breathed in wonder.

"Home," Iráma said with a little smile.

Mariah dismounted, pulling Miguel's greatcoat from the saddle. She pulled it on and Iráma took the reins, leading the horse through the dark entrance. The woman and horse disappeared abruptly into the darkness, leaving Mariah alone on the outside, still staring at the intricate stonework. Her horse nickered from within, and Mariah gathered her courage to follow.

Mariah expected it to be dark inside, but her eyes adjusted quickly. The entrance hall, either carved from or lined with the same stone that made the façade, funneled her toward a dark hall. Iráma had disappeared, but Mariah could hear the horse's unshod steps clopping on the hard floor.

She followed, the hard stone floor unyielding under her boots, trailing her hand along the rough stone wall as the light faded. The hall twisted a couple times before light appeared before her. Without meaning to, she picked up her pace. The hall opened into a large chamber, and the amount of light that filtered down across the stone, nearly as bright as the evening outside, surprised Mariah.

Iráma waited for her while another Wayuu woman led the horse away. Mariah stared at the room, trying to take it all in. It wasn't that she hadn't seen elegance before—she had practically been raised in the extravagant halls of the Casa de la Cuesta—but this was different.

Torches lined the room, but none were lit. Instead, it seemed that the light was coming from the arched ceiling. She looked up, trying to figure how it had been done, but could not pinpoint a source; the circular windows from the facade did not open into the room. The room itself was round with many doors, some of which were open, and the walls between each door had figures carved into them. Most were human figures in all sorts of poses, but none entirely free of the wall behind them. As her gaze swept the room, she caught sight of Iráma watching her with her arms crossed.

"It is an impressive sight, is it not?"

Mariah agreed with a nod.

"Would you like to meet him now, or rest a little first?"

Mariah's stomach growled that it would like some food but she ignored it. "Now, I think, would be best."

Iráma led the way through the door immediately to their left. This hallway was darker than the round entrance chamber and curved slightly, but did not twist like the first one. The passage through the darkness was much shorter. Light from another chamber ahead appeared almost as soon as the light from the previous room vanished. This time, she felt no need to trail her hand along the wall.

They continued through a long, straight hall with the same stretch of darkness. They continued back into the light, and Iráma stopped at a large, ornate door. She pushed it open and motioned Mariah through.

Mariah tried not to appear impressed as she stepped into the large, long room. The pale stone, with its mineral staining of tans and greys, had been smoothed almost to shine along the walls. More of the half-finished statues lined the walls, with halls and doors interspersed among them. As she stepped forward, her eyes rose to the ceiling. The room had the same gentle fading daylight glow as the round chamber, though surely they were far deeper into the mountain.

Unwilling to be caught gaping, she dropped her eyes to the far end of the long chamber and paused. Sitting on a raised stone platform sat a large, gaudy chair draped with pale cloth and cushions; the first decorations she had seen here not made of stone.

Iráma swept past her, stopping a short way from the throne—Mariah could think of no better word for it—and dropped into a graceful, sweeping bow. A momentary twinge of jealousy that Iráma seemed to do everything with such grace and poise struck Mariah, but the feeling passed as she looked back at the throne, unable to make out an occupant.

"My Lord Sophus, I have brought one who seeks your assistance," Iráma said, rising from the bow.

"Bring her to me." A resonant, low male voice echoed through the chamber. Mariah saw a hand moving and from there, the figure seated amid the mass of silk and cushions became clear to her. Iráma turned back to Mariah and gestured her forward.

Mariah walked tentatively forward with her head held high, trying to make out further details of the man on the throne. The nearer she came, the further the illusion dissolved, but he held so still that when she blinked, his figure nearly disappeared back into the draped cloth. The click of her boots sounded unnaturally loud in her ears, and she stopped before reaching Iráma. Sophus stood and gave her an appraising look. His body was draped in pale cloth the same colors as the cloth on his throne, and his skin was even paler. It was no wonder she'd had difficulty making him out. His face, as sculpted and beautiful as any of the statues she'd seen, was framed by light blond hair in short, tight curls that cascaded languorously to his shoulders. Beautiful was a good word for him, Mariah decided, but his smile, and the look in his eyes spoke of a dark place within.

"Welcome, child," he said, and Mariah felt a chill steal up her spine despite his warm and welcoming tone. "I am Lord Sophus, the Noble. And you, my dear?"

"I am Mariah Álvarez... del Mar." Mariah hesitated a moment over the last name. A fear seized her heart when she thought of giving her mother's name of Zyanya.

"A Spaniard! And you speak the native tongue so well, considering. How very interesting." Sophus stroked his chin as he stepped toward her, looking her over. "What is it that you seek?"

Mariah held her ground before him. "I am searching for my husband, and I was told that you might give assistance. That it would only be with your assistance that I would find him."

"Tell me, Mariah, what if we are unable to find him? What is your plan then?" he asked with obviously feigned interest.

"I will continue to search for him until he is found."

"If that is your wish." Sophus sighed and returned to his throne with a flourish of his long, pale robe. "I would gladly assist you, but I fear that now is not a good time for me. If you are willing to wait and stay with us for a few days, we will see what we can do."

Mariah curtsied, flourishing the greatcoat as though it were a skirt. "I thank you for your kindness."

"Iráma, please show Mariah to one of the guest rooms and arrange for something for me to drink in my chambers. Mariah, we will speak again later."

"As you say, Lord Sophus." Iráma gave another graceful, sweeping bow. She motioned for Mariah to follow and swept past her back toward the door they'd come from. The dark part of the hall seemed longer going back than it had coming in. When they emerged into a small chamber rather than the intersection she had expected, Mariah paused. Certainly they'd taken the same passageway? She shook her head. There must have been a turnoff somewhere.

"You'll learn," Iráma said warmly.

"Do they all branch in the darkness?"

"Yes, but at night we use torches if we must walk the halls, and you will learn where the turnoffs are." Iráma continued.

Mariah followed closely, worried that she'd take a wrong turn as they entered another passageway. "Was this place carved straight out of the rock?"

"Not entirely. Lord Sophus carved out most of it himself following the natural passages that were already here. Most of the artwork is his doing, though." Iráma paused to stroke one of the statues with admiration.

"It is very beautiful. I've never seen anything like it before."

They walked the rest of the way in silence until they came to another large chamber with doors lining the walls. These doors all had symbols on them, which Mariah recognized as Greek characters.

"Yours is this one." Iráma motioned to one of the doors.

"Theta," Mariah noted, and the other woman nodded in approval.

Iráma opened the door and stepped back. "I'll have some food sent up to you, and there is clean water within. Please be aware, also, that it is against the rules we live by to send anything downstream."

"Thank you," Mariah said, trying not to let her confusion show as she entered.

"For now, it would be best that you stay in your room unless you have a guide. These halls are very extensive, and more than one newcomer has become lost in them. Often, those who get lost are not found alive," Iráma added before closing the door.

"I'll remember that." Mariah closed the door. She had no trouble believing that she would get lost the moment she stepped out her door without someone to guide her. These caves must be huge. She shook her head. A single person could not have carved them out in one lifetime, especially one who looked as young as Sophus. No doubt he'd had a crew to help him, and he'd planned and directed it. Or perhaps Sophus was a title, and men through the generations had gone by that title, carving and expanding their domain. But what an undertaking, nonetheless!

She looked over her room. It was, of course, made of stone like the rest of the caves and had similar ambient lighting coming from the high ceiling, now colored with the blue hue of just past sunset. The room was nearly the same size as her bedroom back home, and light-colored drapes and tapestries hung on the walls, giving it an almost cozy look. The lightness of the colors made it seem larger and less confining than it really was.

The sound of running water caught Mariah's attention and she searched for the source. Niches and shelves of stone lined the walls, most of which appeared to have been carved, though a couple appeared as natural formations. A couple held books or wooden statues. One held towels, and another a set of two cups. Beside the cups was a niche with a V-shaped bottom that went back further into the wall, and as she looked in, she realized that that was where the sound was coming from. Reaching in her hand, she felt a cool stream of water running over it. She snatched her hand out again, remembering Iráma's instruction about sending things downstream and thought about how dirty her hand must be.

She looked around for something to wash up with, as the cups were too wide to fit back into the hole. She ran her hands over the smooth wood furniture, admiring its beauty as she looked. There was a dresser with drawers and a nice-looking bed frame with a mattress, though no linen had been put on yet. A small bit of excitement rose in Mariah at the realization she'd be sleeping on a real bed, rather than her travel roll or a hammock.

On the dresser sat a large pitcher and an equally large bowl, both of which were empty. The question now was how to get the water out of the wall. Perhaps something to divert the water. She searched through the drawers of the dresser and all the shelves, and found some linen for the bed. Unable to find anything for the water, she set to work making up the bed, wishing she at least had her gear so that she could put on something clean.

As Mariah smoothed the covers, her door opened, and a small, middle-aged woman with dark but greying hair entered backward. She carried a wooden tray with cloth covering what looked like food dishes, and a younger woman followed her with Mariah's bags and some other bundles.

"What news do you bring, *waré*?" the older woman gave Mariah the traditional greeting. She smiled warmly, exuding an overall feel of contentment with life.

"I have no news of your people," Mariah answered apologetically.

The younger woman seemed to slump a little as she set Mariah's bags on the bed.

"It is unfortunate," the old woman said, "that you do not bring news with you. We do not get much here, secluded as we are from the world."

"What do you mean?" Mariah asked as she began unpacking her bags, placing her effects about the room.

"Only that we do not leave, and the few who do leave do not return. Coming here, it is a commitment to stay, to obtain the peace this place can give you. And of course, there is a price to stay here."

"A price?" Mariah had not brought anything of value with her, at least, not valuable to anyone else.

"It is different for each of us," the younger woman replied, taking a seat on the bed. "It's also rather personal for some, and so not something we talk about."

The older woman nodded. "You should get changed and cleaned up—Lord Sophus will probably want to see you soon. Someone will come to lead you to him." She nodded toward the tray.

Mariah's stomach growled as she looked toward the tray.

"I'd eat lightly, though," the young woman said. "Lord Sophus can be pretty intimidating, especially the first time you meet him."

Mariah nodded. The man's strangeness wasn't easily overlooked. As the two women turned to leave, Mariah blurted out her question. "How do you get the water into the pitcher?"

The younger woman giggled. "It's all right, I couldn't figure it out for the longest time, but I was too shy to ask anyone when I first got here." Still laughing, she walked over to the water niche. "There's a lever just on the inside that you can move up to divert some of the water."

Mariah watched as the young woman demonstrated and a small stream of water flowed down and into the indent of the shelf. "I'm glad I asked."

The two women smiled again and left, shutting the door behind them. Mariah washed herself in the basin and realized with chagrin that she hadn't asked their names. Irritated at her rudeness, she tried to pick out the nicest outfit she had. There wasn't much to choose from, as she'd only packed traveling gear. Who'd have guessed she'd need a dress? Not that she'd fit into any of her dresses now.

Tears tried to form in her eyes, and Mariah paused, closing them. *Not now,* she told herself over and over, breathing deeply, until she had managed to push aside the darkness and lock it back up. For now, she needed to keep her head about her. *Maybe later, but not now.*

She sighed at herself and pulled on some clean pants, hesitating over her pistols. She had the distinct feeling that they would be inadequate here, but she holstered the two her father had given her anyway, and strapped on all of her knives. In an effort to keep busy, she brushed out her long, dark hair, then had some of the food, careful to eat slowly and not too much. When no one had come for her, she polished her boots, rearranged the drawers, and finished unpacking.

Her chamber grew darker and darker, until she nearly couldn't see. Why hadn't she brought candles? She stopped herself from answering, knowing that way led to the void of self blame, and she didn't have time for that. Clinging to her composure, she took measured breaths, willing her mind to be still.

Without warning, her door opened and torchlight flickered into her room. A different woman stood in the doorway; cold, aloof, and erect, her features sharp in the light of the torch she carried. Mariah's stomach tied itself in knots when the woman spoke with a voice as cold as her demeanor.

"Lord Sophus has asked for you. You will follow me." She turned on her heel and strode away.

Mariah didn't even have time to grab Miguel's greatcoat as she rushed to hall, trying to catch the woman before she could disappear down the long, dark corridor.

Chapter 16

THE SHORT WALK to their destination surprised Mariah; Iráma had taken her a longer route. Her cool guide gestured to a large, closed wooden door and walked away abruptly, leaving Mariah in the dark. She watched the woman's retreating figure a moment, taken aback—she was the first person Mariah had met here who hadn't treated her cordially.

Light spilled into the dark hall from beneath the ornate door. Mariah swallowed, her mouth dry, as she stood beside it. What might he ask from her? She had nothing of value to give; she'd left her entire world behind to find whatever was left for her future. She rubbed her sweating palms on her pants. The rough, practical texture reminded her of Miguel. The thought of him steadied her as she rapped loudly on the wood.

The door swung open with an eerie silence.

"Come in, come in," Sophus's unbelievably beautiful and melodic voice called out.

She stepped into the light, and the door swung silently shut behind her. She looked around for her host but found herself taking in the room at the same time. It was large, four or five times bigger than her room, though smaller than the throne room Iráma had first led her to. Lavish decor and furniture filled the space, along with statues in random places—some even hanging from the ceiling—and the ever-present figures that seemed to be trying to emerge from the very walls.

What a room! Mariah stepped further in. Curtains, tapestries, and several doors lined the walls. In one corner, portioned off by the placement of the furniture, sat a large desk and bookshelves lining the walls. At least a score of lamps lit the space. The extravagance of it all, especially in a cave miles from modern civilization, astounded her.

"It is quite a sight, isn't it?" a voice said from right next to her ear.

Mariah whirled.

Sophus leaned back, amused.

"It is indeed," she agreed, relieved in a way she couldn't quite define.

"Come now, you said you were a Spaniard." He gave a warm, friendly smile that seemed to show too many teeth. "Let us speak in your native tongue. It has been so very long since I have spoken a good Latin dialect."

"Of course." Mariah switched to Castilian with a smile. "It feels nice to speak it again."

"It is a beautiful language." He motioned her to take a seat among a set of overstuffed chairs. "Come and sit down so we can talk. I trust you found your room comfortable?"

"Yes, thank you," she said, grateful to sit, but still on edge.

He settled himself gracefully onto a chair opposite her. "And the food was to your taste?"

"Yes, everything was fine. Thank you again for your hospitality."

Sophus looked at her thoughtfully for a moment, as though he were sizing her up. His eyes, which had seemed dark and foreboding before, seemed different now. They were lighter, silver with a reddish-brown rim, the color in them almost alive. Finally, he seemed to come to a conclusion and nodded, looking pleased.

"Well, my dear, I am rather excited to have a visitor such as yourself here. It has actually been a very long time since I've had the pleasure of meeting another European. Truly, the natives get a little dull after a while. Come now, tell me about yourself!" Sophus leaned back in his chair, crossing one leg over the other.

"Thank you again." A need to keep the meeting as formal and proper as possible pressed on Mariah. She needed to impress him if she was to obtain his help. "I'm flattered that you think so highly of me, but I must confess I have never been to Europe. I was born near Maracaibo to a merchant family. My mother died when I was very young, my father passed recently as well, and my husband has disappeared on a trading mission. Though I had every creature comfort and a secure future before me in Maracaibo and my father's merchant business, I simply had no reason to live without my husband."

"Ah, young love." Sophus's words contrasted with his unimpressed expression. "And how did you come to learn of me?"

"My old nursemaid, a Wayuu woman, saw my distress and insisted on accompanying me in my search. I think it was a good thing she did, because I really didn't have the slightest idea what I was doing." She smiled and gave a laugh to emphasize the absurdity of it. "Can you imagine a well-off city girl trying to survive a night on her own in the jungle? She ended up taking over and leading me to her village. She was the one who taught me to speak Wayuunaiki and suggested I come to you for assistance in my search."

"I see," he said flatly.

Mariah felt she had just failed an important test. "But you asked me to tell you about myself. Let's see..." She quickly fished around in her head for something about herself that might interest the strange man. "Well, when I was a young girl I rescued this pup from certain death. My dear Tía Olivia, the woman who raised me after my mother died, nearly fainted when I told her, but my father, he let me keep it as long as I cared for it."

She told him some of the episodes with the pup and of her difficulty finding him a suitable name. Sophus's interest increased as she told the story, so she kept on, telling him of the time she'd been attacked on the docks and her dog came to the rescue. "It wasn't until he'd made it back home that night, all battered and beat up, that I found a name for him. I decided to call him Alistair."

"A Gaelic name, if I recall. Means 'defender of man,'" Sophus said.

Mariah grinned. "It seemed appropriate."

"Now tell me, my dear, do you have any unusual talents? What is it that makes you interesting?"

Mariah laughed. "No, not really. I managed my father's business in his absence, so I am skilled in math. I read and write well and can keep a business running." She dug a little deeper. "I'm a decent shot with a pistol." She pulled out the matching pistol set her father had given her and offered them to Sophus, who took them, studying the carving with interest.

"These are lovely. I am rather fond of beautiful things, as I am sure you can see." he gestured at the artistry of the room. "We shall have to try shooting them some time."

"Thank you. They were a gift from my father, and I should greatly enjoy practicing with them more," Mariah said as he returned the pistols, his interest again waning. She would need to do better if she was to ask for his help. "I don't know that those are particularly unusual talents, though most women I know couldn't handle that kind of stress. As for what makes me interesting, well... I'm not sure if you could call it interesting, but I have strange dreams."

Sophus leaned toward her. "What kind of dreams?"

"Well, one dream really, over and over. Usually it is the same, but it has changed over time. Sometimes I almost think I can manipulate it."

"Tell me about it." It wasn't a request but it wasn't quite a command either.

Hope flickered through her. Looking into his perfectly formed, pale face, and the bright silver and brown eyes, Mariah could not refuse.

***

Maracaibo waited, glittering in the distance. Mariah turned her face toward the familiar landscape. Home. The sun shone warm in the clear sky as she stood alone in the fields. She missed the cool rain. Soon though, the rain would come, cool and refreshing. But there was no more time for waiting.

The wind blew an alluring scent into her face, a scent that drew her to its source while chilling her to the bone. She could not wait for Alistair, she couldn't risk looking for Álvaro, and she would not wait for the jungle noise that she knew would distract her.

She raced south on horseback, away from the dangerous edge of civilization and toward the Casa de la Cuesta. She glanced back. Behind her, Alistair defended her retreat with a threatening growl and threw himself into the jungle. The grand plantation house came into sight, and Mariah pulled the horse to a stop.

The sound of her own hard breathing filled Mariah's ears, and urgency filled her chest as she leapt from the horse's back. The dangerously tempting scent clung to the air around her even as she ran up the front steps. She raced through the halls of the house and onto the balcony that overlooked the immaculate gardens.

Muffled dancing music came from inside the house, but Mariah didn't have time to consider it. Desperate, she looked at the shadowy people strolling in the gardens below her. The skirts of her dark, deep red dress moved sluggishly about her legs, the same gown she'd worn so long ago in another life. She searched the couples walking around beneath her, oblivious to anything beyond each other.

There! A familiar shape in a familiar coat stepped into view. He had just the right gait and the distinct cutlass swung at his side. She could hardly believe it.

Miguel! she shouted, waving her arms frantically. *Miguel! Up here!*

But he did not hear her. Mariah lifted her skirts and charged down the steps, but Miguel was no longer there. She raced in the direction he'd gone, but when she turned the corner she came to an abrupt halt.

Mariah stood in the darkness of the night on the docks, sending her dead protector back to the sea, the waves murmuring gently below. The emptiness of the place filling her as the scent of flowers entwined with lavender drifted through the air. Her father was not there, and neither was Miguel.

She stood alone.

A rustle of cloth from the deep shadows behind her made her turn. A figure stood in there, just beyond her sight, radiating negativity at her like a spear. Mariah turned back to the lake to watch the lights of the floating village dance on the water and wait for her beloved's voice.

***

A world of grey and a fading wolf song filled Mariah's mind when she woke. The grey began to take form as she blinked the sleep from her eyes. She lay on a bed in her room, or rather, Sophus's visitor's room. Steady light from the ceiling filled the space as she stretched.

As she brushed her hair, Mariah mulled over the events of the previous evening. She had told Sophus about the dream in general detail, the ways it had changed, and at his urging, the major events in her life that had happened around each change. Then he had switched the topic to books, and they had discussed various authors and philosophies deep into the night. At some point, food had been brought in. Sophus had insisted that she eat but ate nothing himself, claiming a fragile appetite. It had been a pleasant evening of intellectual banter and had woken a part of Mariah that had lain dormant since Miguel had left. Though it felt almost like a betrayal to admit, really using her mind again had felt good.

After finishing her hair, Mariah paced the room, uncertain what to do with herself. While she had been with Sophus, someone had washed her clothes, and it felt good to wear something clean. What she really wanted, though, was to soak in a warm bath for a while. And something more appropriate to wear than her husband's clothes, though she would not have given them up for anything in the world except for the man to whom they belonged. She settled on eating some of the breakfast that waited on her dresser.

As she ate, a quick knock came at her door which opened before she could turn around.

"Don Sophus!" Why had he come directly for her?

"*Buenos días*, Mariah." The beautiful, strange man gave her a wry smile.

A chill stole down Mariah's back at his look, and she had difficulty thinking. She felt trapped by his powerful gaze.

"I... uh... didn't expect... you," she said, trying desperately to fill the silence, to escape the force that seemed to be trying to subdue her. She rushed on, "I mean, it's just that... uh... I didn't think... I mean, I thought that only the other women...."

She paused, closing her eyes. In that moment of darkness she centered herself, taking a deep breath. Opening her eyes, she threw on a gracious smile. "Don Sophus, it is a pleasant surprise to see you this morning. I didn't expect to see you again so soon with all the pressing matters to which I'm sure you need to attend."

A frown flickered across the pale man's face but was gone as swiftly as it had come. He smiled again, the broad smile of a predator who realized he can have fun with his prey. She stood up taller; she would not be easy prey.

"Actually, I took care of much of it last night after you retired."

It must not have been as late as I thought.

Sophus held out a hand to her. "I came to see if you would like a grand tour of my home."

"Certainly." She slipped her arm into his and repressed a shiver as they walked down the cool hall. Despite his rather lean appearance, his muscles were hard and unyielding under his long sleeves. *Fitting,* she thought, *for a stone carver.*

Sophus took the lead with the conversation, explaining to her how the caves had been formed when he found the place, how he was inspired to change them, to make them his own. He explained that the entire society was self-contained. Above the caves, they raised livestock and crops, and there was a water reserve.

He led her to various rooms and through many halls, most of which were punctuated by stretches of complete darkness. When they circled back toward his rooms, Mariah began to recognize things, but they had not gone through the round entry chamber from her arrival.

"So, tell me, how do you get the light in here like this?" she asked, the chill beginning to bother her.

Sophus gave her a large, pleased smile. "That, my dear, is a secret. But I'm sure with your highly educated mind you will figure it out. In fact, I'd be a little disappointed if you didn't."

He led her into the room they had spent most of the previous evening in, and Mariah disengaged from his arm to sit in the same chair she'd used before. She immediately felt warmer as she moved away from him. Had he been the source of her chill? Surely not.

Sophus inhaled deeply as he took his seat across from her. "You are so beautiful. It really is a shame you have nothing better to wear than that."

Mariah looked down at her shabby but clean traveling clothes. She shrugged. "I didn't believe I would need anything better."

Sophus nodded, his pale curls moving carelessly around his face. "I have decided that while you are my guest here, you will have the best that I have to provide."

"That is very kind of you, Don Sophus, but entirely unnecessary."

Sophus waved away her concerns, cutting off her protest. "It is nothing. I already had your things moved to a new room, much closer to mine. I am afraid I have some things to attend to for the next few days, so we will not be seeing each other, but I do look forward to seeing you again once I return." He stood and gestured to his room. "Feel free to use anything here that you wish, most especially my library. Now come, my dear, I will show you to your new room."

Mariah followed him out, trying to discreetly avoid taking his arm again. His use of familiarity with her unnerved her; he had done so twice now and she was not pleased about it. "Don Sophus, if you please, I was sent here to ask for your help in finding my husband."

He looked down at her, compassion in his eyes. "I will be happy to assist in any way I can, however, there are things I must attend to first. I promise we will speak of it when I return."

She longed to protest that she needed to move on if he could not help her, but Doña Olivia had trained her too well to press the matter. Miguel had been gone for months now, and she felt she was so close. The possibility of true help in recovering her husband was worth a couple more days' wait. She tilted her head in acquiescence. "*Gracias.*"

He stopped at a wooden door just as large, heavy, and intricately carved as the one to her host's rooms. Though some distance down the hall, the door was the first along the smooth stone wall.

"Closer is a bit of an understatement," she said under her breath.

He chuckled and pushed open the door, gesturing her inside. She stepped through and gasped.

The room, though not nearly as large as Sophus's chamber, was huge. Fine furniture sat among plush rugs on the stone floor, and tapestries hung on the walls. In the far end stood a large four-post bed with ornately carved posts and hung with rich, draping cloth.

Like many of the larger chambers, this room held statues and carvings in random places, many of people reaching up to matching statues reaching down to them.

"Did you..." She gestured to a nearby set of statues. "These were carved out of the natural formations already here, weren't they?"

Sophus, still standing near the door, smiled smugly, every bit an artist basking in the admiration of his work.

Her eyes wandered back to the statues. "It is a beautiful room. I'm honored with its use."

"It has a beautiful occupant; I am honored for you to use it. Feel free to wander through my home—there is nowhere you can go here that I cannot find you. But, please, be careful in the dark passageways. Many of them are as yet unfinished and have dangerous footings and drop-offs. I would hate for you to get hurt." Sophus bowed and left, shutting the door behind him.

Mariah felt a pang of uneasiness at the repeated compliment, but it was quickly lost to wonder as she took a closer look around the room. It held a few additional doors leading to side chambers; one was a large closet that held her meager supply of traveling clothes as well as a handful of out-of-fashion dresses, another led to a large bathroom that had a tub already full of steaming water. Mariah decided to hold off further exploration in favor of a warm, relaxing bath.

She found some large towels and nice-smelling soaps and oils in the niches on the wall alongside the bath. Once she had scrubbed herself clean and washed her long, dark hair, she lay relaxing in the warm water, thinking over all that had happened since her arrival only the day before.

Her mind wandered, as it inevitably always did, to Miguel. What was he doing? Was he safe? Was he hurt? Was he lost, wandering alone, cold and hungry, or had he found a refuge, a place to stay? Perhaps he was held captive somewhere. Knowing it would break her, she did not allow the thought that he might not be alive. She knew he lived, she was certain of it, more certain of that than anything else. She would find him if it took her the rest of her life, or beyond, if necessary.

The water grew tepid and she got out, wrapping one of the large towels around herself, and dried her hair, working a sweetly scented oil into it. The stone floor beneath her feet chilled her as she dried off. A gentle but cold draft moved across the room, and she shivered as she returned to the closet to dress. The bath had refreshed her, clearing her mind, and she found herself loath to return to her stained and worn clothes. Would her host mind if she wore one of the dresses in the closet?

Mariah searched the shelves and found a long, cotton chemise, which she pulled on. Turning back to the dresses, she inspected them, running her fingers across the material. A few were far older than she'd realized, the cloth crackling in an alarming way when she touched it. She jerked back, afraid to damage anything. Amazed, she examined them without touching or moving them. The dresses appeared to be centuries old, the fabric so faded she could hardly tell the original color or pattern, and the style was just as old-fashioned.

She was pulled from her inspection of the curiously old clothing by another draft that chilled her and a soft, rhythmic, and oddly familiar sound that seemed to come from everywhere at once. She cocked her head and listened, trying to place the source. As she did, the rooms darkened, though she knew it was far too early for evening. Truly, the lighting baffled her. It was obviously sunlight, but a direct shaft opening to the sky was unreasonable, given the intricacies of the caves.

A rumble of thunder growled softly throughout the chamber and she rolled her eyes. *Rain! Of course.*

A shiver drew her mind back to the problem at hand. None of the ancient dresses would work, so she chose a newer dress at random. The dress had a fairly simple cut and was wrinkled, badly out of style, and poorly fitting. Not that she cared. Mariah smiled at it as she looked at herself in the mirror. She'd never been very fashion conscious, unlike the Senoritas de la Cuesta and their cousin.

For a moment, she wondered how they were doing. Likely, they were all sitting in one of Doña Olivia's rooms, doing embroidery. Elisa would be by the door, chatting away, with Selena butting in on occasion. Betania, sitting quietly in the corner where she could get the best light, would make a quiet comment, and the four of them would burst out into giggles. Doña Olivia would smile indulgently, and Miguel would be waiting to escort her home.

She and Miguel would go home together, to their son, and raise him to be a fine man. He would look like his father, marry his childhood playmate, and they would live a happy and peaceful life.

Homesickness filled Mariah, a longing to return to her friends, to their camaraderie, to a place and time where she was safe and where everything was right in the world.

No, they wouldn't be there like that. Even if she could return home, it would never be what it was. Betania had her own family now, a man whom she adored, and a beautiful daughter to raise. Selena had run off. Elisa sulked in her garden when she wasn't unabashedly chasing high society men, or perhaps had been sent off to Spain by now. Mariah's father was dead.

The walls seemed to press in on Mariah as her thoughts followed their inevitable pattern. Mariah had sent the man she loved into horrible danger. Her lungs could not pull in enough air, and her heart raced. A huge, gaping wound lay across her soul that had once been her son. She dropped her knees as she gasped at the pain. Álvaro was dead. Her son was dead. And it was her fault.

She couldn't do this. Not here. Mariah focused on her breathing. The room had enough air, she only needed to relax and inhale. This place was dangerous; she couldn't be seen breaking down. The entire weight of the mountain above her seemed to press against her chest, demanding she submit to her own worthlessness. She took another deep breath and pushed the accusatory thoughts down deep. What mattered now was to keep her wits about her and find Miguel. Focus on the problem at hand. She was here, now. She didn't even know how to leave the labyrinthine caves if she'd wanted to.

What a mess. She took another deep breath and stood, trying to steady her shaking limbs before leaving the closet. *We can do this.*

Mariah returned to the main chamber of her rooms just as the middle-aged woman from before brought in a tray of food. Mariah hadn't seen anyone save Don Sophus since her first interview with him the previous day, so the woman's presence was a relief.

"Good day!" she said as the woman set the tray on a table.

"Good day," the woman returned with a smile. "I hear you are the new one. Lord Sophus must have taken a liking to you to put you in these rooms."

Mariah nodded. "So it would seem. He is very generous."

"That he is, though most of us believe that his gifts are not without a reasonable cost," the woman said, her voice almost playful. "Ah, where are my manners. My name is Wuchii."

"I am Mariah Álvarez Zyan—del Mar." Mariah tried to cover the slip in her name as Wuchii looked at her in shock. She'd have to be more careful.

"Of course." Wuchii's voice turned serious. "Mariah Álvarez *del Mar* it is, then. If there is anything I can do for you, please ask."

"Well... I would like to get to know this place better, perhaps even go outside." Mariah said, unsure what to make of the woman's changed manner.

"Of course." Wuchii gestured toward the door, but then looked back, a friendly twinkle in her eye. "Unless you'd like to eat first."

Mariah's growling stomach gave her away, and she grinned as she sat at the table. "I suppose the cave won't go anywhere while I eat. Have a seat." She looked at the strange food, chose something at random. "It appears that I'm not the first to stay in these rooms. Are there visitors here often?"

Wuchii shook her head as she sat. "No, there has not been anyone in here since before I came, which was years ago when I was still a young and beautiful woman." Her eyes twinkled. "However, I do believe there was one some years before that. There have been a few, here and there, throughout the history of this place."

"What happened to them?" Mariah asked, her interest piqued.

"They either left or grew old and died, same as the rest of us, I'm sure. They're not often talked about and so not much is known about them."

Mariah picked up a roll. "You make it seem as though this place has a long history. How old is it, do you know?"

"Our legends say that it has been here for many generations, since before the white men invaded our lands."

"I've heard of that, but I'm afraid I'm a little confused. When I first got here, Iráma indicated that Don Sophus carved all of this himself, but I don't see how that is possible if it has existed for as long as you say." The same sense of unease as when the strange man looked at her crept up Mariah's spine. "Perhaps it was one of his predecessors?"

"No, Lord Sophus did it. It is his work and his work alone," Wuchii said.

Mariah's irritation flared up. This was just the sort of thing Nana would have tried to imply. *Maybe I just don't understand the language as well as I thought*, she reasoned, trying to keep her temper in check. She'd just ask Don Sophus about it later.

"I think I am finished eating. Don Sophus said the animals are kept outside. Can you show me how to get there? I'm yearning for the sun and some open space."

"I understand that." Wuchii grinned. "It sounds like it is still raining, but I'll show you the way anyhow."

They stood, and Mariah grabbed Miguel's greatcoat. Wuchii led the way slowly, letting Mariah take her time looking at the passageways and statues as they went. She also lit a torch and showed Mariah how, in many of the darkened passages, the stone halls branched. She seemed nervous about the fire though, and when Mariah questioned her about it, Wuchii just shrugged and said that Don Sophus didn't like the smoke staining the walls.

They climbed several sets of stairs and turned so many corners that Mariah lost her bearings entirely. Clear daylight, the smell of wet earth, and the whisper of rain reached Mariah, and she rushed forward. It wasn't the door Iráma had led her through when they arrived, but Mariah didn't care. She ran out into the open air and gentle rain, excited to be outside.

Mariah breathed in the clean air, allowing it to fill her, calming all the turmoil she had so recently pushed aside. With a small smile, she took in the view. The mostly flat ground sloped a little, stretching away to the west and north. Goats and sheep huddled under bushes and overhangs, trying to take shelter from the storm. A few women sat in a distant shelter out of the rain beside several fenced-off areas that appeared to be gardens. Beyond the fences, the world fell away.

She walked forward through the warm rain to get a better look at the rest of the land. The water soaked into her hair and ran down her neck. She ought to have grabbed a hat as well. Behind the door, the small mountain rose to a ragged peak. Walking cautiously to the nearest edge, Mariah peered over—the world dropped precariously away from her at what she was sure was a deadly distance. She quickly stepped back.

"It's like that the entire way around," Wuchii said quietly, walking up behind her, her head thoughtfully covered in her shawl. "There is no way down."

"What about the other entrance, the one Iráma brought me in through?"

"Iráma and Lord Sophus are the only ones who know where it is. Very few people ever leave here, Mariah, and none ever return save Lord Sophus and Iráma."

"I was told that there was one once...." Foreboding settled over Mariah.

Wuchii gave her a significant look. "One way or another everybody leaves this life, but there has only been one who survived the journey."

Chapter 17

MARIAH STOOD IN the rain, enjoying the feel of fresh water on her skin and the smell of the ocean breeze. The desert terrace above Sophus's labyrinth was high enough that she could see the water, but it was too far to hear. To the south, about ten miles away by her estimate, stood another large plateau formation, its slopes angled sharply downward. It couldn't have been more than a few miles wide—she could see the ocean on either end of it. She swept her eyes over the land before her, turning in a slow circle.

With a feeling of testing the bars of a cage, Mariah walked to the northern edge of the terrace, trying to find a way around the large rise that held the entrance back to the labyrinth below. There was none. The rise here sloped more gently than the cliffs on the northern side. Birds sang their random bits of broken melody from the scrubby bushes behind her. She gave the steep slope a rueful look. As much as she wanted to know what was at the top, climbing it was too risky.

She stood, staring northeast until the rain stopped and the sun returned in the western sky and warmed her back. She was drawn to the north. Something nagged at her mind—what did Wuchii mean that only one had survived? Clearly, she hadn't meant Iráma, who came and went as she pleased. The comment was too similar to something Nana had said when Mariah had asked if anyone ever returned from seeking Sophus. *Only one.* From what Mariah had seen, none of these women seemed to want to leave. They seemed content with their lives.

"Wuchii?" she called, turning to see if the woman was still there.

Wuchii stepped from the doorway where she'd been waiting out of the rain. "Yes?"

"Before I left the Wayuu village, where I was told that Don Sophus could help me, I was told of an old legend of the Wayuu being held captive by a strange and powerful man, and then being saved by another...."

Wuchii nodded, watching Mariah's face. "Yes, it is an old tale, and quite true. Lord Sophus would confirm its authenticity, if you were to ask him. It is why we are all here. In return for his assistance generations ago, Lord Sophus declared that any Wayuu woman who wished for a great change in her life, or a different life, or for a life of peace, was to come to him and he would provide it. Each of us came for our own reasons, and many did not expect what we found. However, we are mostly content here."

"But doesn't anyone ever want to leave?"

"We are free to leave any time we wish," Wuchii said carefully.

Mariah chewed her lip and looked at the short woman beside her. "I don't understand. You said that only Iráma and Don Sophus know where the entrance is. I don't see how anyone can leave if they can't find the way out."

"That is a dilemma, isn't it?" Wuchii patted Mariah's shoulder. "If a person wishes to leave, they need only find the door, or ask the Noble One himself and he will render his assistance in the matter. However, with the exception of Iráma, once a woman leaves, she cannot return."

Mariah shook her head. Something about this just didn't sound right. Why would Nana have sent her here if she couldn't leave? Did she think that finding Miguel was a lost cause, or that Mariah could never find joy again after the death of her son and simply wanted her to find peace? No doubt this had to do with the crazy idea that Mariah was key to destroying this whole system, but how was she supposed to do that if she couldn't ever leave?

"There's something else I still do not understand, Wuchii. You speak of Don Sophus as though he himself was the one to carve out all those caverns and free the Wayuu generations ago." Mariah wasn't certain she believed that Don Sophus was immortal. "But he seems so young he can't be more than a few years older than I am. Perhaps you mean that it was his father or grandfather who did all that, and he bears their title?"

"No," Wuchii shook her head. "He is the *same* one. He is generations old; he does not age. I have seen it. When I first arrived as a young, heartbroken woman so many years ago, he looked as young and beautiful as he does today."

Mariah looked thoughtfully at the other woman. Wuchii's greying hair was well kept and her colorful Wayuu dress trim and clean. She hadn't given Mariah any reason not to trust her, but it all seemed so fantastic. There were people who lived to extreme old age—Mariah had seen some among the Wayuu elders—but everyone aged. No one stayed in perpetual youth. *I wonder how he's tricked them.*

"No, I haven't lost my mind, young one." Wuchii's eyes twinkled with mirth, and Mariah blushed.

"The first time I really met with him, he asked me if I had any unusual talents. Does he ask that of everyone?"

"Not that question exactly, but I believe he is always hoping somebody interesting will come along." Wuchii leaned against the heavy wood door frame and crossed her arms. "Those who do pique his interest tend to get more attention from him. Iráma is one such. I've never found out why, but he trusts her so completely that she is his special assistant. He has obviously taken quite a liking to you, putting you in the rooms next to his."

"Is that a good thing or a bad thing?"

"That really depends on you. If you knock some of the other women out from their favored places, you might find some trouble with them, but I doubt that it would be much. Lord Sophus does not tolerate troublemakers in his realm."

A breeze passed though the doorway, and Mariah shivered in her wet clothes. "There is something else bothering me; perhaps you can explain it. My nursemaid, the woman who practically raised me, was Wayuu. She led me to her home village, then from there sent me to Don Sophus for help in finding my husband, Miguel. She seemed very certain that it was only with his help that I would be able to find Miguel again."

"Tell me, how were you received by the elders when you arrived?" Wuchii asked.

"Well, at first they just seemed excited to get some visitors, but then the village elders took to her as though she were one of them. 'Old One,' they called her." Mariah shrugged. "I can't understand why a woman who had such a high standing among her people would leave to help raise another woman's child."

"I remember her, actually," Wuchii nodded, then lowered her voice and Mariah leaned closer. "It was not long before I came here. My family had sent me to live with some distant cousins who resided in the same village as the Old One. I was there when the Old One's charge died just after giving birth to a girl child. The Old One left with the baby's father." Wuchii's voice dropped lower and became more urgent. "I remember him well, a Spaniard merchant, but it is not something that should be spoken of here."

"Why not?" A knot formed in her stomach, but Mariah needed to hear Nana's story from another's point of view.

"There is more to the legend of the Slaver and the Noble One. The Wayuu received the bitter end of the deal, and we remain as subtle slaves to both of them. There is a legend that one of our own will bring about the utter destruction of them both. Born of a line of women whose firstborn is always a girl to continue the line. It is said that when that chain breaks, we will all be freed. Though we all suspect that Lord Sophus knows of this prophecy, we dare not confirm its existence with him. Whatever you do, you must not let him even suspect you may be a part of it."

"If it is so imperative that it not be known, it would have been wiser not to share it." Mariah grinned, trying to convince herself that it was just a joke. "The fewer minds that know it, the fewer the mouths that can speak it."

"Hush!" Wuchii hissed at her. "These walls have ears, and Lord Sophus's are the best of them all. I would not have told you had you not given me the name, and were Sophus himself not here. Know this: Sophus will kill you if he ever learns your secret, or your name."

"What secret?" Mariah whispered skeptically.

"Your firstborn was a son, was he not?"

Mariah nodded—lucky guess.

"The Old One raised you, and your mother, and her mother before her, going back generations. Now the chain has been broken. The Forever line has been broken."

Mariah stiffened and looked again to the northeast. This woman knew about her son, or seemed to; knowledge Mariah did not want shared. Deep inside, she knew it would be a mistake to let Sophus know she was any part Wayuu. She knew, too, that he was dangerous, and she did not want him to have any connection to her past life, most especially her son. The imperative pressed on her to the point that she hadn't even sought out Álvaro in the dream.

Nana had told her that Wayuu surnames passed from mother to daughter and that the Wayuunaiki word *forever* was the name Mariah's mother had passed to her: Zyanya.

Mariah shook herself. Perhaps there was some legend out there about the Wayuu freeing themselves from this admittedly odd situation, and she could understand why people would hold to such a thing. Hope seemed to be a way of life for the Wayuu, and she found both beauty and comfort in it. And, as Nana had told her, everything that begins must end. But it seemed far too unlikely that Mariah should be the one to make it happen.

Besides, she couldn't allow herself to get distracted. Chances were that the entrance was just a loosely guarded secret, and anyone could find it or figure it out. She would just ask Don Sophus when he returned. Until then, Mariah supposed, the best thing to do would be to become familiar with this place. Perhaps peruse some of her host's books, as he'd offered.

"Let's go back inside," Mariah suggested, again shivering as the sun began to set. "It's getting late, and I'd like to see if I can remember the way back, if you'll let me lead?"

"Certainly," Wuchii said with her regular warm smile.

Mariah thought she did a fairly good job of remembering which directions to go, with Wuchii correcting her only a couple of times. She recognized the area around Sophus's chambers and walked with greater purpose as she became more confident. Wuchii left her to herself once Mariah assured her that she knew the way, and Mariah was glad of the chance to be alone. She passed the occasional woman or two as she walked, and they all smiled and greeted her but hurried about their tasks. In her rooms, Mariah changed out of her rain-dampened dress and found a warm supper waiting for her. She settled down at the table and ate.

There was an undeniably dark side to this place despite all that the friendly smiles tried to hide. Perhaps many of them were content to live out their days in peace and quiet, but what about those who weren't? She still couldn't understand the cryptic remark about not surviving the journey when you left.

Mariah found ways to keep herself busy while she awaited Don Sophus's return. The first day, she spent most of the morning working up the courage to go into his chambers alone and look through his library. Once she did, she spent about as much time examining the contents of the room as the collection of books. In the end, she picked a few books and returned to her room where she could read them at her ease. Feeling restless, she then tried to remember her way to the pasture. She was pleased that she'd needed directions only a few times before she found herself beneath the open sky. She spent a majority of the day there, enjoying the sun and unintentionally facing north as she read one of the books she had borrowed.

    The next day was much the same. Mariah continued to explore and spent some time talking to Wuchii, who refused to say anything more about Wayuu legends. Mariah was careful to always take a torch with her into the unlit parts of the tunnels and didn't explore far from the tunnels she had become familiar with. She also managed to need directions only once on her way to the pasture.

    When the third day followed the same routine as the first two, Mariah became irritable and restless, feeling as though she was wasting precious time. She woke the fourth day with Alistair's customary howl flowing through her mind, and a determination to leave. If Sophus had returned, she would request his assistance. Otherwise, she would get a torch and start searching for the exit.

    Mariah washed in the cold water from the wall, appreciating the way it removed all traces of lingering sleep and energized her for her day. She paused at the closet, debating on wearing some of the nicer clothes or her worn traveling attire. After a moment, she chose the traveling clothes, not knowing how the day would end. She stacked her meager collection of belongings on one of the tables and noticed with dismay that the only food she'd have was some leftover fruit. *I will find a way.* Picking up the books she had borrowed, Mariah walked with a brisk pace to Sophus's chambers. She stopped just short of going in, with her hand on the door. What if he was already in there? It would be rude to just barge in. Perhaps she should knock first?

No. Mariah shook her head. *I am determined to do this. I will do it full of confidence, and if he is in there, I will not let him know I feel anything less than sure of myself.* She took a deep breath and pushed the door open.

She stepped into the brightly lit room with her head held high and looked straight forward. When she didn't hear anything after a moment, Mariah looked around tentatively and let out a breath that she didn't realize she'd been holding. The room was empty of anyone but her. She relaxed a little and strode to the shelves to return the books. Content that they had been put away correctly, she swept her gaze around the room once more to convince herself that its occupant had not yet returned. She was both relieved and disappointed to conclude that Sophus was still gone. Feeling a little sheepish, she left the grand room.

Well, there's nothing to do now but start searching. She returned to her room for a lamp, grateful that her room used lamps rather than torches.

Mariah had once heard a riddle about a blind man in a maze. The solution for how he found his way through it was to keep his hand on one of the walls, and he would eventually be led out. She felt very much like that blind man in this labyrinth as she shouldered her gear. But where to start?

"Best place to start searching is where you are, I suppose," she said to herself as she stepped out her door.

She stood outside her door, hesitating over which way to turn. To the left was the way to the pastures, so she chose to go right. She placed her hand firmly on the wall to her left. The stone beneath her fingers was chill and finely textured as she moved forward with sure, even steps. In the first dark passage, she turned left, following the wall. The hallway curved back around, rising in some places and descending in others. It was lit often enough that at the end of one pool of light, the next area could just be seen with an ominous stretch of darkness between.

Before long, Mariah came to a well-lit chamber with four doors. She tried the first door on her left, but it was locked. The second and third were open but led only to small storage rooms. The fourth was another hall. She took a deep breath and stepped into the new tunnel, continuing to follow the wall on her left-hand side, certain she would be able to find the same tunnel that she had come from.

There were more small chambers and more branching tunnels, but Mariah did not stop. Occasionally, there were figures and statues carved into niches at random intervals, but always near a section of light. She continued forward, her fingers trailing over the cool statues as she walked past them.

Her stomach growled, and she slowed, noting the light had begun to dim and the walls had grown more coarse. She leaned against the wall, pleased with herself. Her method appeared to be working well enough. She still had her lamp, unlit, and as long as she followed the wall to her right, she'd be able to find her way back.

Smiling to herself, she sat down with her guiding wall to her back and pulled out the fruit she had brought along.

Movement down the hall caught her eye, and Mariah looked up. The long corridor to her left held gloomy shadows but nothing more. The silence seemed to press on her, but she shook off her nerves and took a bite of the fruit.

Again, she caught movement out of the corner of her eye, but instead of jerking her head up, she moved her head only enough to see through the corner of her eyes. Perhaps whoever it was didn't want to be noticed.

A woman stood in the far end of the corridor, indistinct in the shadows. She seemed to be watching

Mariah. Mariah took another bite of her food and looked back down at her lap. Should she say something?

After another moment of hesitation, Mariah looked back up, ready to greet the strange woman, but she was gone. Mariah was alone in the gloomy corridor.

Mariah's neck prickled. *Time to go back.*

She stood, pocketing the pit to throw away when she returned to her room. Thoughts of ghosts and vampires, haunted caves and disappearing women tried to crowd her mind, but she pushed them away in scorn. There were many women under Sophus's protection; why wouldn't there be some in this random, abandoned corridor?

Mariah placed her right hand on the wall she had been leaning against and walked forward. She refused to give in to the imaginary feeling of being watched by glancing over her shoulder. For a long time, the course seemed familiar.

When the light grew too dim to see by, she stopped and lit the lamp with the flint she had brought. She continued to walk, carefully keeping her fingers trailing on the cold stone wall. Mariah was glad for the lamp; the warm light kept her spirits high and dispelled her dark thoughts.

The ambient lights disappeared altogether, but Mariah pressed on. She knew that, somehow, the light from the ceiling was sunlight. The question was simply *how* did Sophus manage to get it inside? Perhaps she'd crawl into one of the tunnels tomorrow to figure it out.

Mariah turned a corner and stopped cold. There were stairs before her, curving down into the darkness. She had not climbed any stairs today.

A cold nausea clenched at her stomach. How could this be? She was certain she had kept to the wall on her left initially, and the same wall, now to her right, since she turned back.

Mariah ran through her mind all that she had done when she turned around. Then she went very carefully through her memory. Had she climbed a set of steps? *Maybe...?*

Steeling herself, Mariah began the descent. As she neared the bottom she saw a statue, a figure she was certain she had not seen before, carved into a niche in the wall. It was a woman in the pose of a crouching archer, her bow drawn. The lamplight flickered off its grey stone face, making the eyes seem almost alive. Despite her worry, she had to stop and admire the figure.

Slowly, Mariah's eyes were drawn to the darkness behind the figure, and a deep sense of panic began to well up inside her as she realized the space wasn't a niche—it was another hall. A hall with just enough space between the wall and the statue that she could have passed next to the figure and not seen it in the darkness.

Her mind raced as she recalled all the other niched statues she had passed. Were they all tunnels? Unwilling to allow panic to rise in her, she took a deep breath. Obviously, she had taken a wrong turn somewhere. She would just have to go back to a familiar place and start again. Someone would find her.

Except that I haven't seen anyone since I set out, a cynical voice in Mariah's head whispered.

You saw that woman in the shadows, she countered. But had she really? Even that might have been an illusion, or even her own fancy.

Iráma's voice seemed to float out of the darkness as Mariah tried to keep her breathing calm. *These halls are very extensive, and more than one newcomer has become lost in them.*

Returning up the twisting stairs, Mariah laughed bitterly at the memory. *I remembered, Iráma, just like I told you I would.* She was certain she should have reached the top by now, but the stairs continued up. *What is this place?*

The figures carved into the walls and hanging from the ceiling, mocked her. A chill wind blew up from below, and her lamp flickered dangerously. When the stairs turned again to reveal a long, straight stretch of continued steps, Mariah stopped.

She was going the wrong way.

Fighting the rising panic, she decided to return to the archer and try again. She started back down and movement caught her eye. She twisted, trying to see it. The empty stairwell rose behind her, reaching upwards. Another gust of wind echoed down the stairwell, buffeting her, and she reached out to the wall to steady herself but found only empty space. A stone slipped under her foot and she fell backwards, dropping the lamp.

Suddenly, she was tumbling through the darkness. The sharp edges of the steps shot pain throughout her body until she crashed into something solid. The darkness was as complete as the silence, broken only by Mariah's futile gasps for air and the pain bombarding her mind. She tried to call out but couldn't take a deep enough breath. She tried to move, but the pain immobilized her.

As she felt herself fading into unconsciousness, Iráma's warning echoed through her mind. *Often, those who get lost are not found alive.*

A wolf's howl filled her mind as she slipped into the void.

Miguel...

Chapter 18

MARIAH STOOD IN a field far to the west of Maracaibo, a place that was once her home. Fire tore through her body, throbbing in her leg and chest and arm. A chill wind whipped around her, and the sun flickered like a dying torch. The rain beat down, but the world remained dry. To her left, the jungle beckoned her forward, and to the right, home and safety—but a false safety, she knew.

A strange rustling from her left accompanied a cool, beautiful, fragrant scent that soothed the pain. The scent enticed her toward it, promising relief. A pale face materialized from the leaves, like an angel from the darkness with smiling silver-red eyes and careless, tight blond curls hanging around his face. She stepped toward him, but a tugging on her dress and a plaintive whine gave her pause.

Before her stood Alistair, larger than life, pleading with her not to go. He looked toward the north, and Mariah followed his gaze. Something. Something to the northeast waited for her, something she needed to find. Alistair urged her on, but when she tried to walk, she fell in a crumpled heap, the pain resurfacing and crashing over her. Then Alistair was standing over her, bristling and growling at the pale angel who promised relief. The wolf-dog charged at the seraph, and they tumbled into the darkness as the dry rain continued to thunder down.

She tried to stand but found her legs entangled in her dress. The dress was too warm in the dry, hot rain, and it suffocated her. Mariah thrashed about, trying to get free. Finally the encumbering garments tore away and she stood free in breeches, a shirt, and Miguel's overcoat.

Miguel! She turned and looked to the northeast. *I have to reach him!*

She ran. She ran as quickly and frantically as she could, her heart racing and sweat on her face, but the landscape refused to move.

Alistair awaited her in the distance, but as she neared him, he stood and was Miguel. He turned away from her, walking to the northeast, and she gave desperate chase. She stopped abruptly at the edge of the dark balcony and looked over the garden at the couples walking through the darkness, each lost in their own worlds, alone with each other. The dancing music—a haunting Wayuu lullaby— drifted over her, and the pain began to subside. Then she saw the familiar figure in that worn coat and the gait that was just so….

She tried to leap the banister to reach him, but her strength gave way, and she crashed to the floor.

Miguel! Miguel I'm over here! Don't leave me! she called out to him, pulling herself up from the floor. A chill wind helped her to her feet and the otherworldly, entrancing scent enveloped her, giving her strength and easing the lingering pain. She tried to run down the steps, but the wind stole the light from her lamp, and she fell.

When she landed, Mariah stood on the docks of Maracaibo Lake on a moonless night. The lights from the floating *palafitosi* danced on the water's surface, and there below her, she saw the large, lifeless form of Alistair lying on a makeshift barge, wreathed in flowers. The pain in her chest was a sharp emptiness that threatened to consume her, a missing piece that had once been the source of all the joy in her life.

Mariah looked over and saw that she was alone. Yet in the darkness, a force waited, watching her, envying her, hating her. The dancing lights on the water disappeared one by one, and the long, plaintive howl of her beloved sea dog floated across the lake.

I'm here. I hear you. I am coming....

***

Mariah awoke to a bright room. The space before her was pale, and as her eyes and mind focused, the pale draped cloth came into view, hanging above her. She turned her head to the side and recognized Iráma sitting beside the bed.

"You are awake!" the woman said, sounding pleased.

It took Mariah a full minute to process the sounds, realize it was Wayuunaiki, form a reply, translate it, and make her mouth say it.

"Uhhnng...." was all she managed. Mariah closed her eyes, exhausted by the effort.

When she was able to open her eyes again, Wuchii sat beside her in the dim light, carving wood and humming that same Wayuu lullaby. This time, Mariah took more care to form her word.

"Water?" she croaked.

Wuchii nearly fell off her chair in surprise, and Mariah would have chuckled at the comical sight if she'd had the energy.

"Yes, of course! Certainly!" Wuchii hurried to bring some water. "It is so good to see you fully awake. You had us worried for a very long time." She helped Mariah sit up a little and tipped the cup gently onto her lips. "Iráma kept you sedated at first—the pain was too great for you—but after a time, you became feverish. You have been in and out of consciousness the entire time, usually just enough for us to force some broth down you, which is fortunate. The fever finally broke a few days ago, but we weren't sure when you would truly wake up. Actually, this is the second time your fever broke, but you didn't really wake before."

"*Gracias,*" Mariah said slowly as Wuchii lowered the water. Her head had cleared a little, and she could follow Wuchii's speech if she concentrated. She carefully formed her words and asked, "How long?"

"Nearly a month, I'm afraid. You took a very nasty fall down some forgotten stairs. It is a good thing Lord Sophus had returned that day and was looking for you. He has such an uncanny ability to find people, and I'm sure it helps that he knows this place so well. He did build it, after all." Wuchii helped Mariah lay back on the pillows as she continued. "You did some serious damage to yourself, and it seemed to cause a relapse into an illness you'd been fighting. Your upper leg and a couple ribs are broken, but they seem to be mending. You should be glad you were unconscious for the worst of it."

Mariah's fuzzy brain reeled. A month? It was too much time. That meant it had been at least four months since she'd set out, perhaps five. She had lost track of the time after Álvaro—

She stopped herself. She couldn't go there. Not right now. She had to get up. Miguel needed her. She needed to leave.

Mariah tried to swing her legs out of bed but fell back as a wave of pain engulfed her. What had Wuchii said? Broken leg and some ribs. She'd be immobile for months yet, and then she'd be on a crutch if she could even walk again.

"Careful now." Wuchii took hold of her arm. "The fall itself, and even the broken leg, shouldn't have made you so ill. I dare say you'd been seriously ill not long before coming here, and not entirely healed. Your accident has caused a relapse. You need to rest and regain your strength."

Mariah lay back in the bed, tears spilling from her eyes at this added difficulty. It was too much to take, and, with Wuchii's gentle hands settling the blanket over her shoulders, she fell back into blissful unconsciousness.

The room was bright again. For some reason, that irritated Mariah. She inhaled deeply, ignoring the stab of pain from her ribs, and opened her eyes. This time, Don Sophus sat beside her. He had been in her dream, promising her freedom from pain and sorrow. She felt a surge of anger toward him. He had no place in her dreams, they were reserved for Miguel, and Miguel alone.

Mariah decided that she would not be the first to speak, but it was not necessary. He had been watching her, but she had the distinct feeling that he would have known when she woke, even if he hadn't been watching.

"Good morning, Mariah, and welcome back," he said graciously.

Mariah nodded. What had Wuchii said? He had been the one to find her. She knew she should show him gratitude, but she was still grouchy about the bright light and his intrusion into her dreams.

Sighing inwardly, she spoke, her voice low and scratchy. "*Gracias,* Don Sophus. It is good to be awake."

Sophus offered her a cup of tea with an amused smile, and helped her when she struggled to sit. She noted again the chill of his hand through her dress, and how very unyielding his flesh was despite his gentleness. Determined to not be completely useless, she reached weakly for the cup. He hesitated for a moment but handed it to her anyway. She stared down at it, willing herself to have the strength to drink it on her own, and successfully brought it to her lips.

When she had finished, Mariah handed the cup back to Sophus with a triumphant smile. Now, if only there was some food.

"I am glad to see you doing so well, my dear."

Mariah cringed inwardly at the term of endearment.

"Tell me, do you think you could eat something?"

"I think," Mariah said slowly, "that if I could stay awake long enough, I could eat a horse."

"Most excellent!" Sophus walked to the door.

Mariah blinked. She hadn't seen him stand—perhaps she wasn't doing as well as she'd hoped?

Sophus peeked his head out the door and spoke quietly to someone before returning to her side. A familiar rich fragrance swept over her as he neared, and for a moment Mariah could no longer think.

"Food is on the way."

Mariah nodded, trying to clear her head.

"Now," he continued in a more serious voice, "why don't you tell me what brought you to this terrible mishap. If you remember."

Mariah considered lying to him, but the beautiful, muddling scent that she now recognized from her dream seemed to tell her that he would know. She could think of no dire consequences to telling the truth, but she hesitated. *My brain is all jumbled.* Despite her irritation with him, she found herself wanting to please him, which in turn irritated her further.

"I got lost exploring." She explained how she had planned to follow a wall and return following the same wall but had misjudged the niches with the statues. Sophus seemed to accept her explanation, and for a moment, Mariah felt relieved.

"Iráma should have warned you not to wander. It was careless of her," he said with a bit of ire.

"No, it wasn't her fault; she warned me not to go off on my own. Really, she did. Wuchii did, too. Don't be upset with them." Part of her worried that something very bad would happen to the two friendly women if Sophus became angry with them. Mariah placed a pleading hand on Sophus's bare arm. It was firm and far colder than she had expected, and she almost flinched away.

Sophus looked down at her hand and raised an eyebrow at her. Delicately, as though he was handling something very fragile, he removed her hand from his arm and set it back in her lap. "If you insist. Tell me, though, what is it that you were looking for?" He gave her a critical look.

Mariah took a deep breath and plunged in, forming her words carefully. "As you know, I came here for your assistance in finding my husband, Miguel del Mar. The need to reach him presses on me even now. I was told that only with your assistance would I be successful in helping him, but when you had not returned, I felt that I needed to move on. I came to your chambers first, hoping that you, or perhaps Iráma, could show me to the exit. When I could not find either of you, I decided to search on my own. As you know, I misjudged, got lost, and then got hurt."

There, it was out. She wanted to leave. She fervently hoped that Wuchii really was just a crazy woman when she had indicated that the only way to leave was to die.

"I see." Sophus stroked his chin. "Ah, your food is here."

Mariah looked up, but no one had come in. Just as she was thinking that Sophus might be as crazy as Wuchii, someone knocked on the door and pushed it open without waiting for an answer. The wondrous smell of food washed over her, and, though her conversation with Sophus had been exhausting, she wanted more than anything to eat. Mariah didn't recognize the woman, but her disappointment lasted only until Sophus sat the tray before her.

The meal consisted of a bowl of steaming lamb broth and a piece of bread, but to Mariah's eyes, it was a feast. She ate as quickly as her tired body allowed, savoring each mouthful of the rich broth and the glorious plain bread. Her thin, wasted hands trembled as she ate. Gratitude at whatever fate had kept her alive through two such close, prolonged fevers filled her along with the hot broth. Eventually, she would need to work up the courage to see how badly her leg had been damaged. The bone in her thigh ached, even now. She lay back on her pillows, stuffed and comfortable, and enjoyed the warmth that spread through her.

When she opened her eyes again, the room was dim. An urgent need to relieve herself pressed on her consciousness. Somewhat frantically she looked around the room, hoping to see someone nearby who could assist her. Sure enough, Sophus sat in the corner, watching silently.

Anyone but him, Mariah corrected.

She pushed herself up, and by the time she'd managed to get halfway up, Sophus had his arm around her, assisting. His dizzying scent washed over her again, befuddling her brain, but she shook it away with irritation.

"Would you like more food?" he asked, gesturing to a table with some food already set out.

"In a minute, perhaps. It is very kind of you to watch over me, Don Sophus, but right now I would appreciate some privacy. And the assistance of a woman."

Sophus looked at her, confused, as though trying to determine if she was joking.

"Really, this can't wait," Mariah said, giving him a meaningful look.

Understanding dawned on his face, and he nodded, striding away. Almost as soon as he was out the door Iráma came in, moving at a blessedly normal speed.

Iráma lifted Mariah out of the bed and carried her to the washroom where she could relieve herself. Mariah didn't want to think about what had been done during the weeks she had been unconscious. Iráma hummed a quiet, soothing melody, but worry about Sophus gnawed at Mariah. He seemed to be giving her far more attention than a guest deserved, and it bothered her. She would need to talk to him soon and make it clear that as soon as she could walk again, she would be on her way.

Iráma paused in her narrative to ask, "Would you like to bathe, Mariah?"

"Absolutely," Mariah replied. "But what about this?" She gestured to the hard cast that had been put on her leg to immobilize it.

"We'll remove it. The dressing needs to be changed anyway, but you may not want to look."

Mariah tried to follow Iráma's advice as the cast was removed, but could not help herself. Her leg was hideous, the muscles withered and the skin wrinkled. The smell nearly made her sick, and she wrinkled her nose, trying to breathe through her mouth. Mariah was afraid to move the leg but had to admit that it felt wonderful to air out the skin.

Iráma helped her to the bath. Soaking in the warm water felt glorious, and she knew it would feel even better to be clean and wearing clean clothes. Iráma seemed to sense her mood, and once they were both certain Mariah wouldn't slip under the water's surface, she left to direct someone to change the bed linens. When she returned, she washed and oiled Mariah's hair and helped her out.

Mariah stood on one leg, leaning on a second woman, before a large mirror while Iráma helped dry and dress her. She looked at herself critically. The signs of her recent pregnancy remained. The skin of her belly still sagged a bit, striped where her skin had stretched with her growing child, and her breasts—full before—now hung, reduced and listless.

She looked over the rest of her body. She was thin and boney, her hips and elbows and wrists jutting out at strange angles, and she could count her individual ribs. Her high cheekbones cast shadows on her sunken cheeks, and her hair fell limp and lusterless.

Once she was dried off, Iráma placed a new dressing and hard cast on the leg. The bandage across Mariah's ribs had also been changed. She tested out the rest of her joints one by one as they waited for the plaster to set. Some had sharp pains, and all had the dull soreness of muscles that hadn't been used for too long. The pale remnants of bruising all across her body ached, too. All in all, she was a mess.

Iráma finished dressing her in a thin gown and soft robe, and then carried Mariah back to the table as though she weighed nothing.

When Mariah tried to protest that she could walk, Iráma scoffed and said "Nonsense. Your leg is broken, you're recovering from a prolonged fever, and you would be better served using what little energy you have left to eat."

"There's food?" Mariah brightened.

Iráma shook her head and chuckled in a way that reminded Mariah of Nana as she brought over the food. Mariah was delighted to see a bowl of broth—almost a soup this time, with small bits of meat—fruit and more bread. She ate the entire bowl of soup while Iráma patiently watched.

"How long before I am able to walk, do you think?" she asked between mouthfuls.

"Assuming the bone is healing, you shouldn't put weight on it for at least another couple of weeks." Iráma leaned back in her chair. "In the meantime, though, it is important that you exercise your other muscles so that the flesh does not weaken further and begin to die."

Mariah handed the other woman a piece of bread which she took, munching on it thoughtfully. Tall and slender, with smooth skin and long, straight black hair, Iráma had an air of strangeness about her. She moved with a careless, catlike grace, as though every move she made was a dance, and her eyes seemed focused on something only she could see. Mariah wondered what had brought her here and why she continued to return.

Mariah finished her meal. As she set her spoon down onto the empty tray, Sophus returned. Iráma stood and left, taking the tray with her in a single, smooth movement. Mariah leaned back in her chair, acutely aware of the disadvantages of being immobile.

"Why, yes, I did enjoy my meal, thank you." She grinned, anticipating Sophus's question. He paused, his mouth open to speak, and just as he started to ask another question Mariah answered it, too. "I'm feeling quite well and rather refreshed. I am treated very kindly here."

Sophus smiled, catlike. "Am I allowed to speak yet, or will you be answering all my questions before I ask them? Am I so predictable?" he asked playfully.

"Not after the first two questions." She returned the smile. "I do know, though, that you'd like to talk. However, I do have a request for you before we begin."

"You need only ask." Sophus eyes twinkled.

"Would you mind moving me to the couch? This chair is most uncomfortable—"

Before Mariah could even finish her sentence, Sophus had swept her up into his arms. The way he seemed to be on the other side of the room one moment, then swinging her through the air the next, dizzied her. His beautiful, entrancing scent didn't help much either, and she found herself again irritated. She shoved her ill mood aside as the cold, hard arms set her gently onto the soft couch. He sat across from her in a matching cushioned chair and crossed his legs.

"Now then, what is it that you would like to ask?" Mariah said before an uncomfortable silence could set in.

"Such directness, my dear. It is a trait I'm beginning to like about you. You do not seem to be intimidated by me." Sophus's smile showed too many perfect white teeth.

Mariah's heart tried to beat a little faster but she took a deep breath to calm it.

His smile changed to one of amusement as if he knew what had just happened. "I understand your need to find this man of yours, and I've come to like you. I want to help in any way that I can, truly I do. However, as I'm certain you've come to realize, you will be in no condition to go searching for him for some time. Given the urgency of your quest when you arrived, I am afraid he is most likely lost to you."

Mariah shook her head. She wouldn't believe that; she would never give up on finding Miguel, he was all she had left. She would go on, even if it meant dragging herself out of there with her bare, weak arms.

"Please, hear me out," Sophus continued. Mariah looked back at him. "What I would like is for you to remain here until you are healed enough to continue on. Should you wish to continue your search at that time, I would be happy to render whatever assistance is necessary."

He leaned closer. "There is something I wish to share with you, though. I am a rather... unique individual. I have lived an extremely long life, and though I am often surrounded by kind, sweet women"—he gestured toward the door—"I find it a lonely existence. If you decide you do not wish to continue your search, I ask you to consider staying with me. I have found you to be a most intriguing person with a certain intelligence that I have not come across for longer than living memory. In return, I would give to you a life without pain, without sickness, without weakness. I would take away the frailties of your mortal body and give you youth eternal.

"Please do not answer now, wait until you are well." He locked his eyes on hers. "This is not an offer I make lightly. It is also not an offer I have ever made before."

Chapter 19

"I... DON'T KNOW what to say," Mariah stammered, taken aback. She had been willing to accept that the Wayuu believed differently than her, but this was more than she had bargained for.

Sophus shook his head. "I don't want you to say anything now, just to think about it as you heal."

"I think... I'd like to rest now," she said weakly. She certainly did need to think about it. Could she really spend months trapped in some cave with a man who not only believed in eternal youth but thought to share it with her?

Sophus stepped over and picked her up, his annoyingly calming scent washing over her. His arms were as hard and cold as ever, harder than flesh should be. His entire body seemed to radiate cold the way a normal person's radiated heat. The strangeness was undeniable.

She considered his face as he walked her to her bed, thinking of how the angles seemed just right and every feature was perfectly proportioned to the others. His pale golden locks were glossy and smooth enough to elicit jealousy from any woman. Mariah felt without reserve that he deserved the word *beautiful*. Yet there was something sinister about him. The expression in his eyes and the way he smiled made her think of a predator, a very cunning predator who liked a challenge to his intellect. She would need to be on her guard.

He laid her gently on the bed and this time, she felt as frail as she appeared.

"*Gracias*," she barely managed to say as he straightened. She was more tired than she had realized.

"*De nada, mi corazón.*" He gave a sly smile as he left.

It's nothing, my heart. Mariah bristled. The familiarity was getting out of hand. She appreciated his kindness and hospitality, but even if he did have the power to grant immortality—she cringed as she adjusted her leg and pain gripped her for a moment—and yes, even the freedom from her constant pain, she would never accept him. Behind his smiling eyes, she saw nothing but danger.

As the next few weeks passed, she grew anxious to begin walking on her own. She spent a great deal of the time in her host's company either playing chess or talking, their topics ranging through everything from philosophers and theology to literature and science.

The lovely and intricate chess set in Sophus's room had caught Mariah's eye, and the next thing she knew they were concentrating over the beautifully carved board. She wasn't surprised when he won, but she insisted they play again so that she could divine his strategy.

When she was not entertaining the blond man she read, slept, and ate. The dressing on her leg was changed every few days, and finally Iráma claimed the leg to be well enough for Mariah to begin walking with assistance.

"You will need a crutch of some sort," Iráma told her as Mariah hobbled around the room. "You are not to put any weight on the leg for at least another week, and then only lightly."

Mariah nodded, already enjoying the freedom of moving around on her own. She leaned on the chairs, the table, anything she could use to support herself as she hopped one-legged from one side of the room to another. It tired her, but her strength had been returning and she was restless and eager to begin building her muscles in earnest.

As Iráma finished cleaning up the mess from the old cast and dressing, Sophus appeared in the door, holding a long stick.

"Lord Sophus." Iráma nodded to him without looking up from what she was doing. He watched her walk lithely from the room before turning to Mariah.

"I have brought you a gift." He held the stick out to her ceremoniously. It had been smoothed and polished, and near the middle there was a branch that had been cut away, creating a handle. One end was branched and wrapped in padded cloth.

"*Gracias,* Don Sophus." Mariah took the crutch from him and set it beside her.

Sophus helped her position it under her arm to see if it was the correct length. It fit perfectly.

"It is my pleasure, Mariah. Try it out, and please, no titles, just Sophus." He gestured for her to go.

She limped around with the crutch, quickly getting the feel for it and ecstatic at her newfound freedom.

"Infinitely better than hopping." She reached the other side of the room, looking over her shoulder with a triumphant smile. The quick movement overset her balance, and she tried to lift the crutch to catch herself, succeeding only in catching it in her voluminous skirt. She squeezed her eyes shut, bracing for the impact of the floor, but instead found herself in cold, firm arms.

He helped her back to her feet. The spike of fear from the fall released its hold on her as she balanced carefully between her foot and the crutch. Sophus remained behind her, his hands steady beneath her arms.

"I'm quite all right now," she said, expecting him to give her some space.

He didn't move.

Oh dear, Mariah thought, *this is not good.*

She cleared her throat and tried to move from Sophus's arms. His breath on the back of her neck chilled her as he moved his face closer to hers. *Not good, not good, not good,* she thought frantically as his strange scent immobilized her and set her heart to pounding. She tried unsuccessfully to push his arms away; she could sooner have pushed away the arm of a statue. His face brushed against her hair, and his chest pressed against her back as he inhaled deeply.

"You have a most appealing scent," he whispered in her ear, his low, soft voice trying to draw her to look at him.

She refused. If she turned toward him, all would be lost. She stopped struggling and stood limp, staring straight ahead. "Don Sophus, this is really most inappropriate. As always, your kindness is extremely appreciated, but I must request that you leave for now," she said as stiffly as she could.

Sophus released her with a resounding laugh, his hands hovering until he was sure she was stable.

"You know," he said as he reached the door, "I could make this all go away. Think about it."

She refused to turn until she heard the door close. Scowling and muttering to herself, she continued hobbling around the room until she had worn herself out.

The next morning as she ate her breakfast, Sophus returned looking very pleased with himself.

"I have something for you." He took a seat across from her.

"Don Sophus, you've done so much already. I don't believe I could accept any more of your generosity," Mariah responded, hoping to avoid any further advances.

"It is nothing, my dear. Actually, I had meant to give it to you before your accident," he said with a mischievous glimmer in his eyes.

She stood as gracefully as she could manage, which in her mind, equated to that of a cow rising from the ground. "All right then."

"No, no, please, it can wait until you are finished," Sophus protested once she was up.

Mariah rolled her eyes. "I'm up, I am finished." She tried to not let the sarcasm through.

"Wonderful!" he said, practically leaping up from the chair, which, oddly, didn't move when he stood. Mariah had begun to get used to his idiosyncrasies, even his silvery eyes with the red-ringed irises and cold, hard skin.

He led her to the closet and gestured inside. Mariah had not seen the inside of it since before she'd been hurt, as Iráma or the other women had always chosen her clothes and helped her dress. Now, as she peered into the side room, she hardly recognized it. It was filled, top to bottom and front to back, with clothing of every color, style and cloth.

Mariah stepped back, overwhelmed. Even at home she had not had such an array. She hobbled through the small chamber. He'd even included a small selection of breeches and shirts. *This must have cost a fortune,* she thought.

She turned back. "I really can't accept this."

Sophus shook his head. "Whether you accept it or not is your choice, but know it is here should you wish to use any of it during your stay. Now, I have a request for you. Put on something nice, comfortable, and warm. I think you might enjoy spending the day out of doors; perhaps we can shoot those pistols of your father's." Sophus backed out of the closet. "I'll be right outside your room once you are ready."

Mariah sighed when she heard the door to her room close. He was always around, always so close. She needed a break from him, but how could she get it?

She chose a nice, simple green dress and a green shawl with gold embroidering to go over it. The dress hung more loosely than it should have, though she was no longer quite so gaunt. No doubt as that improved, the clothes would fit better. Settling and tightening all the layers of the dress exhausted her, and she took a moment to rest on the chair before pulling on her shoes. Her leg remained both stiff and sore, but the improvement encouraged her.

Last, she brushed out her hair, pleased to see some of its original luster had come back. She watched her reflection in the mirror, only partly pleased to see her old self returning. How could she politely ignore him?

She picked up her pistols. *Perfect*, she thought. She could ask him to carry them for her as they walked, which would help to keep at least one of his hands occupied.

Her plan worked well at first, but it was a long walk to the pastures, made longer still by her lame leg. When they reached the stairs she realized, with chagrin, that she had miscalculated. Her hurt leg already ached from the exertion, and her good leg would not be able to jump up each of the many steps. Sophus swept her up into his arms before she had a chance to protest.

Exhausted, her body tried to pull her into unconsciousness, but she fought it. She would not fall asleep in his arms, no matter how relaxing his scent. She concentrated on her breathing and counting each of the steps as they went, refusing to relax or allow her eyes to close. The breeze from the open doorway filled her lungs as they neared. The smell of impending rain from the overcast sky stirred her to wakefulness.

"I'm fine now; you can set me down," she said as they passed through the doorway.

He set her on a bench and handed her the pistols. "Prime these while I set up a target, would you?"

"Certainly." She took the equipment, and the familiarity of the task heartened her. The feel of the guns reminded her of her father, and the smell of gunpowder brought back memories of Miguel. Happier times. She found herself smiling.

"Ah, that is what I like to see." Sophus helped her to her feet and handed her the crutch. "You light up when you smile like that."

She offered him the gun. "Would you like to shoot first?"

"Why don't you go first?" He took the first pistol. "It has been such a long time since I've used a gun; I'm afraid they've developed a bit without me."

Pleased at the chance to show off her marksmanship, Mariah aimed the second pistol and shot, hitting the target nearly dead center.

Sophus nodded his approval. "Well done. Do you think you can do even better?" He took the spent pistol from her and held out the unshot pistol, hilt first, the muzzle directed toward his chest.

She reached out to it, a word of caution against ever pointing it at himself on her lips. When she touched it, the unthinkable happened: the gun fired. The weapon fell to the earth as Sophus crumpled.

"Don Sophus!" she cried, dropping down beside him, her crutch flung to the side. Mariah touched his arm, steeling herself for the sight of blood as she rolled him over. Instead, she was treated to booming laughter.

"No harm done, *mi corazón*," he assured her, sitting up. "Your worry is touching, however."

"I thought you were killed." Mariah sat heavily on the ground, her bad leg outstretched. How had the gun gone off? She hadn't even touched the trigger. "What happened?"

"I was shot, of course. Firearms are so temperamental, you know."

Mariah's head spun. "But, there is no blood. I've shot a man before; they bleed so much...."

"Have you now?"

"You must not have been hit," Mariah said, still trying to wrap her mind around what had happened.

Sophus turned toward her and pointed to his shirt. The ragged hole over his chest was singed where the gunpowder had hit it at point-blank range. "Oh, it hit me, I can promise you that."

Mariah's mind raced. There was no way he could have tricked her. She was certain the shirt had been whole, and she had loaded and primed the gun herself. She had seen him shot. What if Nana and the others were right? None of the tales had made sense because she hadn't actually believed. But accepting, however it had come to be, that Sophus was immortal made everything fall into place.

It was too much to think about at once, and she asked him to help her back to her room. He picked her up before they began down the first flight of stairs, and her exhaustion overcame her protests. She was asleep before they reached the bottom.

***

Mariah woke with the feel of the warm sun on her skin, the smell of damp earth in her nose, and the distant bleating of sheep in her ears. She stretched before opening her eyes, feeling rested, warm, and comfortable and unwilling to admit to herself that she had awoken. Sighing, she opened her eyes to the clear, brilliantly blue sky. It had been two months now since she had started walking again.

Her muscles had returned, but not nearly as fast as she would have liked, and her leg still pained her with every step. Mariah often felt too restless to focus inside, and so she had begun spending most of the day out in the pastures. She especially enjoyed being out in the sun because Sophus seemed to avoid it, though she often caught him standing in the doorway, watching her. The daily trek through the twisting halls and winding stairs had helped to speed her recovery, and the sunlight and warm air lifted her spirits. She had also found a nice remote place on the northern side of the pasture where she could sit, leaning against a rock, and stare off to the north. It provided a good view of the low hills in the far distance. Was that where she would find Miguel?

Mariah sighed again at the lengthening shadows. This evening, like most every other evening, she would be obliged to spend with her host. Typically, they played chess or conversed on any of the vast range of interests that they shared. Mariah wondered idly what he would choose to speak about tonight. Perhaps he would tell her more about himself.

Mariah had come to terms with the idea that he was, in fact, immortal, but only recently had been brave enough to ask about it. Her mind wandered to a conversation they'd had a few days before.

"I would hardly know how to describe it anymore," Sophus had said. "It has been centuries since I was human, and I was human for such a relatively short time that I don't really remember much of it."

"What do you remember?" she had asked, trying to imagine what it would be like to not recall so much of her past

He smiled, leaning back. "My first memory is the change. It is a very vivid memory. Our kind are equipped with some amazing weapons, one of which is the venom from our teeth. It is that distinguished substance that changes the mortal into something extraordinary. The venom is introduced, usually through a bite"—Sophus gave her a sideways glance to gauge her reaction—"and works its way through the body, burning out the imperfections, pushed along by the heart. A strong heart is required, for if it stops beating before the change is complete, then death follows swiftly."

"And you imagine my heart is strong enough?" Mariah teased. She found the topic fascinating and wondered how much of it she could take at face value.

"Of that I have little doubt." Sophus reached over and caressed her hand.

"Were your eyes always silver?"

"No, the silver is a distinct feature, one that marks us as Immortals. As for the outer ring, it is said that the more human blood one consumes, the brighter the red will shine." He smiled again, inwardly amused. "It is not, however, a sign of power. Mine are a softer red, for I like to limit my diet and often partake of the blood of the animals that sustain the household."

A vampire then, just as Nana tried to tell me. Mariah smiled politely. Miguel had told her a story of blood drinkers once. Sophus hardly seemed to fit the picture of a grotesque monstrosity surrounded by foulness and death that Miguel had painted that night, so long ago. "What happened after you were transformed?"

"After my new birth, I had immense strength, vision, hearing, speed. Everything that I once was had become enhanced. Even my thoughts, dreams, and desires had become grander. Anything I wanted, I obtained; everything I desired, I had. It was a good life."

"Was?"

"As with every young person, I had not learned the value of patience, of self-control or even self-denial. Power betrayed me and nearly destroyed me. It was a hard lesson to learn. So, instead, I took to learning. I learned all the things that I had not had time for as a mortal. I became an artist and a scholar. As I am certain you know, all the art here is my own. I am especially fond of working with stone." He wore the smile of an artist who loved and found great joy in his work and Mariah found that smile to be—for once—almost human.

"Can you show me?" she'd asked.

Sophus stood and went to a wall, considering it. Mariah followed, carefully maneuvering her crutch around the furniture. As she neared, Sophus touched the wall and pulled down, curling his fingers. Mariah was shocked to see the indents left behind, dust crumbling from his fingertips.

"How...?" she asked. The stone looked like someone had clawed into lightly chilled butter.

Sophus had smiled broadly. "The strength of the Immortal."

A bird landed on a short, stubby tree beside her and chirped, bringing Mariah back from the memory. She pushed herself up to a stand and looked once more in the direction she was certain would lead to Miguel. Sophus may have consumed her evenings, but the rest of her time belonged to the man she loved. Soon, she would be strong enough to ride, and she would ask Sophus one last time for his help. Then, with or without his help, she would leave to find Miguel.

She gave a rueful look to the smooth cane in her hands. She had traded in her well-worn crutch for the cane only that morning and was still getting used to putting more weight on her leg. The bone ached in the cold of the cave and still stung to walk on, which was yet another reason for her long days in the sun.

She limped back to her room. *Limping on two legs is far better than hopping around on one*, she thought, grinning at the relative speed with which she had returned. She changed into one of the nicer gowns Sophus had brought her—he insisted she look nice in the evenings—and rearranged her hair.

As she put the finishing touches in her hair, the worn bag of *arras* sitting limply on the corner of the dresser caught her eye. Gently, she picked it up and sat on her bed. She opened the bag and spread the contents on the quilt, counting them as they came out. Thirteen coins glinted in the fading light, more beautiful and precious to her than jewels. Miguel had given them to her at their wedding, a symbol of love and a declaration that he could and would always take care of her. She picked them up, inspecting them one by one, Miguel's tales of how he had obtained them flitting through her mind. Some of the tales were elaborate or humorous while others had merely been change for food, but each had come with such a detailing of the country of origin that Mariah could almost imagine herself there with him.

So engrossed was she in her memories that she did not hear Sophus knock before he entered the room, and so full of longing and heartbreak that she did not care when his shadow fell over her treasures. He stood in silence, waiting for her to speak first.

"It has been over a year now, since I last saw him," she said without looking up. "Since I sent him away."

"Your husband?"

Mariah nodded, her throat too constricted with emotion to answer as she ran her fingers over the precious coins.

Sophus watched her for a moment then sat on the bed across from her. "I know it must be hard for you, but perhaps telling me about it would help ease the pain a little." He reached out for her hand, but she drew it away, instead picking up the coins and returning them to her bag.

"That is an unusual collection of coins. Perhaps you can start there?"

Mariah nodded, taking a moment to collect herself and her thoughts. She could see no reason not to ask Sophus yet again for his help now instead of later.

"Miguel was a sailor before I met him. These were mementos of his travels that he gave to me when we were married, in place of the traditional gold *arras*.

"Shortly afterward, my father went off to war to assist with the Wayuu uprising. He wrote regularly, until one day he simply stopped. I've had that dream I told you of off and on for years, but it was then that I began to dream it in earnest." Mariah tightened the drawstring on the bag and stood to return it to the dresser. "In it, I always felt that someone I loved was in terrible danger, and the feeling grew as the dream changed and time passed. When we finally received another letter from my father, it came in the middle of the night and was covered with blood. In it, my father sounded as though he'd given up on life and was preparing to die, insisting that we enjoy our lives and not go in search of him.

"I didn't listen." Mariah choked up, clutching the bag to her stomach rather than setting it down. "I sent Miguel out to find him. My old nursemaid, the Wayuu woman who sent me to you, insisted that I shouldn't, that things wouldn't turn out well, but I didn't care. I sent him anyway." She paused to regain her composure, swallowing hard and fighting to keep tears from spilling. Fighting to remember to hide that she'd had a child, even though he was gone.

"Eventually, Papa returned, but without Miguel. He was dying and delirious. He told me something about being prepared to die and a replacement being required."

"And your husband was the replacement," Sophus said, his voice thoughtful.

"Yes," Mariah whispered. "Papa told me not to seek him out, but I have no life without him. He is my heart, all my joy and my life. There is nothing for me otherwise."

"Oh, dear." Sophus shook his head and moved to stand beside her. "I do so wish you had told me all of this detail about a replacement earlier, when you first came. There may still have been time then, but I'm afraid it is far too late to help him now."

"What do you mean?" she asked, looking up at the beautiful blond man.

"You know of the Wayuu legend of the Noble One and the Slaver?"

"Yes...."

"Then you should know that your father had been sent as a sacrifice to Theron, the Slaver. This is why your nursemaid sent you to me. I am the only one Theron fears; I am the only one to whom he would listen. All those who are sent to him die, some more quickly than others. I am so sorry, but I'm afraid it is far too late to save your Miguel now."

Mariah shook her head. What he said was simply not possible. "No. He's still alive, I am sure of it."

"Mariah," Sophus gently took her hand, "I know your husband is dead. I promise you Theron would not have kept him alive. It is a shock, I know, but you need to believe me and not hold to false hopes. Let him go."

She just shook her head again, gripping the bag of *arras* more tightly, pressing it to her. Mariah had lost everyone dear to her; she couldn't let Miguel go as well.

"My dear, I know this is a bad time, but please, consider my previous request. Join with me. Live without pain, without death or illness. I could fix all your wounds, remove every pain in a moment, and we would live forever."

Mariah pulled her hand from the cold grasp and turned away. "I have no use for forever without him."

Sophus reached out to touch her hair, but she jerked away, and he let his hand fall.

"At least stay here until you have finished healing. Then you may leave if you wish."

Mariah only nodded, clinging to her composure with her chin up as silence filled the room between them. After what seemed like a very long time, Sophus stood and left.

As soon as the door clicked shut, she crumpled. Dropping to the hard stone floor, her dress billowed out around her, she wept until her tears ran dry.

Chapter 20

MARIAH STAYED CURLED up in bed all of the next day, facing the grey stone wall, lost in its blandness. Wuchii had convinced her to move to the bed, but she did not eat the food that was brought to her nor did she otherwise respond to anyone. She remained in her catatonic state the following day, clutching the worn bag of coins to her as though they were her hold on sanity or life.

When Mariah still had not moved by the third day, Sophus had Iráma look in on her. When Iráma pulled on Mariah's arm to roll her onto her back, Mariah jerked away violently and returned to her vigil of the cold stone wall.

"She was fine the last time I saw her. What happened?" Iráma asked.

"She told me the man she'd been following after had gone to Theron," Sophus said, irritation coloring his smooth voice.

Iráma's voice became sympathetic. "So he is dead after all. That would explain it; she held out so fiercely for him. There's nothing wrong; she just needs time to grieve. You usually don't see this part. We come to you after the first shock of death has worn off. She is resilient and will come back to herself with time."

"I had such high hopes for her," Sophus said with a snort. "I even offered her immortality. It's a shame—she would have been so useful, but I can't change her like this. I can barely abide the moping of mortal women. I need a companion who is strong."

"She *is* strong, Lord Sophus," Iráma replied, more sternly now. "Her loyalties run so deep that cutting her hope like you did hurts tremendously. It will take time for her to recover, and all you can do is wait for her fire to return. When it does, it will burn far more fiercely than before."

"Well, we shall see, I suppose. It would be a shame if, in the end, she was just another one of you."

There was a pause before Iráma responded. "Have you told her everything then? Does she know the darker side of your offer?"

"There is no darker side, Iráma. You eat the meat of your carefully managed flocks; I drink the blood of mine. What is the difference, I ask, between you milking your goats and me mine? At least I have devised a way to not kill my sheep unless they wish it, and they offer their blood willingly without the inevitable fatality of suffering my bite."

"Your generosity is self-serving."

"And yours is not? You house and tend dumb animals; I rescue lost people and give them a life of peace and happiness within halls of beauty. What I ask in return is a pittance, by comparison. You dole out death but I give life. And yes, I have told her."

"We are your menagerie," Iráma said carelessly. "I pity her, should she accept your offer."

"She would be my prized pet, that is for sure. Ah, but I had such plans for her. Perhaps she will be useful yet." Sophus sounded satisfied and walked out.

"Lord Sophus," Iráma whispered once the door was closed and he was long gone, "I should warn you, she hears you just fine."

**

Mariah did hear, but she did not care. A part of her mind registered everything that was said and stored it for future processing. Mariah's will had gone out of her. It was too much effort to move, to think, to breathe. Her body, however, rebelled against her depression, and a part of her mind fought against the numbness, keeping her chest rising and falling and her heart beating.

On the fourth day, Wuchii came and sat beside her, running her fingers through Mariah's glossy black hair.

"I know how you feel," she said softly. "The pain of loss. It is still sharp, especially when I'm alone at night. Like you, I don't remember much of my mother, for she died when I was very young. I had brothers, though, and a father. And a husband. My brothers and father died one by one in battles. Each time, I felt a part of me die as I tended their bones. When my husband was killed, I was left alone. There were many people around me, the people of my village that tried to reach me, but I would not be reached.

"I was heavy with new life when they brought his body back for the funeral. I, too, would have turned my face to a wall and died, but I had a child to bear. I held on for him, lived my life for him. When he was born, he was so perfect, but he was anxious to travel. Before he was three days old, he joined his fathers in Jepira, the land of the dead.

"Then, I did turn my face to the wall to die, but my spirit was too strong. It would not let me die, and so the elders sent me to the village of the Old One, who, in turn, sent me here. Though death may be a beautiful release from the sorrows of this world, I realized I had a purpose to fulfill and distances yet to travel before I could sleep. You, too, have a destiny to fulfill, child of Zyanya.

"Time is needed, but time I have." Wuchii leaned back in her chair. A comfortable silence fell between them.

Mariah rolled onto her back, and Wuchii smiled.

"You need not be whole yet, but you do need to eat. Come, let us get you up."

Mariah allowed herself to be herded around the room, eating as she was told, bathing and dressing with Wuchii's help. When she was finished doing a task she simply stopped, standing and staring into space until she was told to do otherwise.

Mariah knew that time passed but time had ceased to have meaning for her. She slept as little as possible, for sleep brought with it vivid dreams of dashed hopes, tearing open anew the pain of her loss. Dreams that insisted she was wasting precious time here, that he still lived, that he was searching for her.

Despite herself, Mariah began to improve. Though she wandered the halls aimlessly, a woman always trailing silently behind, she no longer slowed to a stop at random places, staring into space until someone suggested that she continue. She began to eat when she noticed hunger, which happened with increasing frequency. She began to get out of bed, bathe, and dress without being convinced, and then even began choosing her own clothes. At first, she just picked the first thing in her closet that her hand fell on, but then she began taking care what she chose. The pain in her leg never really went away, though she grew more adept at ignoring it.

One day as she walked by a table, a book lying open on it caught her attention. She stopped and looked at it for a long time, before picking it up and starting to read.

There was a knock at her door, and when she looked up, an elderly woman rushed in, falling to her knees at Mariah's feet.

"You must forgive me! I didn't know you'd survived," the woman cried, a coughing fit wracking her small frame.

"Please, stand up." Mariah took the woman's hand and helped her up. Turning the woman's face toward her, Mariah gasped. Maachon, Muusa's grandmother, stood before her. Excited to see a familiar face, Mariah gently led her to a seat. "What do you mean? You've never been anything but kind to me, *abuela* Maachon. How is Muusa? Is she well?"

"Your son, I didn't know. We had already left the village. The Old One told me you had died of your fever," Maachon said. "I swear, I would never have done it. The Elder's council would never have condoned it."

Coldness stole over Mariah's heart as she brought Maachon a cup of water. "Drink this," she said softly, forcing herself to wait until the old woman had finished before asking the question that burned in her. "What about my son?"

"Muusa's son had never been strong. When he succumbed to the call of his fathers to join them in Jepira, the Old One came to Muusa, asking her to nurse your boy."

"Muusa's son died," Mariah repeated. As she began to suspect what Maachon would say next, the coldness in her heart solidified into rage.

"The Old One said that you had succumbed to a birth fever, and begged us to take your son back to your home. I didn't know you had lived—I wouldn't have taken him, I swear it. To steal a child from his mother, it is not done! But we did as she asked, and he is there, even now, with your Betania. They loved you so and were so grieved to hear of your passing. When I returned to my people and heard you'd come here, I knew I had to make it right. Even if it meant my death."

Mariah no longer heard what the woman's words as the ground gave way beneath her feet.

Álvaro lived.

Mariah grasped the table to keep from falling.

Nana had lied to her.

With an animalistic cry, Mariah swept the ewer and basin from off the table top. They shattered across the stone floor as surely as Mariah's life had been shattered by the Old One's lies.

How could Nana have ever said she cared for her? That woman cared more about a legend than she had for Mariah or even for Ayelen. For all her talk and years of service and false love, had Nana just been biding her time until she could force Mariah here? Mariah had planned to take her son and return home, so Nana had stolen him. Had Nana manipulated her all along?

Mariah's knees buckled, and a sob stuck in her throat. Álvaro was alive. Mariah had lost track of the days. How long had she been here now? What would he look like? What would he be doing?

Mariah felt as though a fog had lifted from her brain, a fog she hadn't noticed come, a fog she hadn't even been able to see. The door stood open before her, and suddenly everything seemed so clear. Why was she still here? Miguel—she thought his name with difficulty, swallowing down a sob—was lost to her, but

Álvaro still lived, still needed his mother. She would go back to him.

Mariah calmed Maachon, helping her get her coughing under control and assured her that all was forgiven. Asking another woman to help Maachon, she sent them to find Wuchii for food and rest. Closing the door, Mariah considered her ill-fated first attempt at exploration as she paced the room. That had been immensely foolish. She ought to have started in a place she knew was near the entrance—the throne room, the first place Iráma had taken her when they arrived—and started from there. She even knew where to find it now.

For the first time since she had arrived, she donned all her knives and pistols, callously cutting access points into her dress. She paused to look at her father's pistols and smiled.

"These will be yours," she said softly, thinking of her son. "I will teach you to shoot as your father taught me. His legacy will live in you."

Carefully, she cleaned, loaded, and slipped them into her belt. Mariah packed some warm clothes and threw on Miguel's greatcoat, as comfortable as though it were his arms around her. The more she thought about it, the more certain she felt that she knew exactly where the entrance was. Last, she slipped the pouch with the thirteen *arras* into a pocket and strode from the room.

The throne room was in the opposite direction from the one Mariah had taken when she'd gone exploring. She walked directly to it and stopped in front of the closed door. Turning her back to the door, she looked down into the dark corridor directly across the hall. When she had come in, they had walked in a straight line to this room. When they left, again going down the corridor, they had arrived in a vastly different chamber.

Mariah grabbed a nearby torch and lit it, walking forward with confidence. Halfway through the darkness, the tunnel did, indeed, branch the way Iráma had said, but it was angled so that the branching would only be seen by someone coming from the throne room. She laughed derisively, realizing that the smaller chamber must have been merely a room behind one of the closed doors in the large round room.

Cunning, she thought, taking the path to the round room.

When she reached the room, she recognized it as one she had passed through often on the way to the pastures. She shook her head again and admired the deceptive architecture. The room was built skewed so that a person passing through from one end to another would think it was just another peculiarly shaped chamber. One side bowed away, the wall lined with the odd-sized but grand doors and statues, neither of which was uncommon in Sophus's labyrinth. The other side had a deep overhang with more statues lining the edge of the complete darkness beyond.

She strode forward to the dark side of the oblong room and stood behind one of the beautiful stone seraphs, taking in the view. It was exactly as she had remembered it. From the center of the darkness, the room seemed perfectly round, curving into the distance with a bright, arched ceiling. Behind her was freedom. Mariah took one last look at the grandeur and turned to the darkness, her torch before her. There were walls guiding her way, but the torch did not light them well, and within a few feet, the darkness before her was complete. With her head held high, Mariah started into the void.

Iráma materialized out of the darkness, walking toward her. She slowed as she neared.

"Now is not the time to leave," Iráma said with a quiet but urgent voice. "You have found your purpose again I see, but danger is coming."

Mariah opened her mouth to argue, but Iráma cut her off.

"You will die if you leave now. Return to your room and stay there until someone comes to get you. Tell everyone you see to do the same." She set her hand on Mariah's shoulder. "I will help you leave after our visitor has gone."

"Why, what is going on?" Mariah asked, skeptical of the strange woman. "Who is coming?"

"Death," the tall, graceful woman answered, and walked on.

Mariah hesitated. Freedom was just on the other side of the darkness. But Iráma had never been anything but a friend to her; why would she lie now? Mariah returned toward her own chambers, pausing only long enough to tell anyone she saw what Iráma had said.

Undercurrents of unease and excitement flowed through the labyrinth as the other women rushed to follow Iráma's instruction.

"What is going on?" Mariah asked Wuchii when they passed in the hall.

"It sounds as though another immortal has come to pay Lord Sophus a visit. This has not happened in living memory, but we have all been warned that it is certain and painful death to be about if one comes by. Quickly now, go." Wuchii shoved Mariah in the direction of her rooms then ran off in another direction.

Iráma stood beside Mariah's door, her casual stance marred by nervous, jerky movements as she opened the door.

"I ought not to do this for you," Iráma said carelessly, as though she was speaking of gossip that she didn't care for. "Lord Sophus will be angry if he finds out, but I think you need to see our visitor. I have been instructed to lock you in your chambers, but if you decide to solve the riddle of the way Lord Sophus has lit his home, you might find something worth seeing."

Mariah stepped into her room, and the lock clicked behind her. Why would Iráma care now about Mariah knowing how the rooms were lit? Mariah set her packs beside a couch and looked up at the lit ceiling. She had long ago figured that it was some network of mirrors but had never cared enough to confirm it.

Why not? she thought, looking for things she could climb to reach the lip in the wall that the lights reflected out of. Though she still had some issues walking, she had grown used to the pain, and her leg was strong enough. She could probably climb something to get up there.

With some effort, Mariah dragged various bits of furniture around, stacking them under a light on the wall nearest to Sophus's chambers. Once the makeshift tower was complete, Mariah stood back and took in the sight, deciding that designing architecture was not for her. Steeling herself, she climbed the pile, peered over the lip into the light, and found herself blind.

Fool girl. Shaking her head, she reached her hand in to block the source of the light and found a very straight tunnel large enough to crawl through. She hoisted herself onto the ledge and felt the cracking of glass beneath her. Moving her skirt aside, she found a broken mirror. Mirrors had been set up along the ledge, one at each turn to send sunlight through the labyrinth and light the way.

Why had Iráma wanted her to see this? Perhaps she wanted her to see their visitor. But why?

As Mariah sat on the ledge, the remnants of an overheard conversation came back to her.

"*Have you told her everything, then? Does she know the darker side of your offer?*"

"*There is no darker side, Iráma. You eat the meat of your carefully managed flocks; I drink the blood of mine. What is the difference, I ask, between you milking your goats and me mine? At least I have devised a way to not kill my sheep unless they wish it. And to answer your question, yes, I have told her."*

"We are your menagerie," Iráma had said. *"I pity her, should she accept your offer."*

"She would be my prized pet, that is for sure. Ah, but I had such plans for her. Perhaps she will be useful yet."

Was Iráma trying to warn her of something? Sophus was immortal, impossibly beautiful, drank blood, and was most likely a vampire. She'd already figured all that out. Perhaps he was really a hellish demon sent to destroy and kill for lust? He didn't seem the type.

Though she had gone to church as appropriate, she had never believed most of what was taught. Even that tale Miguel had told her on that night so long ago did not seem to fit very well. She accepted that Sophus was immortal and could believe that he was a vampire, but a twisted hellish demon was not an accurate description. It was as Sophus had said: he provided beauty, life, happiness, and peace for the troubled. Being immortal, he had probably even freed her mother's people from slavery as the legends said.

There was the issue of drinking blood, as Iráma had pointed out. *But,* Mariah rationalized, *in the months I have been here I have known of no deaths*

As Mariah pondered, she began to hear voices. The first she recognized as Sophus's. The other was Iráma, probably reporting back to him. A sudden determination welled up in Mariah to heed her friend's suggestion and see what it was Iráma had wanted her to see. Knowing Sophus's penchant for mazes, Mariah returned to her room for a ball of twine and something to clear the broken glass from the ledge. Tying the twine at the entrance, she crawled through the tight tunnel. The dazzling light from the mirror darkened as rain began and a clap of thunder echoed through the caves. She paused until she could hear the voices again, then followed them through the turns

"Because having a straight passage between the walls would have been too simple," she muttered as she moved backwards from a dead end. Turning a corner, the voices sounded clearer. Certain now that she'd found Sophus's main chamber, she peeked her head out as the echo of rainfall sounded through the cave.

Sophus sat languidly on his favorite and largest chair, sloshing a goblet of red liquid. *Blood,* Mariah concluded. The air currents pulled the tangy metallic scent toward her. There was no one else in the room, though another goblet of similar liquid sat on a table beside him.

He really does drink blood, she thought absently. *No wonder I've never seen him eat.*

Mariah jumped a little when the door opened, and she held her breath as Iráma entered and dropped into her graceful bow.

"My Lord Sophus, your visitor has arrived." She gestured back to the door, signaling for the guest to come in. "May I present your old acquaintance, Lord Theron."

Mariah stifled a gasp as Theron walked in. He was beautiful, more beautiful than Mariah had ever imagined a man could be, more so even than Sophus. His glossy black hair fell to his broad shoulders. He was tall, well-muscled and well-proportioned, obviously more than a match physically for Sophus, who looked slender by comparison. Eyes that ought to have been green showed silver instead. They looked pained as he stepped forward to clasp Sophus's offered hand, smiling cruelly, a familiar dimple forming.

His handsome features were more pronounced and defined, than she ever remembered them and made him look all the more amazing. Mariah could hardly breathe. The sound of the rain thundered in her ears. Or was it her own heartbeat?

"Drink?" Sophus offered, mischief in his voice. His guest declined and Sophus happily drank both drinks himself while Theron twitched. Sophus gave a wicked smile, gesturing for him to sit.

"Your hospitality comes at too high a price. I will stand," Miguel said coldly.

Chapter 21

MARIAH COULDN'T move. She couldn't breathe. Miguel lived, but how? Sophus had insisted that he was dead. She should have known him for a liar; things never felt quite right around him. How could she have allowed herself to trust him?

She feasted her eyes on the sight of her husband below her, heart aching with the joy of being so near. He was everything she remembered of him, but also *more*. He had changed since the last she had seen him, riding off in the rain, but in a way she could not explain. And his eyes. She could see them well from here—they were silver with a blood red border rather than the tawny red of Sophus's, the eyes of immortality. Eyes that appeared to be in *pain*. Her heart went out to him, and she wanted to leap down from her hiding place and hold him, comfort him.

"You never did trust me much, did you, my old friend?" Sophus asked, chuckling.

"I did once, but as I said, your *generosity* has far too high a price," Miguel answered briskly.

No, not Miguel, Mariah thought. *Theron. But how?* The timbre of the voice was right, exactly what she remembered, but the speech itself was not as Miguel would have spoken. It carried an odd accent that reminded her of Sophus and used words and cadences that Miguel would not have.

What is going on?

"Come now, I'm sure you went to great lengths to acquire this new pet, though it is shameful that you would do so to a fellow immortal. Did you really think I'd take him from you so soon?" Sophus asked, sounding hurt.

"One can never be too careful with you," Theron replied with Miguel's voice.

Mariah was entranced by the almost musical quality of her husband's voice. He made Sophus seem dull by comparison.

Miguel inhaled deeply, twitching as though having difficulty keeping control of himself. "It was not so hard, really. It seemed after so many years of bad luck, always being sent men too old and sickly to survive a transformation—men useful only for a meal—things changed. I was blessed with this fine specimen who succumbed to me easily enough. It would seem you have a new pet as well. She does smell lovely."

"She does indeed. You know what an effort it can be to get good help, what a hassle it is to train them. I would appreciate you not killing any this time," Sophus said with exasperation.

"I would hate to be so rude. I would not have come if I was not certain of my control."

"It is more like you would not have risked letting him so far away from you. You do appear to be having some trouble controlling him as it is." Sophus gestured toward the twitching hand.

Mariah took it in stride. In a world with immortals, vampires, and ancient prophecies involving her, what was the addition of mind control? She almost laughed.

"My strength grows with familiarity, as well you know, which is part of the reason I took so long to come." Theron shrugged. "It always saddened me that you could not experience this. It is amazing to see the world through another's eyes, see what they see, and experience what they experience. Her blood sings to this poor fool, an incredible feeling, one which I have not experienced before. You would be wise to ensure they do not cross paths, else I'm afraid he might take over and kill her. He fights fiercely, you realize."

"I imagine he would, and that this is the reason you have waited so long to visit. He really is a fine-looking creature," Sophus said. "He probably has a wife back home that he longs for."

"That very thing." Theron raised Miguel's hand, showing the glint of his wedding ring. "He has caused no little trouble over it."

Pride and love filled Mariah to know he hadn't ever given up. *Keep fighting, Miguel!* Her mind raced.

She would need to return to Maracaibo before he did, she could meet him—

"Perhaps he would be easier to control if you had him return and find his bride. With any luck, he'll kill her. People are always so much easier to control once they're broken."

"That might be just the way," Theron mused, finally sitting down.

Mariah paused. Surely Miguel wouldn't kill *her*. Not after fighting so hard. Certainly, if he only saw her... She turned her attention back to the conversation, hoping they would give away how she could best them.

"I imagine you did not come just for the advice on doing what you've done for centuries. However, I could not fault you if you did. You may have the raw talent, but my way takes work and practice, and practice will always trump raw skill."

Theron bristled. "I did not, in fact, come here for your advice, however good it may seem. I came to reclaim what is mine."

"The natives? You can have them; they have begun to bore me anyhow. After a few centuries, you begin to see the same things over and over. I have taken to starting wars with the Europeans just to stir things up a bit."

"You know I could not care less about your pathetic cattle," Theron growled. "I have come for my limbs that you so kindly removed and hid. The danger to me has long since passed, as has the time to return them."

"Ah, Theron, you never did trust me as much as you should have," Sophus stood and wandered the room. "I have kept them safe and hidden, as I said I would."

Suddenly, faster than Mariah could see, Miguel crossed the room and held Sophus in the air by his collar. Mariah held back a gasp at the unimaginable speed of it. "I want my body back," Theron growled. "I will have it back if I have to find it piece by piece. I will have it back if I must tear you limb from limb."

"How ironic that would be." Sophus shrugged, unperturbed by his dangling feet. "Especially since I am the only one who knows where your orphaned limbs are hidden. Pull yourself together, Theron." He raised an eyebrow before continuing. "If you dismantle me, I promise to remain silent on the matter, and you will never be whole again. Now, if you would return me to the floor."

Theron lowered Sophus to the ground, pushing him away with disgust.

Sophus smoothed his clothes, disgust on his face. "I believe you have overstayed your welcome."

"It was not much of a welcome." Theron scowled as he turned on his heel and stormed out, smashing the door in his fury.

Mariah felt the stone around her shudder and backed down the tunnel to return to her room, her mind racing. Miguel was alive! Sophus knew he had gone to Theron and that Theron would not have killed him.

It took far less time to get back than it had to find her way, and she quickly returned the furniture to its proper place, her heart pounding. She dismissed the idea of racing after Miguel. She could never have caught up to him with her weak leg, even if he'd been mortal. Once she was sure everything looked normal, she collapsed onto a couch with a book in hand and tried to look bored. Her heart continued to pound, waiting for Sophus to come in, angry at her for spying. When he did not come, Mariah's heart calmed but her mind raced, trying to process all she had seen and heard.

Miguel was alive, but he was changed. She should not have given up on him; even now he fought to return to her, and that knowledge filled her with a fierce joy. Outside, the storm continued, thunder echoing through the tunnels. He fought to return to her, but she was not in Maracaibo, she was trapped here. Iráma had promised to help her leave—perhaps she could go, even now. On horseback, she could make it home to Maracaibo in under a week.

"With any luck, he'll kill her. They're always so much easier to control once they're broken."

The impact of the words began to hit home. She shook her head. No, Miguel wouldn't kill her. He couldn't.

"... would be wise to ensure they do not cross paths, else I'm afraid he might take over and kill her...."

She was certain it was *her* scent Theron had spoken of. Mariah saw again the pained look in Miguel's silver eyes, almost that of a caged and tortured animal. She had seen boys do that once, cage an animal and tease it until it broke loose and attacked one of the boys. The animal had escaped, but the boy bore the mutilating scars for the rest of his life.

"With any luck, he'll kill her."

Could the bloodlust really be so strong that he would kill her and not even realize what he was doing? They couldn't have known she was watching, so why would they have lied? Perhaps they meant to demoralize Miguel. Either way, it wasn't worth the risk.

The wind whistled from beyond the overhead passages as the storm reached its height. There had to be a way. Sophus had referred to Miguel as an immortal, and Mariah could see the change. As she thought about it, she realized how like Sophus Miguel had become. The strength, the speed, the beauty, the silvered eyes. If Theron could change Miguel into an immortal, perhaps Sophus could do the same for her.

The world around her fell into silence.

In fact, he had already offered.

Miguel could not kill her if Mariah could not die. If they could not die, they could be together forever, as they had promised each other they would be. Hope blossomed in her chest.

And what of Álvaro? He was alive, and the knowledge of it filled her with joy. She could go back to him. She ought to go back to him; she was his mother. But she had come so far to find Miguel, and she was here now. It would be a waste to leave at this point, on the cusp of victory. Could she live with herself, knowing she had abandoned her son? Would Miguel hate her for it?

A good mother would have gone back to her child, but who had ever shown her how to be a mother? Mariah shut the book with a snap. What she did know was that she could not live with herself, haunted for the rest of her life by dreams that compelled her forward, knowing that success had been within reach but she had not taken the final step.

To look her son in the eye and tell him she could have brought his father home, but hadn't, was not something she could ever face.

Álvaro was with Betania and Benito. They were good people and could care for him a little longer. She was so close. She couldn't turn back now.

Mariah strode with purpose to the closet. She put on the most attractive and appealing dress Sophus had bought for her, red and black. She did her hair so that it framed her face perfectly, added the necessary adornments, and returned the weapons to their hiding places.

"I am coming, Miguel." She kissed the bag of coins and hid it, along with Miguel's greatcoat, behind a panel in the closet.

She returned to Sophus's chambers, through the hall. She found his rooms empty, though the shattered door had already been cleared away. Mariah picked a couch that gave her a good view of the open doorway and lounged in it, hoping to look alluring as she read a large book.

She didn't notice him enter; he was just suddenly standing before her.

Mariah peered up over the book, looking through her lashes. "I heard your guest left."

"He has indeed," Sophus said, testily. "Do you have a purpose for being in my room?"

"I wasn't aware I needed one," she said blithely. "But, since you ask, I do have a request for you."

Sophus waved her away. "Iráma has already told me you have found the way out. Leave if you wish."

Mariah stood, letting the book tumble down from her lap. It hit the floor with a thud, and Sophus looked back to her. She locked eyes with him.

"I no longer wish to leave." She walked toward him. "I have seen the power your kind has, the fear you instill in people. I accept your offer of immortality, if you are still willing to give it."

"I am indeed." He grabbed her waist and pulled her toward him, his befuddling scent washing over her.

***

Mariah burned. Her heart raced, first with fear and then fighting the poison that now attacked it. It fought to live, to survive the fire racing through her veins, burning away her imperfections, her pain, her mortality.

As she burned, she found herself in a peaceful place, a field near her home. She heard herself screaming, burning as though she were in a furnace, a burning that did not stop though it seared her skin, her muscles, her nerves. But those were all parts of her body. Here, she did not have a body; here, she was free. Here, there was peace.

A gentle breeze blew, but Mariah felt it as she never had before—she felt the very particles of the air collide with each cell of her skin, felt each hair on her head move as the wind whipped it around. She turned her face to the sun and basked in its warmth. She looked down and saw her body, pale and sinuous, gliding with such ease and power that she felt that, if she tried, even gravity could not hold her down.

She smelled the rain in the air and the salt in the breeze—Mariah loved the rain. Someone fumbled through the undergrowth of the jungle nearby, and she turned her back on the clumsy oaf in disdain. His familiar, attractive scent had no power over her now. Elsewhere, her body burned, and her heart struggled to continue on, her voice screaming silently, her throat too raw to make noise.

In the distance, Miguel shone in the sunlight, magnificent and perfect, with his silver eyes bordered in red, matching her own. She did not try to run to him; she simply wished herself there and she was. They stood, staring at each other, reaching for each other, but Miguel twitched, turned back toward Maracaibo, and was gone.

Mariah knew where to find him.

She stood on the balcony of the garden of Casa de la Cuesta, a haunting Wayuu lullaby drifting over her. She turned. Nana watched her with a satisfied smile. A flare of anger rose in Mariah, but Miguel walked by, and she followed him instead. Nothing could stop her. This time she would reach him.

In the distance, in a cold, dark cave, Mariah's dying heart sped up in one final effort to live as the burning venom, having consumed the rest of her body, turned its full force on the noble muscle. Her body had long since stopped trying to scream. Screaming was useless.

Miguel stopped at the entrance to the garden, and Mariah reached out to him.

I'm here! she said, but her hand passed through his shoulder as he entered into the garden. Mariah followed him in, but as she stepped through the gate, she stepped into darkness.

Below her, the lights of the floating village danced like stars on the water. Mariah could see through the dark water, could see the fish swimming in the darkness. Nearer her was a funeral barge where Miguel's lifeless, mortal body lay surrounded by flowers. The scent of the flowers drifted up to her; orchids, roses, lilies. And lavender. The barge moved out, floating on the waves, almost dancing among the lights. The lights went out one by one, and she was left alone on the dock in the darkness of her dreams. A darkness that held no mysteries for her.

Mariah saw, through the darkness, a new, perfectly glorious Miguel step forward, but before she could step toward him, the silvery-red-eyed figure, who had lurked for so long in the deep shadows, filled with loathing, malice, and hate, stepped between them, her golden hair glinting in the moonlight.

In a distant, cavernous room filled with reflected sunlight, Mariah's heart finally succumbed.

As Mariah's mind returned to its new, perfect, immortal body, a voice that chilled her drifted back with her across time and space. The voice of the silver-eyed shadow.

"*I saw him first. He will always be mine,*" Elisa snarled.

Thank you for reading Amaranth Dawn!

IF YOU ENJOYED IT, PLEASE LEAVE A REVIEW
Reviews buoy my spirits and stoke the fires of creativity.

NEED MORE DAUGHTER OF ZYANYA?

You can find the rest of the series on Amazon.com

Aura of Dawn – a Prequel
Amaranth Dawn – Book 1
Aeonian Dreams – Book 2
Abiding Destiny – Book 3 (forthcoming)

ABOUT THE AUTHOR

Morgan J Muir fell in love with reading fantasy as child, and could never get enough of it. She is a mom of three crazy kids and lives in northern Utah. You can find more of her stories at morganjmuir.com

Made in the USA
Monee, IL
28 March 2021